THE DAUGHTERS
OF NIGHTSONG

THE DAUGHTERS OF NIGHTSONG

AN HISTORICAL NOVEL: THE NIGHTSONG SAGA, BOOK TWO

V. J. BANIS

THE BORGO PRESS

MMXII

I am deeply indebted to my friend, Heather, for all the help she has given me in getting these early works of mine reissued.

And I am grateful as well to Rob Reginald, for all his assistance and support.

CONTENTS

PART ONE

CHAPTER ONE

She was young and painfully beautiful, her sleek black hair flying behind her and her face—normally an opalescent tint of ochre—reddened to the blush of a peach from running.

"Is he here yet?" she cried, in a single gasp of breath as she burst into the tea shop.

The woman behind the counter wrestled with a tray of tea cakes shimmering behind a veil of steam. "I will be with you in a minute, please," she said.

"Ohhh!" It was a wail of anguish. "Su Lin!"

The tray slid neatly into a glass fronted case, and Su Lin looked up, mock surprise unable to hide a mischievous glint in her eyes.

"Ah, it is you," Su Lin said, smiling rather too broadly for mere workaday greeting.

"Hasn't he come?" the girl asked, alternating anxious glances at Grant Avenue outside, the main thoroughfare of San Francisco's Chinatown, with looks of desperate pleading, a frantic ransom flung down before Su Lin.

It was more than the tea shop owner could bear; the hand she brought to her mouth was inadequate to stifle an impertinent giggle.

"Is he here?" April demanded, finishing the question on an ascending squeal as Su Lin nodded and darted her eyes in the direction of the curtained doorway that led to the rear of the shop.

April dashed toward the doorway, but she paused just in front of it, for a final nervous glance at the street—even if she hadn't been followed, one never knew who might just wander by at an inopportune moment—before she went through the curtain.

"David," she cried. The young man had leapt up, rather too quickly, from the chair in which he had been seated. Its falling provided a crescendo to her cry as she threw herself into his arms.

"Darling," he sighed, when words were once again possible, "My darling April."

* * * * * * *

It was so difficult for them, these two young people in love, belonging to warring clans. "Like Romeo and Juliet," she was fond of saying, and he would smile a trifle sadly, because he knew she had never read the conclusion to that bittersweet tale, and because he sometimes feared the description might prove prophetic.

Their first meeting, mere chance, had been outside this very shop. After that, the meetings had been not merely by chance. Soon they had begun spending a part of nearly every afternoon together, with the connivance of Su Lin, whose husband would no doubt have beaten her for thus encouraging a romance between the lovely half-Chinese girl, and the handsome white youth whose clothes so determinedly proclaimed, "Nob Hill Wealth."

"A romance," he would have told her, had he the knowledge, and had he deigned to explain the beating, "inevitably to be as tragic as any literary mating."

For David MacNair, the inevitability had been written on that first day. From that time on, her image had been indelibly stamped upon his consciousness, so that no matter where he was nor what he was doing, *she* was always there, hovering just on the fringes of his thought—the almond shaped eyes, the skin like fresh sweet cream, the hands like delicate flowers.

He would remember for all his life—and longer, if the soul

existed—the first time he had met April Nightsong; he would remember too, but darkly, as the dark shapes are remembered when the light has proven them innocent, rushing home afterward to share the news of this, his life's most thrilling moment.

His mother had been in the hall when he'd burst into the house. He'd grabbed her about the waist and whirled her around.

"David," she gasped, disapproving because Mrs. Steinmetz was in the hall and had seen what was surely a vulgar display on his part. "What's gotten into you? You haven't been drinking, have you?"

David laughed and whirled her around again. "Oh, Mother, I am very drunk, but not on father's liquor."

"Really, David, I don't understand."

"The most wonderful thing, Mother," he cried, so happy that not even her habitual primness could dampen his spirits.

"David...."

"I have just met the girl I am going to marry!"

She gave him a cautious look. "And where, may I ask, did you meet this ravishing creature?"

"Outside a charming little tea shop in Chinatown."

His mother shook her head and turned away. "Well, just so long as you haven't gotten interested in a Chinese."

His mood plummeted. She'd given him a brutal reminder of the futility of his attraction. He wanted to cry out the truth about the Eurasian girl with whom he'd fallen immediately in love, but he was forced to hold back the happiness bursting like rockets inside him.

In San Francisco, in 1887, Orientals, no matter how exotic and alluring, were regarded as no better than the dirt in the alleys.

Though his mother had chided him afterward about his announcement, David became noncommittal, hiding his pain behind a cryptic smile, purposely cloaking the entire matter in boyish mystery. He had never been open with his parents, and though they liked it no more this time than before, they did not find his attitude unusual.

So the love April and David shared had become a private thing. They were aware of the disapproval of those strangers who saw them on the rare occasions when they strolled the streets of Chinatown hand in hand. David and April closed their ears to the jeers and insults of the more outspoken of those who passed them. They found all they needed of the world in each other's eyes.

Perhaps it was this ostracism that made David more adamant in his defiance of convention and strengthened his need to be with April, nurturing his attraction into a love so all-consuming he'd willingly give up his world for her happiness.

"Oh, David," April said as they talked in the rear of Su Lin's tea shop, "I am so miserable when we aren't together. Meeting like this in the afternoon isn't enough."

The differences in their cultures was a subject they both tactfully avoided; as if, April thought bitterly, it were an infirmity, though she did not voice the thought aloud.

"But you are not yet seventeen, April," David said, letting her name roll lovingly on his tongue. "Your mother would never permit you to go out in the evening without a chaperone, and especially not with me, chaperoned or not."

"I know." She let her shoulders droop dejectedly. "She won't ever let me do anything, except what she wants me to do. How I hate San Francisco. I hate America, I hate everything about it. I don't want to stay here, David. I want to go home to my own people in China where I belong, where I would be treated with the respect owed to the daughter of a Mandarin prince."

David frowned. She'd told him of her background, of how her mother had forced her to flee China and of her royal father, but David never understood any of it. Why had Mrs. Nightsong abandoned her husband and male child, left a life of palaces and luxury to bring her daughter to a land where she'd be despised and rejected?

"You are certainly beautiful enough to be a princess," David said. "I have never seen anyone more beautiful." He turned her toward him and took her in his arms. "I know I am being extremely forward, but I can't help myself, April. Every time I think about you I want to hold you, protect you, keep you safe forever and ever." He paused. "I've been thinking. I've decided that I am not going back to school next month. I'll never go back to school...ever. I don't care what my father says. We'll go away, somewhere where we can love each other openly without all this sneaking around and hiding in out of the way places, always afraid someone will see us."

"China," April said, her face glowing, her eyes dancing with excitement. "We could go to China."

David gave her a patient smile. "We would only be reversing roles. There, I would be the outcast." He saw her hurt and immediately hugged her close. "I'm sorry, April, I didn't mean to offend you."

"No, it's all right, David," she said easing away from him. "I am a half-caste." She shrugged. "As long as I live here in this terrible country I will always be looked upon as an undesirable." She looked up at him and her face brightened. "But home in China it would all be different. I was born in China and from the very beginning of my life I have been a Chinese, regardless of what my mother is. My amah insisted that I be brought up as a Chinese princess, much as my mother hated it. That is why the Dowager Empress is so angry with Mother for having taken me away, for having separated me from my royal father and brother."

She looked at him pleadingly. "I must go back, David. All the while I stay here I will be punished for having left Prince Ke Loo, my father, and worse still for having left China."

It all seemed so much longer than only six years ago when her father had taken them from their palace in Kalgan and brought them into The Forbidden City.

She'd been frightened in the Imperial Palace in Peking and it had been exciting for her to make the escape, though she never understood why her mother had left Prince Ke Loo.

April sighed as she leaned her head against David's chest. Once, what seemed an eternity ago in Kalgan, she had sat in her own little garden, dressed in a lovely soft kimono of flowered silk, and complained to her amah that nothing ever happened in her life.

As long as she remained away from her homeland, that magic kingdom of the Dowager Empress, she would be punished. She would never be able to escape the Dragon Empress. After all, wasn't the Empress called Celestial Goddess? And didn't she rule the world as well as the heavens, as the amah had told her often enough?

"Yes," April said in a tight, frightened voice. "I will be punished forever unless I do as the Empress wants and return to what I am and to where I belong."

David felt a pressure inside his head, like the welling up of a force so determined it made his eyes blur. He held April closer. "I don't know how, or even when, my darling," he said, "but one day I will take you home to where you will be happy."

"Where we will both be happy," she said, clinging to him. "My father will protect you, David. He is a very powerful man, a cousin to the Empress herself, and amah told me that Li Ahn, my little brother, is an heir to the throne. Oh, David, they would welcome us." She pressed closer. "When, David? When can we leave?"

"Soon, my darling. I will have to make arrangements, of course, and we will have to be sensible and make plans. We'll need money, and your mother...."

April looked up sharply, her eyes fearful. "We must never let Mother know we are even seeing each other, let alone planning to elope. I told you how much she hates your family. And you must not tell your father about us either, David. You haven't, have you?"

"No." He felt cowardly. "But darn it, April, you told me that Father knew you and liked you. Surely he'd not object to our being together."

"He'd try and stop us, just as Mother would. There's a feud between them. They'll do anything to spite each other. You and I marrying is the last thing they would approve of."

She turned reflective. "They knew each other in China, from what I gathered. It all has something to do with a scent mother stole from the Imperial Palace, the Empress's exclusive scent. When we were put ashore here in San Francisco, we had nothing but the clothes we were wearing, and the Empress's perfume. So Mother went into competition with your father's cosmetic firm. She wants to duplicate the perfume—*Nightsong,* she calls it— but so far none of the chemists have been successful."

"Your mother's firm seems to be doing all right," David said.

"Empress Cosmetics is making us wealthy—but there's something about that perfume—I don't think it's just the money, though mother says it will make us a fortune—I think it's something to do with your father, with outdoing him in some way."

"You're probably right about that. I heard him and mother talking the other day—or rather, shouting, as they usually do. She mentioned your mother's products, she said all the women were raving about them, and he said she didn't have to remind him, that he knew his P.M. Cosmetics was second rate and had little hope of being anything else but second rate. He said he had to have *Nightsong.*" David looked embarrassed. "I thought at the time that it was some kind of magic formula."

April squeezed his hand. "It is, if it can be duplicated. When we were in The Forbidden City, Mother took care of the Empress's personal creams and scents and powders. It was forbidden for anyone but the Empress to wear them."

"And your mother took them?"

April nodded. "She would have been executed if the Empress had caught her." April's mouth turned down. "Of course, Mother isn't Chinese. She doesn't understand the importance of such things. She deserves to be punished."

"Hush, April. You shouldn't say such things about your mother."

"Why not?" April said, looking petulant. "She's treated me horribly all of my life." She felt a sudden stinging behind her eyes. "Because of her I was forced to stay in a terrible place where the Chinese smoked opium, and I was locked in my cabin all during the voyage from China, because of her. And when we lived with her Uncle Richard they were both so mean and cruel, always making me work and study." She turned her eyes up to his. "I told you how she let everyone think I was her servant because she was ashamed of me."

"Surely she had her reasons?"

April stamped her foot. "How dare you take her part, David MacNair!"

She let the tears come and fought against his efforts to take her in his arms, but after a minute she collapsed against him.

"I am not trying to excuse what your mother did to you, my darling. I am sorry if I've upset you. Only...."

"Only what?" April sobbed, searching for the handkerchief in his breast pocket. "She's selfish and mean and contemptible. All she cares about is her silly cosmetics company and men."

"April, don't say that!"

"Well, it's true. She ran away from my father and took up with Mr. Bates, which was why they kept us away from all the other passengers on the boat. Then, when we came here, she met that rich Mr. Hanover."

David's eyes widened. "Walter Hanover? The one who lives near us on Nob Hill?"

"Yes. Mr. Hanover moved us out of my Uncle Richard's and set Mother up financially. There was some kind of disagreement about money, I think; then my mother met your father and seduced *him.*"

"April!"

She was too angry and hurt to be stopped and she resented David's taking her mother's part. "It's true," she said again, more petulantly. She wiped her eyes and softly blew her nose. "I know because I heard your father in her room one night. He stayed with her until it was light. I stood at my window and saw him leave." A new flood of tears streamed down her cheeks. "Oh, David, please take me away from here."

"Yes, April," he said, recovering. "Of course I will. We'll start making plans right away."

* * * * * *

That night April prayed, but not to the incomprehensible god that her mother had spoken of to her, nor to the gods of China where wisdom was honored more than saintliness. No, she prayed to a woman she'd never met. She prayed to the Dowager Empress.

"I will come back," she promised silently. "I will remain your subject and I will return to China and to you...to my homeland."

CHAPTER TWO

Lydia Nightsong saw her daughter leave the house and hurry down the hill, hair swinging freely. She knew April hadn't told the entire truth when she said she spent her afternoons with Kim Lee, the old tutor who lived over the bake shop. Lydia had run into the old Chinese one morning and had playfully admonished him for indulging her daughter with all his romantic tales of China. The old man hadn't understood, saying he hadn't seen April in several weeks.

In one way Lydia was relieved that April wasn't spending all her time with Kim Lee. The old tutor lived with too many fantasies, embroidered too many Utopian tapestries of the China he dreamed of returning to one day, a China that no longer existed. It was wrong to fill the young girl's head with romantic pictures, clouding her eyes to the truth. The China Lydia knew was a hard, cruel place where people groveled at the feet of the rich and where killing, cruelty and torture were traditions. They were an enigmatic race who would gladly lay down their lives to give honor to a friend, and on the other hand just as willingly feed a newly born infant to the dogs if it happened to be a female child.

She knew; she'd seen all the pagan horrors with her own eyes, horrors she tried so hard to keep from April. Now, however, Lydia thought perhaps she should not have protected the girl from all those terrors. Perhaps if April had seen what Lydia herself had seen, things would be different now and April would be more content with her life.

Lydia could understand a little of April's unhappiness. It was far from easy being even part Chinese in San Francisco, where oriental labor was bought for a penny and where their number and reputation made the Caucasian population uneasy, an uneasiness that grew into prejudice and distrust, ultimately to hatred. April was extremely beautiful; yet in spite of her loveliness, she could not hide the fact that she was part Chinese, and bigotry invariably trumps beauty.

Lydia turned from the window and drew on her gloves. If April weren't visiting old Kim Lee in the afternoons, then where was she spending her time? Her daughter, surly and resentful for so long, had actually been pleasant of late. Almost friendly, Lydia thought as she tucked the papers she'd been studying into her reticule.

Well, she couldn't think of April now. There was too much to be done. Empress Cosmetics was operating again. This time it was her own money that was financing it and she was making a handsome profit. For the first time in her life she was learning how it felt to be rich, to not have to worry about money. Those earlier years as a missionary's daughter in China, hard as they had been, had been a comfort when compared to some of what she had endured since.

"The carriage is here," the housekeeper said, breaking into Lydia's memories.

"Thank you, Nellie."

She would be glad to be rid of her memories, Lydia told herself as she tied her light half-cape about her shoulders and started out of the salon with its lead glass windows and its perfect view of the city from atop Nob Hill.

Outside the air was hot and damp from the previous night's fog. A summer sky of delphinium blue hung over the harbor where *Balclutha,* the three-masted sailing ship, was laying at anchor after having just completed another trip around Cape Horn. When it sailed again, it would be carrying cases of her latest beauty creams en route to her new markets in the south while the new railroads carried her Empress Cosmetics to the north and east.

A trolley clanged as the carriage started down the hill, making the horse whinny and grow skittish. The wheels sank into the trolley track grooves, making the carriage lurch sideways before correcting itself. Lydia gripped the arm rest to steady herself. She felt a familiar pang as she passed a large three storied house with tiers of leaded windows and gingerbread trim. There were several such mansions on Nob Hill but this one was particularly unwelcome to her eyes, though she found she could never keep from looking at it.

She never wanted to see Peter MacNair again and why she'd purchased a mansion within a stone's throw of his she did not know. Of course Nob Hill was convenient and it did represent the epitome of success and respectability, a respectability she had coveted greatly. Why should she have to feel intimidated and live elsewhere simply because the MacNairs had their mansion on Nob Hill?

Lydia drew back in her seat as the front door of the MacNair house opened and Peter MacNair stepped out into the bright of the day. He was as handsome as ever, so tall and muscular, with sandy brown hair that spilled carelessly over his forehead. She watched until he'd brushed back his hair and clamped his hat on his head before dropping the curtain back into place. She could close her eyes and picture how his dark brown eyes turned black when he scowled and the way they smoldered with passion when he looked at her.

She would never allow him to look at her in that way again, she vowed, as she felt the familiar need stirring deep inside her. She had made her success, she had built her fortune, but the price had been high. She'd lavished all of her love on April, a daughter who did not seem to notice or appreciate it. She had a son, too, however, still in China. Perhaps one day, now that she had the money to afford it, she would return to China and bring home the child she'd been forced to abandon. Perhaps he would be more appreciative of his mother's generosity.

The carriage drew up in front of the gleaming white and

pink marble facade of Empress Cosmetics. Lydia found herself wondering if it had all been worth it. Yes, she said to herself, quickly and with determination, thrusting any doubts from her mind and climbing down from the carriage.

The interior of Empress Cosmetics was as luxurious and impressive as its outside, all mahogany and leather, hand carved paneling and rugs so thick they deadened even the heaviest footsteps. Muted Tiffany shades softened the light of the desk lamps, giving the impression that one had walked from harsh reality into a world of make-believe merely by entering the offices.

"You're late," Mrs. Clary said good-naturedly. "Morris has been biting his nails." She helped Lydia off with her cloak and followed her into her private office.

"Sorry, Evelyn. I spent the better part of the morning going over those new proposals from New York. Did you have a chance to check on what the railroad would charge for shipping that many cases?"

"Too much," Mrs. Clary said as she laid her report on Lydia's massive desk. "It's bad enough that they overcharge their customers, but when they find that the customer is a woman, the price goes higher."

Lydia bit down on her lower lip and tugged at a stray curl of red gold that had managed to get loose from its pin. "I found when I began this venture that the world of business is not very tolerant of female executives. You should know that by now, Evelyn."

"It isn't fair."

Lydia picked up the report and frowned at the high cost figures. "Nothing is fair, Evelyn, but thank goodness we can afford to pay their blackmail. Tell Shipping to send the Marshall Field order by Pacific Rail. I've already told them I want the Wanamaker shipment to go by boat. The *Balclutha* will take it tomorrow." She threw down the report. "Now, what's Morris biting his nails about?"

"The *Nez!*"

Lydia gaped at her. When she recovered from the surprise she said, "He found one?"

"From Paris, supposedly. He wouldn't tell me anything except that. From the look of him, he's ready to jump out of his skin with excitement."

"Tell Morris to come in. You'd better sit in too, Evelyn. If he's found a true *Nez*, we'll have cause to celebrate."

A *Nez*. It wasn't a particularly attractive title for a man with such unique talents—at least she wouldn't take too kindly to people referring to her as a "Nose." But in the cosmetic business, a *Nez* was as rare as peonies in winter and the most valuable asset a perfume manufacturer could have. He was the equivalent of a taster in a scotch distillery. A truly fine Nez—and there were only a handful in the entire world—could not only tell, by sniffing, which blossoms a perfume contained, but how many blossoms, when the flower was grown, when harvested, and the composition of the soil in which it was grown.

It took true genius to be a *Nez,* and Lydia had to remind herself not to become too anxious or expect too much. They had searched for a long time for someone who could duplicate the Empress's perfume. Was it possible that the search was ended, that Morris had finally located the man?

Morris Hurley, Lydia's head chemist, was a little man, lean and spare. His sandy hair had gone thin, so he wore it very long on the side and brushed carefully across his large bald spot. He had pale eyes that were watery with excitement as he hurried into Lydia's private office.

"Well?" Lydia said when Mrs. Clary had closed the door.

Morris put his fingertips on the top of the desk and leaned forward on the tips of his toes. He looked as if he were fighting to keep himself from pouncing on her with joy. "His name is Andrieux. Raymond Andrieux," he said, badly imitating the French pronunciation. "I've checked and he's the very best, Mrs. Nightsong. He'll come high, but from all evidence, he's worth whatever the cost."

Lydia's eyes narrowed suspiciously. "If he's so good, why is he so available?" she asked.

"Ah, but that's the rub," the chemist said. "He isn't exactly available. Let's say he is unhappy where he is."

"Which is where?"

Morris glanced at Evelyn Clary, then at Lydia. "I don't know if you are going to like this, Mrs. Nightsong, but he's with P.M. Cosmetics."

"Peter MacNair?" Lydia groaned. "I should have suspected he'd be involved in some way. Why is it every time I turn around that man is standing in my way?"

Mrs. Clary said, "Perhaps because he enjoys placing himself there." She gave Lydia a knowing grin. "He certainly has spent a great deal of his time trying to speak with you, Lydia. I remember...."

"That will do, Evelyn."

Lydia remembered without any help how persistent Peter had been when she had been almost destitute and laden under debts she thought she'd never be able to pay. Peter's attentions, she'd learned, were not for her; they were for what she'd taken out of China. She could close her eyes and still feel the cat that brushed against her, frightening her half to death that dark, horrible night when she'd stolen into the Dragon Empress's vault and taken her personal perfume, a perfume created exclusively for the dowager's imperial use. Peter MacNair knew as well as Lydia that whoever succeeded in duplicating that fragrance would corner every perfume market in the world.

"Nightsong," she mused, as she turned back toward the windows. That was the name she intended to give the duplicate perfume when it was marketed, a name she'd chosen for herself when she'd immigrated.

She frowned as it occurred to her that even the name she'd chosen—Nightsong—had originated with Peter MacNair. That night in Peter's hut, when he'd made her get out of her wet clothes and dressed her in a silk robe, was suddenly clearly etched at the backs of her eyes. She could see the wall of his rough bedroom where some artist, centuries before, had done a painting—a branch of a plum tree in full blossom and a bird on a branch, singing to the slightly curved rim of the moon as it started to rise above the horizon. It was little more than a few deft strokes of the brush, really, in the manner of the Chinese artists, and yet it seemed to capture the scene in all its eloquence. Lydia remembered, too, vividly gazing at the exquisite painting and fancied that she had only to listen to hear the nightingale's song to the moon, that she could actually catch the fragrant scent of the pale blossoms.

"I call it *Nightsong*," Peter MacNair had said, coming to stand behind her. Taking hold of her....

With a shiver she threw off the memory of that night, not really knowing whether the shiver was one of pain or pleasure.

Nightsong. It had given her so much trouble, it had caused deaths and on more than one occasion attempts on her own life and the life of her daughter. The Empress had never forgotten her transgression and Lydia knew that even today that evil woman still wanted her dead. And all because of a perfume, a perfume that seemed to be cursed, as if within its haunting fragrance lay some power for evil, the blossoms of some dark flower as destructive as it was intoxicating. Perhaps that was the secret of its desirability.

For a brief moment she was tempted to turn and tell Morris to forget this *Nez,* this Raymond Andrieux, to let him stay with Peter MacNair's company. But that would be foolish, she told herself. In one devious way or another Peter would succeed in getting the perfume away from her. If Raymond Andrieux was the only man capable of duplicating it, then he had to be on her side, in her employ.

"When do I meet this Monsieur Andrieux?" she asked, turning to Morris.

"Perhaps dinner together. I could arrange...."

"No," Lydia said, cutting him off. "This is a business matter not a social one. And I think the fewer people who see us together, under the circumstances, the better. You're sure you've checked him thoroughly?"

"Thoroughly," Morris assured her.

"Then arrange for him to come to my home late Thursday morning when I know most of the business people on Nob Hill will be in their offices."

* * * * * * *

Raymond Andrieux came as a complete surprise. He was an extremely good-looking man, tall and young and well-built, with deep green eyes, chiseled features of perfect proportions and a wide, agreeable smile. Like so many Frenchmen, Raymond had a thick head of deep black hair that waved down across his forehead. He had a sensual look about him. His masculinity was overpowering, yet it was toned by smooth delicate olive skin and graceful eyebrows as dark as his hair.

His eyes laughed when he took Lydia's hand and touched it to his lips. *"Enchanté, Madame."*

He was as charming as he was handsome, Lydia noted after chatting for half an hour. She liked his friendly nature. She admired his self-assurance. She didn't think him callous or brazen, but she was certain he was the type of man who did whatever he set out to do, regardless of who got hurt in the bargain. She was not sure she liked that, but she respected it.

"And your obligations to Mr. MacNair?" Lydia asked.

Raymond shrugged. "But what obligations, Madame Nightsong? There are none. I feel he brought me to America under false pretenses."

"False pretenses?"

"He represented to me that he had a scent that was incapable of diagnosis, a scent he claimed would revolutionize the perfume industry. Unfortunately, he has nothing but ordinary essences that are, forgive my bluntness, commonplace, *très de deuxième qualité,* very second rate."

Lydia hesitated, then got up. "If you'll excuse me a moment, Monsieur Andrieux, I have something that may interest you." She started out of the room just as April appeared in the doorway.

April said, "Oh, I'm sorry, Mother, I didn't know you had company."

"April," Lydia said, smiling as she turned to Raymond. "My daughter, Monsieur Andrieux."

"Mademoiselle," he said, letting his eyes move slowly over this ravishingly beautiful young woman.

He looked at her in a way that made April frown. It was as if he were thinking impure thoughts as he undressed her with his eyes. She blushed and managed, "How do you do." Even the touch of his lips on her hand made her want to pull back.

Raymond smiled at Lydia. "Very beautiful," he said. "So like her mother. But I must confess it is difficult to believe that you are mother and daughter."

April didn't care much for the fake smile. And she hardly looked anything like her mother. There was something false about the man, she decided, as she turned to her mother. "I was just going out."

"Very well, but try to be home early. I'm not going into the office today. Perhaps you'd like to go to the theatre this evening. Bernhardt is appearing as Camille at the California Theatre."

Raymond said, "Magnificent performance. You will not regret seeing it."

April said, "We'll see. I must hurry, Mother. Very nice meeting you, Monsieur." She let him kiss her hand again but disliked it intensely.

"Charming girl. Charming."

There was something disturbing about the way he hooded his eyes as he looked after April. "Well," Lydia said when they were alone, "excuse me, please. I'll only be a moment."

She removed the small vial that she'd guarded all these many years, the bottle that contained the essence made especially for the Dowager Empress of China. Lydia uncapped it as seldom as possible for fear its intoxicating aroma would gradually vanish.

When she handed the vial to Raymond he looked questioningly at the tiny bottle. "Oriental. Chinese to be precise. Sung Dynasty, I would say." He carefully lifted the stopper and sniffed. His brows knit together as he studied the aroma. He smelled it again and gradually his face began to light up.

"Magnificent," he breathed. He smelled it again briefly before he recapped the vial. "But the essence is definitely not Sung Dynasty. Very new. It was concocted no more than ten years ago, perhaps less."

"Do you think you could duplicate it?" Lydia asked, trying not to appear too anxious.

Raymond shrugged. "It is possible. Unfortunately, the oriental blossoms are sometimes difficult to identify. It's a question of how the essential oils were extracted and distilled. On first guess, I would say that what we call the *enfleurage* method was employed, but it is merely a guess. I would need a laboratory to find out for certain."

Lydia beamed as she took away the vial. "I have whatever you will need, Monsieur Andrieux," she said. "And, I'm familiar with the Chinese method of *enfleurage.*"

He let a sly twinkle spark his eye. "If we are to be working together, perhaps you would honor me by calling me Raymond." He reached for her hand.

"Raymond," she said, feeling a slight tremor run through her as his lips touched her skin. "And you don't think Mr. MacNair will prove a problem?"

"As I said, Madame, I am not interested in the MacNair products, while with you I find myself surrounded by magnificent temptations."

She was not altogether displeased with his flirtatious manner. It had been a long time since she'd appreciated a man looking at her the way Raymond Andrieux was. "If you don't have to rush off, perhaps you'd care to stay for lunch, Monsieur...."

He raised a warning finger.

"Raymond," she said with a laugh.

"I'd be delighted."

"I'll put this away if you'll excuse me," she said, clasping the vial.

She was so elated she scarcely felt the floor under her feet.

She was certain he'd be able to duplicate *Nightsong* and from then on there would be no limit to what she could do.

As she replaced the vial in the safe she kept telling herself that Raymond had to reproduce the essence...he just had to.

When she turned to leave the room Raymond Andrieux was standing blocking the doorway.

"I am sorry," he said. "I was looking for some place to wash my hands."

Lydia felt suddenly nervous, yet she could not deny that a part of her was flattered. "Yes, of course," she stammered. "It is the second door down that hallway."

He didn't move.

There was no mistaking the look in his eyes. She'd seen it before in other men's eyes.

"We haven't discussed pay," Raymond said with an immodest smile.

"I doubt if that will be a problem. My company turns a very nice profit. I am sure we can agree upon a figure."

He eyed her brazenly and she found herself enjoying their little game. Raymond said, "Of course money is of importance but there are other things."

He took a step toward her. "I would be very reluctant to even consider analyzing the perfume without some kind of an understanding." His smile was intoxicating. "I have the exceptional talent of remembering a fragrance once I've inhaled it. It sticks inside my head. I have difficulty getting rid of it until I've copied it."

Lydia felt a sudden tightness around her heart. "You mean...?"

He nodded. "The talent is not unusual for a true *Nez.*"

With a faint smile she said, "Are you blackmailing me, Monsieur?"

Raymond chuckled. "Of course. My price will be high."

"And if I don't meet your price, you'll reproduce the scent for Peter MacNair."

He shrugged. "Possibly."

Raymond simply extended his hand to her and instinctively

she reached for it. A moment later, without her knowing quite how it happened, he was holding her hard against his chest. He felt the warmth of her breath on his cheek and when he turned her face to his, he tasted the sensual loveliness of her mouth.

"You're trembling," he murmured.

"I can't help it. This isn't exactly what I'd planned for our first meeting." She tried to laugh but the moment was too important for levity.

"Ravishing," he whispered as he kissed her hair, her throat, her eyes.

The intensity of her reaction startled her and she could feel it invoking a response in Raymond as he pulled her tighter against him and pressed his body harder against hers. Her lips parted, perhaps to protest, but in the next instant she was lost to him. She seemed to have lost her senses to everything else about her, even to where they were standing, and yet she was acutely aware of everything about this handsome Frenchman.

She felt his hardness, the pulsing of his need for her as it pressed against her thigh. Suddenly a flash of memory blinded her—she saw Peter MacNair standing naked before her in a Chinese hut. He seemed to be beckoning to her, smiling encouragingly as she felt his hot, wet lips kissing her mouth, her face.

Like lightning shattering the dark, suddenly it appeared to her as if all the secrets, all the wonderments were made clear and all problems resolved.

Raymond moaned softly as he took his mouth from hers, bringing her back to the moment. "Forgive me, Lydia, I cannot help myself. You have blinded me to all reason," he whispered, more to himself than to her.

Yes, she thought. Pray God forgive us both, for she knew that he was no more to blame than she. Some strange need was drawing them together, changing his hair to brown, his face to Peter's face. Her body longed for his body as some suffocating sweetness robbed her of all rationality.

She moved away from him slightly, keeping her eyelids lowered. As she undressed she didn't want to look at him; she knew that this was not Peter MacNair. Suddenly she bit her lower lip. She didn't want it to be Peter MacNair. She looked up sharply and stared into Raymond's handsome face. Wantonly she stepped out of her clothes and opened her arms to him.

A moment later naked flesh pressed hotly against naked flesh and Lydia whimpered with an almost delirious delight as Raymond's hands moved down her back, tracing the curve of her spine, outlining the fullness of her hips, her buttocks and still lower. He lifted her into his arms and carried her to the bed. As he lowered himself on top of her Lydia felt his breath, urgent and hot with passion and desire.

He ravaged her with his lips and tongue as she moaned softly and writhed against him. His hands fondled and cupped her breasts as he sucked the pouting nipples between his teeth, nipping them, causing tiny sparks to course through her.

She loved the feel of his firmness, his strength, the mat of hair on his chest as he made hot, passionate love first to one breast then to the other. A moment later he moved downward, easing apart her thighs as he rained kisses on her middle, igniting her like a torch as he manipulated her from one height to another.

When she felt the first scorching touch of his lips against the center of her being she was sure the world had stopped its rotation and that all life had ceased to be. He made love to her, first gently, tenderly, then pressing deeper, deeper, urgently, demanding. She knew it would be impossible for her to deny him anything.

Wave after wave of delicious pleasure washed over her as the almost forgotten ecstasy of sexual passion blotted out everything but the sensuous delights of physical love. There was a strangely sweet aching inside her that was gradually increasing in its intensity. An instant later something far deep in her soul exploded like a huge skyrocket and she felt herself flying off into space, leaving everything mortal behind.

Slowly she returned to the living and felt the tangle of bedclothes beneath her. She clung to him weakly, blissfully grateful for the fantastic pleasure that he'd given her. She sighed a deep sigh of relaxation and opened her eyes.

It took a moment or two before his face came into focus. A tiny gasp caught in her throat as she turned her head on the pillow. She felt the stinging at the backs of her eyes as the pangs of disappointment wracked her brain. She shut her eyes and silently spoke his name.

"Peter."

CHAPTER THREE

"No, April," David said as they walked along the low lying coastline. It was mid-afternoon and despite the fact that the sun had stayed stubbornly behind the bank of clouds, the day was warm. "I've been giving it a lot of thought all week and I seriously think the right thing to do is for us to go to your mother. I've tried approaching the matter with Father but we never could communicate. He's too busy to listen to me and Mother is visiting in Los Angeles."

"My mother doesn't care what we do," April complained. "She has a new employee, a man she is spending all her time with, Raymond Andrieux. He's French," she said, making a face.

David shook his head. "I still think we would be making a mistake by eloping to China."

"You don't love me," she pouted.

"You know that isn't true. As much as I want to marry you and travel to your father's home in Kalgan, I think I should at least meet your mother."

"She'd never permit us to run away together. She hates your father. You're the last person she'd want me to marry."

"I am *not* my father," he said stubbornly. "Once she gets to know me I know I can get her to like me."

April's disappointment made her petulant. "I suppose all women swoon at your feet."

"Stop, April. You're behaving like a child."

"Me?" she cried. "You're the child, afraid to do anything

without mama's consent."

He stepped in front of her and put his hands on her shoulders. As usual, he felt a sort of shattering turmoil that affected every inch of him each time he looked deep into her lovely eyes. "We're arguing," he said giving her a gentle smile. "It's our first."

April threw herself into his arms. "Oh, David, why do we have to have other people in our lives? Why weren't we born alone on a deserted island where we'd have only each other?"

He chuckled softly at her naiveté. "That sounds wonderful, but hardly realistic."

"Why do we have to be realistic? Why can't everyone leave us alone?"

"Because people weren't meant to be left alone." He held her quietly for a moment. "Come on, let's go to your house and you can introduce me to your mother." He saw her fear and added, "It's only fair that she meet the man you are to marry, April. That way she won't have to face a stranger when we bring her grandchildren to her."

April smiled at first, then laughed. She took his hand and started to run toward the hill.

They found her mother sitting at the writing desk in the morning room. Lydia was engrossed in a letter and did not look up when they came to the doorway.

"Mother," April said, her voice tight. "I'd like you to meet someone."

Lydia stopped writing and raised her head. When she saw the handsome young man standing so tall and straight beside her daughter her breath caught in her throat. For a moment she thought she recognized Peter MacNair as she had seen him so many years before.

"Mother," April said nervously, leading him into the glass-paneled room. "This is David."

"How do you do, David," Lydia said as she stood up and put out her hand to him. Even when their hands touched and she had a clear view of his face, she could not rid herself of the uneasy feeling that stirred inside her.

"I am very pleased to meet you, Mrs. Nightsong. April talks about you all the time."

"Oh? You have known April for some time then?"

"Since the beginning of the summer. We met in Chinatown."

"I see."

An awkward silence followed.

David cleared his throat and said, "I'm fond of April, Mrs. Nightsong. Extremely fond."

"As am I," Lydia said with a charming smile.

David swallowed hard and said, "We would like to consider ourselves engaged to be married."

Lydia's smile slowly disappeared. "I see." She motioned toward the adjoining sitting room and moved toward it. "You realize, of course, Mr...."

"MacNair. David MacNair."

"Mr. MacNair, that April...." Her voice stopped. "MacNair?" she said, whirling around to face him. "Peter MacNair's son?"

"Yes," David admitted.

"How dare you!" She glowered at April. "How could you encourage him knowing...."

"But I didn't know," April argued. "Not at first. And then when I learned, it didn't seem to make any difference."

Quickly David put in, "And it doesn't matter, Mrs. Nightsong. April told me that you were not particularly fond of my father, but that's something between you and him. I'm concerned about my life and that life includes April."

"It most assuredly does *not* include April, young man, nor will it ever! Now kindly leave this house and you are never to see each other again. Is that understood?"

April clenched her fists and stood up to her. "No, that is not understood. I love David, and he loves me. All my life I've had to do what you want me to do. Well, I'm not going to anymore." She grasped David's hand. "David and I are going to be married whether you approve or not."

Lydia stood with her spine stretched straight and taut, every nerve in her body tingling. She folded her hands in front of her and turning to David, said as calmly as she could, "My daughter is sixteen; you are not much older. I am certain your father would not condone this marriage any more than I do. If you are wise, young man, you will leave this house and put all of this nonsense out of your head." She knew she was being cruel, but it was for April's own good. A marriage into the MacNair household was unthinkable on both sides.

"As you can see for yourself," Lydia said, speaking slowly and deliberately, "April is a Eurasian and as such is very susceptible to the attentions of those who are not."

"Mother," April gasped.

"Now kindly leave, Mr. MacNair. I suggest you go home and forget you ever met us. I intend to do everything possible for April to do the same."

David and April looked helplessly at one another.

"Go!" Lydia ordered, pointing to the door.

He started away. April clung to his hand. "David," she cried.

As he hugged her to him he whispered, "I'll be waiting at the tea shop tomorrow." He gave Lydia a cold nod and walked out of the house.

April collapsed into tears and fled up the stairs.

* * * * * * *

Peter MacNair was blazing with anger when he burst into Lydia's offices at Empress Cosmetics. Evelyn Clary jumped up from her desk and tried to block the door to Lydia's private office, but Peter put his hands on her waist and lifted her easily out of the way.

"I know she's in and I intend seeing her," he said. He shoved open the heavy oak door and stormed into the office.

Lydia looked up sharply. When she saw who it was she threw aside the pen in her hand and said, "How dare you barge in here? Get out!"

"Not until I've given you a good piece of my mind," Peter

stormed.

Lydia picked up a book and threw it at him. "Get out of here." The book almost hit Evelyn Clary who had come up behind Peter.

"I'm sorry," Evelyn said. "I tried to keep him out."

Peter grabbed Evelyn's arm, turned her around and hurried her through the door, slamming it behind her.

Lydia had almost forgotten how handsome he was, now that she was seeing him up close again. Even his good-looking son paled in comparison. There were tiny age lines at the corners of Peter's eyes and his face had a more worn look, but it only accentuated the flecks of rust in his eyes and the sandy brown hair that spilled over his forehead.

"Will you please leave?" Lydia ordered. "We have nothing to say to one another."

"Like hell we haven't." He leaned on her desk, putting his face close to hers. She found his nearness unnerving but she held herself firm. She was sure she knew why he'd come. Knowing him, he'd use any excuse to see her, even the unhappiness of his son.

"How in the devil did you get to Andrieux?" he demanded.

Her eyes widened in surprise. She had been sure Peter had come about David and April.

"Get to him?" she said innocently. "I don't know what you mean."

"You know perfectly well that I brought Raymond Andrieux here to work for P.M. Cosmetics."

"My dear Mr. MacNair," Lydia said imperiously. "I cannot be held accountable for any ex-employee of yours who finds himself dissatisfied with his employer and asks for employment elsewhere."

"Did he duplicate the Empress's perfume?"

"Nightsong." Lydia gloated and said no more, leaving Peter to draw whatever conclusion he wished.

She felt wonderful. For years she'd wanted this moment when things were turned around and she held him at a disadvantage.

Too often she'd been subjected to his villainy, his cruelties; now, she could understand the pleasure it must have given him to see her suffer.

A quickening of her pulse began as she thought of what would happen if he were again to take his revenge upon her. She recalled the brute strength of him when he made love to her, the animal prowess of his body, the ferocity of his passions, the marks his hands left on her skin as he held her hard on the bed.

"Then he's already duplicated it?" Peter demanded.

But unlike Peter's, Lydia's joy in seeing him suffer began to fade. "No." Was it possible, she wondered, for a woman to despise a man and want him at the same time?

Peter's expression softened as he straightened. "You know, Lydia, instead of fighting each other we should join sides."

"And with my perfume, become the biggest cosmeticians in the world," she finished.

He laughed and scratched the back of his neck. "Yes, something like that." He looked at her standing so tall and so lovely in the shaft of sunlight. "You are still the most ravishing woman I have ever seen, Lydia."

"And I still have *Nightsong* and intend to keep it exclusively for myself, so kindly save your Scottish flattery for your wife."

"You know perfectly well that I'd divorce Lorna tomorrow if you'd agree to marry me."

She gave a little toss of her head and settled a steady gaze on him. "I told myself a long, long time ago, Peter, that I would never again put myself in a position where I would have to accept the terms dictated to me by a man—any man."

"Any man?" Peter asked, pointedly. "Does that include Andrieux? From what I surmise, it wasn't exactly an increase in salary that lured him away from my company." The minute the words were out he was sorry. It always ended like this between them, bitter words, accusations, insults, threats.

"What do you mean?" she demanded.

"You know perfectly well what I'm talking about. Dinner almost every night at Claridge's, the opera, that opening at the

California Theatre on Bush Street, even taking in the vaudeville show at the Emporium."

Lydia gasped. "You've been spying on me."

"Oh, don't flatter yourself," he said, but it was true. He had hired that odious detective, Ramsey, when Andrieux packed up and left with little or no explanation. "People talk. You haven't been exactly discreet."

"You should talk of discretion," she charged. "I have no apologies for taking on Raymond, especially when I found out you hired him just to keep him away from my company. My chemist found him in Paris originally and then Monsieur Andrieux disappeared mysteriously, I understand, only to reappear just as mysteriously at P.M. Cosmetics. You knew he was the only *Nez* capable of duplicating *Nightsong* and you tried to secret him away from me. You're contemptible."

He surprised her by laughing. "And what in hell did you expect me to do, take him by the hand and lead him to you?" He planted his feet firmly and said. "Look, Lydia, I know perfectly well that when *Nightsong* goes on the market you're going to make bushels of money, which means stiffer competition for me. I don't mind the competition so much as I mind what all that money is going to do to you."

"And what will it do to me?"

"You're a woman. You don't know how to handle a company as big as the one you'll wind up with. It takes a man to handle that kind of an operation."

"Too bad you aren't peddling egotism, you'd make a fortune."

"But it's true. Even if you do find yourself capable of running a huge corporation, what kind of reliable, self-respecting executives would work for a woman?"

"Raymond Andrieux doesn't seem to find working for a woman so demeaning."

"Not all of your key men are going to be interested in sleeping with you."

If he had been within reach she would have slapped his face. Her temper flared out of control. "Get out of here before I really tell you what I think of you." She was glad to see she had provoked a glaze of pain in his eyes, but it quickly disappeared. Peter MacNair was not the kind of man who showed he could be hurt.

"I know perfectly well what you think of me, Lydia, and all of it is wrong!"

Their eyes met and held. Peter looked at her, her skin like alabaster with a glow that seemed lighted from within, her eyes bold and flashing. Her figure was still superb, the waist tiny, the breasts and hips lusciously fuller and rounder, a feast for any man's eyes and something more as well.

He had a sudden urge to seize her in his arms, to tear the clothes from her lovely body and make wild, passionate love to her right here on the floor. It was an effort of will that restrained him from doing exactly that. He knew if he closed his eyes he would again see her naked, her long legs and arms spread wide, her ripe, full breasts trembling with the force of her breath.

But it wasn't only her beauty that he wanted. She had the Empress's perfume. He longed to possess them both, but thus far he had failed miserably. He clenched his fists as he told himself that he wasn't finished with her yet.

Still, it was not only her loveliness that made his blood race, there was something more, something deeper, more difficult to put his finger on. Despite her independence, despite the intelligence and courage she must have had in order to find her way out from under the all-seeing evil eye of the treacherous Dowager Empress, he found Lydia had a touching vulnerability that made him feel oddly as if he wanted to protect her, especially against unscrupulous men like himself.

Peter said, "What I told you about my behavior in China was the truth, Lydia, whether you want to believe it or not."

Their eyes held. He looked at her, wanting never to look away, afraid that this might well be the last time he'd ever look at her again.

With a great effort he unfixed his gaze, turned slowly and walked out of her office.

CHAPTER FOUR

Raymond Andrieux took off his sleeve guards and visor and got up from the stool beside the lab table. He picked up the Sung Dynasty vial and replaced it in the safe, smiling smugly to himself. A more unscrupulous man would have no compunctions about leaving the beautiful Lydia Nightsong and making his own fortune by reproducing her tantalizing perfume.

He had no such ambitions—yet. All his life he'd been lazy and it was much more interesting to spend other people's money than spend his own. Depleting one's own financial reserves only resulted in poverty, while depleting another's money gave him greater security.

He had been left a bit of money when his father died, but he was too selfish to touch any of it. Instead, he spent the funds belonging to his father's cosmetic firm, running it into ruin. It made little difference to Raymond because the company belonged to the estate executors, not to him, so what did he care about their money? It wasn't his fault that they had put him in charge in order to retain the family firm name.

Raymond had luck and courage and always prided himself on being clever. It didn't require much energy to be crafty; all he found necessary was a simple disregard for everyone else and a quick mind for opportunity.

He was not called *Le Nez* for nothing, either. Not only did he have a nose for scents, he had a nose for people as well, and especially for women. It was a talent he liked boasting about. He could tell if a woman had something weak in her makeup;

just by getting close to her he knew just what temptation she couldn't resist.

Lydia Nightsong was a determined woman whose purpose was to try and buy her daughter's affection. In the week or so that he'd spent with them he was quick to see April's dislike of her mother and Lydia's obsession with trying to impress her child with her success.

And there was something else about Lydia which he had yet to figure out. Raymond had known many women who wanted wealth because of the luxuries it provided; Lydia didn't seem to enjoy the affluence in which she lived. She wore handsome jewels but could afford better. She made do with a maid and a housekeeper when she could easily afford three times as many servants. So it wasn't a love of money that drove her, and it wasn't only her daughter she wanted to impress. There was some other underlying reason for this compulsion to duplicate *Nightsong* and Raymond was sure it wasn't the fortune it would make.

He glanced at the locked safe and then at the beaker resting on the laboratory table. He'd succeeded in copying the Empress's fragrance but he didn't intend telling Lydia just yet. There were a few things he had to find out about her and then there was the price to be settled upon. She'd promised him anything and money did not seem enough.

When they were finishing their coffee in Lydia's drawing room Raymond helped himself to a balloon of brandy and said, "I'm getting very near to the duplication."

Lydia's cup clattered on its saucer. "Oh, Raymond, how wonderful. When?"

"Very soon, I think." He carried his glass back to the velvet settee and settled himself across from her, stretching his long, trim legs out in front of him. He was disappointed when her eyes didn't move over him. He knew he was extremely handsome and woman constantly admired him. Yet, for all their secret love-making he always got the impression that Lydia was envisioning herself with someone else.

He felt annoyed when she lowered her eyes and got up to refill her coffee cup.

"We haven't agreed upon my price, you realize."

Lydia came back and sat down. "As I told you, Raymond, you have but to name a figure. It was agreed that I would pay you whatever you asked."

Her heart was pounding faster as she saw the way he was looking at her. She saw the lust in his eyes but all she could think about was that the scent would be duplicated. At last she was close to what she'd set out to accomplish, to have her revenge for what Peter MacNair had done to her in China. She'd make her great fortune and show him and the world that despite all the efforts to destroy her, she had bettered them all. With Raymond Andrieux's help she would have her triumph and whatever the cost, it would be worth it.

"I wasn't thinking in terms of money," Raymond said, watching her carefully.

Yes, he could even have her, Lydia told herself as she sipped her coffee. She didn't love him, of course, but she could not deny that he was the only man other than Peter MacNair to arouse her sexually.

Lydia raised her eyes to him. "A price does not always have to be money."

His slow, steady smile brightened his face. "You're a very curious woman, Lydia," he said.

"Oh? How so?"

He kept his gaze level. "Nothing seems to disturb you."

"Perhaps that is because I have had too many disruptions in my life already. I've learned how to deal with just about every situation."

"Toward what end?"

"I beg your pardon?"

Raymond sat forward. "What do you want, Lydia? Why are you so determined to succeed? You don't seem to really enjoy any of this," he said, motioning to the tasteful luxury of the drawing room.

Lydia looked wistful. "I have not had a very attractive past." She paused, not wanting to look back. "April has had a particularly difficult time of it. It's better now that Empress Cosmetics has begun making money. Still, even now I feel I could never make up to her all she's been made to suffer."

"No," Raymond said slowly. "I am a very intuitive man. There is something deeper, even deeper than April."

Lydia looked up sharply, then lowered her eyes just as quickly for fear he'd seen the truth in them. "April is my only reason for whatever I do."

"She's an exquisite creature," Raymond said softly.

Again Lydia looked up quickly. There was something unnerving in the way he had spoken.

He saw her questioning look and said, "I can understand why you would want to give her the world. She is a charming young lady."

"It has been hard for her, living here in San Francisco. There is a great dislike for Orientals. Her father was Chinese."

"I assumed as much. You never told me of your husband."

Lydia grew uneasy. "There isn't much to tell," she said evasively. "My parents were missionaries. They both died of cholera and I was left alone. A Mandarin prince, Ke Loo, took a fancy to me and we married."

"And is your husband dead?" he asked.

"My husband," she said, a bit too sharply, "is in China—and, I assure you, of little consequence in my life."

He made no reply, and she was embarrassed at having spoken so rudely. It was a subject on which she was more than a little sensitive. Why should her life be affected, after all, by a cruel Mandarin who lived in a palace thousands of miles away, a man she had always hated and feared? Too, she could not help a certain feeling of guilt for the son who had been left behind in China, now a prince in his own right, but more, far more to her than that.

Raymond got to his feet when April came into the room. She was dressed in yellow silk—the Imperial color of China. She looked cool and expensive, he thought, a prized China figurine, fragile and alive with brilliance.

April's appearance surprised Lydia. Since the angry scene after David left that day, she only saw April at meals, and even then the girl sat sullen and ill-tempered. Of late however, April seemed less hostile, as though she had resigned herself. Yet Lydia wasn't completely sure her diagnosis was right. There was a strange light in April's eyes and she had a conspiratorial air about her now that prompted Lydia to study her more closely.

Raymond said, "Have you changed your mind and decided to join us for coffee after all, April?"

April smiled charmingly. "I was finishing the book I started, but the ending depressed me so I thought I'd try and take my mind from it by joining you."

"And what book is that?" Lydia asked.

"Just a book," April said, dismissing her. "Tell me about Paris, Monsieur Andrieux. At dinner you mentioned a great fair which is planned."

"Ah, what a grand affair it will be. You must let me take you there."

Lydia said, "An exposition?"

"Yes. It will open in 1889." He gave her a cool smile. "Perhaps we can introduce *Nightsong* to all of Europe then."

She beamed in anticipation.

"France cannot possibly be as beautiful and enchanting as China," April said abruptly, spoiling Lydia's pleasure.

Raymond chuckled and said, "It would be disloyal of me to agree and impolite of me to argue. Let me just say that I would like to show you my beautiful country and let you decide for yourself."

"Only if you'll permit me to show you mine," April countered.

"But this is your country," Lydia reminded her gently.

Without a glance at her mother April said to Raymond, "I was born in China, you know. I believe one's homeland is the land where one was born."

Raymond shifted uncomfortably. "Let me tell you about the Paris exposition," he said, pointedly returning to safer ground. "They are right now building a steel tower that will be the tallest structure in all the world. Eiffel's tower, they call it, after the architect who designed it. It will have hydraulic elevators that will carry the people all the way to the very top, with places where you can eat and shop, observation platforms—even a weather station is planned. And the fair itself will surpass any other ever held, even your centennial when the telephone was introduced."

"It sounds very exciting," Lydia said, her earlier excitement having been cooled by April.

"It is in Paris at the exposition where we will have the Empress Cosmetic exhibit and introduce *Nightsong*. And we must create new creams and lotions and powders." He grew more serious and added, "You must begin thinking of expansion, Lydia. You will find you have outgrown San Francisco in the next year, even America. *Nightsong* will enrapture the whole world." He smiled at April. "It will even enchant your beloved China."

April's face clouded with anger. "The Empress will never permit her personal essence to be capitalized upon. She will kill whoever dares attempt it."

Lydia grew uneasy, remembering suddenly that what April said was much more than the ranting of a jealous child. More than once the Empress's long arm of revenge had stretched itself across the ocean that separated San Francisco from the Forbidden City in Peking.

"What April says is true, Raymond," she said aloud. "I suppose I should have mentioned it, but there have been attempts on my life...Chinese assassins obviously in the employ of the Dowager Empress. Your connection with her personal scent may have put your life in danger too."

Raymond laughed. "Oh, no, you don't, Lydia. You cannot scare me off now that I am so close to making us both a fortune. I have never been afraid of any woman's threats, not even those of an imperial dowager empress."

April said, "My Empress does not make idle threats, Monsieur Andrieux."

"Every woman makes idle threats, little one," he said tolerantly. "But then you yourselves are women and put importance on such things."

April felt her patience with him beginning to run out. She wondered if all Frenchmen were so egotistical and complacent. David wasn't like that. He understood when she talked of the mysterious powers and the omnipotence of her magnificent Dowager Empress.

"I'm going to bed," April announced. With an imperious toss of her hair she turned and walked out of the room in a swirl of yellow silk.

Ascending the stairs to her room, she shut her eyes and tried to put Raymond and her mother out of her mind. What did they matter now? Hadn't David given her his word that they'd be married soon and that he'd take her home to her father and to China?

Let them have their expositions and their steel towers and their dreams of money and success. David was making the final arrangements; she was to meet him tomorrow night and after that nothing her mother did would ever matter to her again.

* * * * * * *

Lorna MacNair's face was creased with agitation as she knocked impatiently on her son's bedroom door. When he didn't answer she knocked again and said, "You're not asleep, David, don't pretend to me that you are. I want to talk with you, so kindly open the door this instant."

She was about to knock again when she heard the latch being unclasped and the door opened. David stood looking sleepy as he pulled himself into his robe. "I was asleep," he insisted. "What time is it?"

"It isn't late and whether you were asleep or not makes no difference to me. I will have words with you, young man." She put the flat of her hand against the panel of the door and pushed it wide. "Sit down, David," she ordered, nodding to the leather tufted chair under the reading lamp.

She started to pace back and forth at the foot of his bed. Suddenly she stopped and whirled on him. "How dare you do this to me?"

David's eyes went wide as he stared up at her. He knew what she meant. One more day and he and April would be away. Why had she found out now? Where had he slipped up?

"What are you talking about, Mother?"

"Don't you dare anger me any more than I am by pretending ignorance," she warned him. "April Nightsong. You've been seeing her."

She knew, he could see it in her face. His only defense would be the truth—but it needn't be the whole truth, he told himself. "All right, so I've been seeing April, Mother, what's the harm in that? We meet sometimes in the afternoon."

"She's Chinese!"

"So?"

Lorna started pacing again, running her hands through her hair. "Good God, David, have you completely lost your senses? How can you possibly humiliate me this way by running around with such trash?"

He knew he was wrong to lose his temper but it was unavoidable. He would permit no one, not even his mother, to insult April. "Humiliate you?" he spat. "April is the finest, most decent girl I've ever met."

"She's Chinese, for God's sake!"

"I wonder, Mother, if it is so much that she's Chinese as that she is Lydia Nightsong's daughter."

Lorna turned abruptly, pulling off the spectacles she only wore in the privacy of her home. "What is that supposed to imply?"

"April told me all about her mother and my father."

"What about Peter and her mother?"

"Now it's my turn to warn you not to play the innocent,

Mother. When I first met April she didn't know who I was and when I told her we laughed about her having met Father. He used to come to their house on Van Ness to see her mother. She'd been too young to think, at the time, that they were anything but just friends. Then a man started watching her house. He even talked to her once, asked her questions about Father and how often he came to visit and whether he stayed all night."

"I forbid this!" Lorna said, the color draining from her face. She didn't want to think of the payment Mr. Ramsey had demanded of her for his reports. She put her hands over her ears. "All right, so your father was on more than friendly terms with Lydia Nightsong. That was over and finished long ago and it has nothing whatever to do with you and this Chinese girl. I forbid it, David! Do you hear me? I forbid it!"

One moment she stood as stiff as a rail, the next she wilted, like a flower hiding from the sun. "Oh, David," she said coming behind his chair and putting her arm protectively around his shoulders. "Why can't you be more like your sister and brother?"

"Susan's all business, just like father. And even at eleven, Efrem's still a boy. Which would you prefer I be like?" he asked sarcastically.

"At least they know what society expects of them."

"Society?" David scoffed. He stood up, feeling uncomfortable under the touch of her arm. She had never been particularly demonstrative and the falseness of it now made him uneasy. "Holy cow, Mother, this is 1887. The world is changing. A whole new century is coming up. A guy's got to be modern if he's going to get along."

"Paying court to a Chinese is not what I would consider being modern. Taboos will always be with us and a liaison between a Caucasian man and an oriental girl will always meet with disapproval from both sides. Her people will no more welcome you than we will welcome her."

He thought about the scene he'd had with Mrs. Nightsong. He knew it was useless to argue with these closed minds. What did they know about love? They were far too old to understand this blind, raging obsession he had for April. Every second he was away from her was torment.

Well, tomorrow night things would be different. They would be away where no one would ever find them and once they reached the protection of April's father's palace in Kalgan, they need never have to worry about anyone keeping them apart again.

"Very well, Mother," David said, feigning resignation. "If you forbid my seeing April ever again, there is very little I can do about it."

"Then you will stop seeing this girl?"

David shrugged. "What choice have I? I will see her tomorrow, of course. It would be the gentlemanly thing for me to do." He put on a beaten expression and hated himself for the sham.

Lorna smiled sadly and patted his head. "One day you will thank me for all of this, David." She went to the door and opened it. Before leaving she stood with her hand on the knob and looked back at him. His head was down, his shoulders slumped. Her heart went out to him; but it was all for the good, she told herself as she closed the door.

Outside, as she went toward her room a slow smile curved her lips. Lydia Nightsong hadn't gotten her husband and neither would she have her son.

She shivered slightly as she thought of the payment Mr. Ramsey would again expect of her for his information about David and the Chinese girl. With a deep sigh she squared her shoulders and told herself that it would be worth it.

"What was all the loud talk?" Peter asked when Lorna came into his bedroom. It had been a long time since they shared a bedroom and whenever Lorna came to him, which she did all too often, it lowered her even further in his esteem. To the world she was a tower of strength and of social decorum. To Peter, his wife was little better than a moneyed tramp. He knew full well that his appeal for her had always been physical. He had used that fact to his advantage—and still did—but it did nothing to increase his respect for either of them.

"A misunderstanding with David," she replied. "It's all straightened out."

She gave him a seductive smile, putting her spectacles on the nightstand. "I thought perhaps you would like some companionship," she said.

"Not tonight," he answered sharply. He threw back the coverlet and slipped into a robe. "I have some reports to do."

She watched her husband go out of the room. It was a blatantly masculine room, all leather and brass and mahogany so dark it was nearly black. Such a room could easily have overpowered a man, but it paled before Peter MacNair. The sight of him, his long legged stride, his splendid body, never ceased to stir up those tantalizingly sensual urges that churned inside her. Despite the coldness of her manner, Peter inevitably roused a desire within her, a desire she was often at pains to keep concealed until her natural demands grew unbearable.

Afterward, when she'd groveled at his feet, she would burn with shame at the memory of how she'd writhed and moaned and clawed like a common whore, like a woman enslaved by her husband's sexuality.

It disgusted her to think that she was so enslaved to his masculinity. She would have preferred to hate him without reservation. She knew he had bought her with his pounding loins and sexual endowments. And she'd willingly exchanged her father's wealth for the feel of Peter's naked, muscular body.

Socially he was beneath her, of course, and she seethed with scorn for him when he denied her as he just had. It gnawed at her when he turned to other women, which he did all too frequently, according to Mr. Ramsey's reports. It especially enraged her when he was with Lydia, whom she knew was more to Peter than she or any other woman could ever be.

Lorna sat looking at the closed door to the study. Her hunger for him filled her with both joy and despair. After several minutes she picked up her spectacles from the nightstand, gave them a hard push against the bridge of her nose and quickly returned to her own bedroom.

CHAPTER FIVE

April moved cautiously through the fog, clutching her shawl tight under her chin. She hated San Francisco with its damp, murky gloom that constantly crept over it from the ocean—the ocean that separated her from her beloved China, the homeland she wanted so desperately to see again.

Not too long ago, at the beginning of this now ending summer, China had been beyond her reach, far on the other side of the horizon; but David would take her there after they were married, and there they would live happily forever after.

The long rows of wooden buildings lining Market Street faded into the mist as she made her way toward the Embarcadero and the bay. Up ahead a light gleamed dully through the fog bank. It had to be the place where David said he'd be waiting. She quickened her steps.

"April!" David called at the sound of her footsteps. He rushed forward as she appeared out of the fog and gathered her lovingly into his arms. "My dearest," he whispered, touching his mouth to her hair, her eyes, her lips. He felt bold and safe in the swirl of mist that hid them from the disapproving eyes of outsiders who couldn't understand the depth of their love.

"David. Oh, David," April cried as she clung to him.

"It's all right now, darling. We will never be apart again. No one will separate us now." He smiled down into her lovely face and kissed her again to make sure she was real and not some exotic apparition that had drifted out of the mist. When he released her he noticed that she'd come empty-handed. "Your carry-all?" he asked anxiously. "You haven't...?"

She saw the fear in his eyes and said quickly, "I left it at the railway depot earlier. I was afraid Mother would catch me leaving the house with it tonight."

He took her in his arms again. "You gave me a fright. There for a moment I thought you'd come to tell me you'd changed your mind about eloping."

"I could never live without you, David, surely you must know that." She let him kiss her again, then gently eased him away and glanced around. "Someone will surely see us and think me one of those ladies from the Barbary Coast."

He laughed softly and kissed her again. "And how would you know about such places?"

A hurt expression clouded her loveliness. "I've been accused of being such a woman by passersby, people who taunted me, told me to go back there where I belong."

He held her close. "Let them say and think what they like. They shan't ever hurt you again, April. I'll see to that." He tightened his arms around her. "You're shivering," he said.

"Just excited, and a little chilled."

"Come inside. We can have some soup and then take the cable trolley to the depot to collect your reticule." As he led her toward the lighted tavern he said, "And before this night is done we will be husband and wife and on our way away from this terrible city. The sailing ship leaves at eleven o'clock. I have already arranged for the Captain to marry us when we board. He's expecting us within the hour." He dug into his coat pocket and produced travel permits and tickets. "Passage for Mr. and Mrs. David MacNair all confirmed for one-way portage to Shanghai."

"You're sure I'm not talking you into something you may one day regret?"

"As long as you are with me, April, I will never be sorry about anything."

"You won't miss your family?"

David shrugged as they moved toward the tavern. "I'll miss

them least of all. There's nothing here for me. My whole life is with you, April."

Several of the men sitting at the wooden tables that were strewn about the smoke-filled room looked up as David and April entered the tavern. April saw their looks of disapproval as she threw back the hood of her cloak. David ushered her to a table away from the bright lamps hanging from the central rafters.

He squeezed her hand. "This will all be behind us very, very soon."

The hot soup and beef pie filled the emptiness that had gnawed at her all day, but the greater part of that emptiness was filled by David's presence beside her.

She knew her mother would be furious when she found the note April had left, but why should she care about her mother's anger or disappointment? She was doing no more than Lydia herself would do. Her mother had always done whatever suited her. She had forced April to abandon her homeland and the people who'd nursed her and reared her and cared for her. Had she even once considered April's wants or needs or desires?

Her mother had dragged her from the Forbidden City to that awful opium den, then to the Embassy with all its strange people who had forced her to dress as they dressed in their constricting, uncomfortable clothing, and eat their bland, tasteless food, who laughed at her shyness, her timidity, all the things her own people prized so dearly.

Her memories were faint, but in her girlish innocence all she could concentrate on were the happy times in Kalgan where her amah had fussed and doted upon her. She remembered too her aloof, regal father, an imposing man who had little to do with her but who was responsible for providing all the oriental luxuries April so dearly longed to have again.

The hushed whisperings of Chinese unrest didn't frighten her; her people had always been unhappy with the white foreigners who ravaged the land and exploited the innocent. She was the eldest daughter of Ke Loo, a royal prince, and she was a princess. Her royal relatives would see to her protection, as well as any needed protection for her husband. The people of China would not dare harm them.

April ate the last of the beef pie and leaned back, looking about the ugly room. "I'll be glad to be away from all this," she said. "And you will adore China, David. Oh, I suspect you'll be a little homesick at first, but I will make you forget. You will grow to love China as much as I do."

He took her hand, indifferent to the hostile looks of the other diners. "Of course I will. And you needn't worry about my missing San Francisco and my family. Father never approved of me anyway and Mother has always tried to run my life for me."

He glanced at his pocket watch. "If you're finished, we should be going. It's getting close to the time."

April pulled her hood over her long, black, silky hair, casting her face into shadows. They ignored again the muttered insults as David threw several silver coins on the table and led April to the door.

"And don't bring her back in here," the surly proprietor called after them.

There was a strange, ominous feel to the night as they walked along. The clang of the trolley bell hurried them to the corner just as the trolley itself loomed out of the fog. David and April hopped aboard, glad to be away from the tavern and all its unpleasantness. They sat huddled close together, oblivious to the city stirring faintly about them, lost as they were in their own private world. They were young and so deeply in love that nothing mattered in all the world except themselves and their dreams.

What did they care about the whispered uprisings far in the north of China? What did all that political nonsense matter to her and David? Besides, hadn't her old tutor, Kim Lee, said there were always those who were discontented?

Kim Lee had spoken to her of the small band who called themselves *I-ho-chuan*, the Righteous and Harmonious Fists Society—the Boxers, as they had come to be known—who were gradually gaining converts, and the White Lotus sect, whose only purpose was to overthrow the Manchus, her father's family; but they had to be foolish, insolent peasants to think they could uproot her father's dynasty, the Empress herself, all of the great Manchus who'd ruled China for almost three hundred years.

As they sat holding tight to one another, neither April nor David could imagine anything blighting their future together. Nothing would ever blemish their happiness, certainly not some insignificant political malcontents.

* * * * * * *

Lydia heard the commotion in the foyer. She started out of her chair just as the doors to the sitting room were flung apart and Lorna MacNair stood framed in the doorway. They had never met but Lydia knew the woman.

"Where are they?" Lorna demanded, shaking a crumpled piece of paper in Lydia's face as she stormed forward.

"Who do you mean?" Lydia asked.

"You know perfectly well. My son and that half-Chinese daughter of yours."

Lydia stiffened and clenched her fists. She felt the first twinges of fear and put her hand on the back of a chair to steady herself.

"My daughter is in her bed," she answered, but she could see the truth in Lorna's face.

"Not according to this," Lorna said, throwing David's note at Lydia's feet.

Lydia hesitated but the urge to read the note was stronger than her refusal to stoop before this woman. She lowered herself gracefully and unraveled the paper, turning her back to Lorna.

"You may rest assured that April and I will never humiliate you, Mother," she read aloud. "Don't try to find us. David."

The words blurred as Lydia's hand began to tremble. She turned suddenly, throwing aside the note. Gathering up her skirts, she ran to the staircase and to April's room. Her heart stopped for an instant when she saw the empty bed and the note folded neatly on the pillowcase.

"I love him," it said simply. "I am sorry if I disappoint you but, like you, I must do what I must do, go where I belong,"

"Go where I belong," she read aloud. She stared at the words for a moment until their full impact struck her. "Good God!"

Lorna MacNair was standing at the bottom of the staircase. "Well?" she asked.

"She's gone...with David," Lydia said, hurrying past her to ring for the housekeeper.

"This is all your fault," Lorna hissed. "If you'd stayed out of my family's life my son would never have been corrupted."

Lydia turned on her, eyes flashing. "I no more welcome your son into my family than you welcome my daughter into yours," she replied.

The housekeeper appeared in the hall. "Nellie, go out and hail a hack, please," Lydia ordered. "I'm going out."

"Out?" Lorna asked, as the housekeeper pulled a shawl around her shoulders and went out the door. "Where are you going? What do you know?"

Lydia was tempted to repeat Lorna's bad manners by throwing April's note at her, but she handed it to her instead.

"What does it mean, go where she belongs?" Suddenly Lorna gasped. "Dear God, not to Chinatown?" She put her hands over her mouth as if to hold back a scream.

Lydia paid her no mind as she went toward her downstairs bedroom to fetch her cape.

"You know where they are," Lorna accused as she hurried after Lydia. "I demand that you tell me."

"I do not know where they are, but I have my suspicions. I only hope they prove to be right."

As Lydia started toward the foyer, the front door again crashed open and Peter barged in with Nellie, the housekeeper, in his wake. He glowered at his wife. "What in hell is going on?" he demanded. "When I got home a few minutes ago Susan said you were screaming something about David and that you were coming here. What's this all about?"

"Oh, Peter," his wife said, throwing herself against him.

He held her away, turning to Lydia instead. "What is it?" he asked, more gently than before.

Lydia kept her eyes averted as she pulled on her gloves. To the housekeeper she asked, "Did you manage to find a carriage?"

"My carriage is outside," Peter told her. "Tell me what the devil's the matter."

"David and April," Lydia said as calmly as she could. "It appears they've eloped."

"Good God!"

His exclamation angered her without her really knowing why. She hesitated, wondering if she should tell him where she suspected the young people were bound, wondering if she should seek his help. Peter knew of the dangers that lay in wait for them if indeed April was foolish enough to take David to her father's house in China.

Lorna decided for her. "She knows where they are, Peter, but she refuses to tell me." Lorna clung to her husband's lapels.

He loosened her grip. "Do you, Lydia?"

She nodded quickly. "April wrote in her note that she must go where she belongs."

"China," Peter gasped. "Good Lord, no!"

"China?" Lorna said, not understanding. "How will they get to China? It's across the ocean. It's thousands of miles away. And what will they live on? Where will they go when they get there?" A thought struck her. She looked up at Peter and said, "The company's Chinese representative. David must have written him...."

"Oh, be quiet," Peter snapped as he reached for Lydia's arm. "Come on, we can take my carriage. I only hope we can find the ship before it sails...if it hasn't already."

"But what about me?" Lorna wailed as the two of them hurried out the door.

"Go home," Peter called back over his shoulder. "With any

kind of luck I'll have David home with me soon."

Lorna stood gaping at them as they got into Peter's carriage and started off toward the docks. Even when the fog had swallowed them up she still stood in the light of the doorway, shoulders sagging, heart aching.

CHAPTER SIX

Lydia sat huddled in the corner of the closed carriage. She hadn't wanted to go with Peter but she knew he was the only one who understood the dangers and could help her. She would have to forget for now how he'd abandoned her in China, sold her—for the price of his own passage to America—leaving her a slave to a Mandarin prince for over ten years. If she hadn't saved herself and April from that cruel, selfish barbarian, their bones would be rotting in China this very day, victims of the executioner her husband had set upon them.

How could she believe Peter MacNair when he told her he'd done it for her own good? Still, it was true enough that they had been in the middle of that accursed country, surrounded by millions of Chinese who'd been goaded by the Empress into killing every white they could find. Her mother was dying of cholera, her father just dead; there had been no chance, Lydia knew, of her reaching any of the distant seaports.

At least with the Mandarin prince she had survived—for a while, Lydia told herself, even if it had been almost as a slave, a concubine. She would never have been able to escape from Ke Loo's heavily guarded palace. He had wanted her too desperately at the beginning to ever permit her to slip away from him without his going after her. She told herself she should be thanking Peter MacNair rather than cursing him.

Peter had said he'd tried to find her over the years. Had he lied to her again about that? He could have been telling the truth, she knew. She had, after all, left no trail for anyone to follow when Ke Loo carried her off, no trail a foreigner could have found. Kalgan, where Ke Loo had taken her, was so isolated a city she'd lived virtually a prisoner in her husband's palace, bearing a son as well as April. It was ten years later that he'd taken them to Peking, to the palace of the Dowager Empress in the Forbidden City, where he deserted her and April in favor of another, a Chinese courtesan.

Yet, she still wanted to hate Peter MacNair even though it was increasingly difficult to do so in retrospect. A part of her wanted to believe the things he'd told her, his explanation for his seemingly cruel, selfish actions in China, his feelings for her and his interest in her when he found her again in San Francisco.

Hard as she tried, she could not quiet the voice inside her that whispered that she was being foolish to rely on and trust this man, for all his handsome good-looks, for all his charms, and the smile that played havoc with her heartbeat every time she looked at him, as she was looking at him now through the concealing darkness of the carriage.

If only there weren't so many facets to the man, Lydia said to herself. It would all be so simple if he were a scoundrel, plain and simple. But Peter MacNair? No woman could ever feel entirely safe and secure in his affections. She'd seen the way he'd looked with disdain at his own wife, the way he'd treated her, humiliated her in front of another woman, a woman Lorna MacNair knew to be her one-time rival. Peter was unlike any other man who had crossed Lydia's path, she told herself, with one singular exception perhaps: Ke Loo, her Mandarin husband.

The two men were alike in that they were both arrogant and heartless and neither would stop at anything to get what they wanted. But unlike Ke Loo, Peter had a soft side too; he would take a woman by force, if necessary, but he would be tender as well as wildly passionate in his lovemaking.

Lydia closed her eyes as her insides began to ache. It might have been only last night when she lay in Peter's arms, feeling the heat of his mouth upon her, his hands searching, discovering, his body so hard, so heavy atop her own.

"Damn," Peter swore, slamming a fist down on the cushioned seat between them.

Lydia's eyes flew open, her reverie splintered into a million fragments.

"Damn," Peter said again. "How could they be so foolish?"

Lydia looked at his handsome profile. Even etched as it was in anger, its chiseled silhouette thrilled her.

She wanted to touch the soft full lips with her fingertips, press her mouth against his cheek, listen to the words of love he'd once spoken to her.

She calmly collected herself. "They are children, Peter," she said. Just speaking his name tugged at her heart.

"Children be damned," he growled. "You were no more than April's age when you managed for yourself in China."

Her beautiful thoughts raced away when she remembered her tears, her misery, the harshness of the Mandarin's sexual assault when Peter left her in his clutches.

He felt her sudden coldness and turned to look at her. "You were only about seventeen. You had sense."

"Sixteen," Lydia corrected with an icy edge to her voice. "And I did not choose my fate, it was chosen for me."

"You still hate me for that?" he said as he looked at her with a hurt expression.

"I will never forgive you for what you did."

"For God's sake, Lydia, what will it take for you to believe me, or has China become a part of you also? Do you live by their ancient belief that revenge is a sacred duty?" He noticed the way she flinched. He'd touched a nerve, he saw. "Damn it, Lydia. Revenge isn't some child's playtoy. It's a damn bomb that could just as likely go off in your hand."

She drew her lips into a thin line and narrowed her eyes when she turned to look at him. "Vengeance makes grief bearable," she said in an even voice.

She watched the steadiness of his gaze upon her, the intense concentration that gathered around his eyes, the change in his expression and she felt suddenly powerless before him. Even as

Peter grabbed her arm and pulled her roughly against him, she felt herself void of any weapons of defense.

He kissed her hard on the mouth, crushing himself against her breasts, hurting her, holding her so tightly she felt her bones would crack. She knew he was leaving black and blue marks on her arms where his wide, thick, powerful fingers encircled them, but the heat of him, the pressure of his kiss made her weak with desire for his love.

"Damn it, I adore you, Lydia. Don't you know that?"

She opened her eyes and saw his face. She felt so vulnerable she wanted to cry out from the pain of it. How could she allow him to manipulate her this way, she asked herself as she felt the rage begin to mount? She slapped his face as hard as she could.

To her utter amazement he raised his hand and slapped her in return, then pulled her back into his arms and began kissing her wildly as she struggled against him. She felt his hands on her breasts, pulling at the bodice of her dress. Something began to tear as she felt a scream catch in her throat.

The trapdoor in the roof flopped back and the driver said, "We're at the docks, Mr. MacNair. Do you know which ship it is?"

Lydia and Peter flew apart, back into their own private hells.

"Look for the first one with its deck lanterns lighted," Peter said gruffly, adjusting himself on the seat.

The moment the carriage stopped Peter was out and up the ramp of the sailing ship, its deck alive with sailors and stevedores.

"You can't come aboard," one of the ship's officers told him, blocking Peter's way at the top of the gangplank.

"I must see the Captain," Peter demanded.

Lydia came up behind him, holding her cloak tightly around her. "A young couple," she said to the officer. "A Eurasian girl and a young American boy. We've got to find them."

The officer gave a scornful smile. "Oh, yeah. They just came aboard a little while ago," he said. "They're in the steering house with the Captain."

The Captain was an old sea mongrel who delighted in lecturing young, headstrong people such as the two before him. He felt it his duty to talk at length about anything that would help to cool the young, sensual heads of his charges.

When the door to the steering house burst open and Peter and Lydia hurried in he was just reaching for his Bible. "You don't barge in like that," he scolded. "I am the captain of this vessel and I am getting ready to marry these two young people."

"There'll be no marriage," Peter said firmly.

"You can't stop us!" David cried. He and April clung tightly to one another.

"I can and I will!" Peter said, his voice deadly calm.

"April, you must come home," Lydia said, and at the very same moment, April cried, "Leave us alone."

"Look here," the Captain said, "This is my ship. I say what goes on here."

"If you want to sail on the tide, Captain," Peter said, "I suggest you permit us to remove these two young people. Here is my identification. I am not unknown in the more influential circles here in San Francisco. Your ship could be detained while this abduction is investigated."

"Abduction?" The Captain sputtered. "Sir, there is no abduction here. These young persons came aboard of their own volition."

"And by the time that's proved to the harbor master's satisfaction, your ship will be well behind schedule, which I'm sure will not please her owners."

The Captain cleared his throat. He had been at his business since a boy, and he had learned never to argue with a threatening sea, but always to ride with the waves. He shrugged at David and April and slammed shut the Bible. He was glad to see the whole kit and kaboodle of them off his ship.

As they went down the gangplank toward the waiting carriage, David balked. "You can't do this," he railed at his father.

Peter shoved him forward. "I already have."

CHAPTER SEVEN

The old Chinese tutor sat up when he heard voices on the other side of the door. The pipe had been headier than usual; it had never sent him into a second dream before. He remembered leaving Chin Chou's in a wonderful euphoria of colors and sounds and walking the same streets and alleys back to his place over the bakery shop. He didn't rightly recall how long he had dreamt the second dream, but his mind cleared quickly when he heard the man mention April's mother.

A carriage clattered past. Kim Lee pressed his ear to the door and listened.

"Ke Loo has been smiled upon by the Gods and our gracious Empress again orders that the stain of his American wife be removed. The other efforts to kill all failed; ours must not fail."

"Ours *will* not fail," the second voice assured the first.

The old Chinese heard them move toward the door and scurried into the alleyway, hiding himself in its shadows. He pressed himself tight against the wall as the two men came out of the silk shop and went past him down the street. He recognized the thinner of the two; he was a highbinder, one of the many Chinese criminals hired as assassins. Highbinders had only one purpose in their life and that was to satisfy the murderous desires of those who hired them. If they succeeded they were pardoned of their earlier crimes committed in China and allowed to return to their homeland. If they failed they were killed in the place of their intended victim.

Only members of the Chinese nobility were permitted to send

criminals—highbinders—out of China on their deadly missions and if the highbinder refused his commission he forfeited his head to the blade of his benefactor's high executioner.

Kim Lee found himself trembling as he inched along the wall, moving as quietly as a murmur. These were assassins sent on a mission for the Dowager Empress herself. Once before, a few years ago, the Tongs had killed one of April's relatives, her great uncle, the man who owned the tailor shop on the next street. April's mother had shot the Tong. Now two more had been sent to deal with the woman. He had to warn April that her mother was again in danger.

As he let himself into his cozy flat over the bakery, the opium dreams started to overcome him. He lay down in the darkness of his room and let the clouds crowd around him and carry him off into sleep. There would be time enough tomorrow to warn young April. Now he must sleep.

* * * * * * *

"I forbid you ever to see David MacNair again."

April sat pouting, curled up against the headboard of her bed. The satin pillow she cradled in her arms was wet from her crying.

"I won't stop seeing him," she sobbed. "There is nothing you or anyone else can do to separate us. We love each other. I could never give him up."

"You will!" Lydia demanded.

"Why?" April asked scornfully. "Tell me why, Mother. Just because you can't have his father you're jealous of me for having his son."

"That's a lie," Lydia insisted angrily.

"No it isn't. I wasn't too young to know what you and Mr. MacNair were doing when he came to visit us at the house on Van Ness Street, that house that Mr. Hanover paid for."

"That will be enough, young lady."

"You disgust me," April growled. "All my life you've never

once considered me, what I wanted. All you ever thought about was yourself and what man would give you money."

"April!"

"It's true. There's a name for women like you, Mother. And I tell you here and now, whatever you do, you'll never keep David and me apart. You may have stopped us this time, but there will be others. You won't be able to leave me alone for a second, because if you do we'll run away again."

Lydia felt a rush of despair. Everything she had done in all her adult life had been done for this child. How could she make April understand that they would long since have been dead if she hadn't sacrificed herself for her daughter's well-being? How else could she have satisfied her ambitions for them both?

Ambition had become a habit, then an addiction; now, if anyone asked, Lydia could not truly tell what her original ambitions had been, except that she had this driving need to reproduce a perfume. To do so meant financial security, so that it would never again be necessary for them to submit to a man, any man, merely to survive.

Yes, she had had to submit to men in return for their assistance, financial or otherwise. And yes, there had been a time when it had been necessary to pretend that April was her maid, and not her daughter. But it had been done for the best of reasons, and none of it had been any more pleasant for her than it had been for her daughter. Surely April was old enough now to understand that.

"Darling, I know it's been difficult," she said aloud, trying to be gentle. "But Empress Cosmetics is a success now, and Raymond is close to duplicating *Nightsong*. There is nothing you can't have."

April wiped her eyes and turned down the corners of her mouth. "I can't have David. If you truly wanted me to be happy you'd let me have the one I love."

Lydia shook her head slowly. "It's impossible; surely you know that. Not only am I against it, the MacNairs are against it as well. What kind of a life would you have with David? How would you live?"

"We'd go to my father, as we planned," April said, jutting out a stubborn lower lip.

"Do be sensible, April." Lydia believed it was bad enough that her daughter felt herself abused and hated by her mother; she could never have her learn the truth about the father who truly despised her, who did in fact want nothing more than to see his girl child dead...drowned as a newborn infant—those had been his orders at her birth.

How could she tell April this? How could she destroy the girl's admiration and love for her father, a father she had never really known? Lydia could not bring herself to shatter the girl's dreams completely. In time perhaps, when April was older and Lydia had had more time to make up for all the heartless things she'd been forced to do; perhaps then she could tell April of the terrible fate that would befall her if either of them returned to China.

Lydia said, "China would no more accept David than San Francisco accepts you."

"Father is a Mandarin prince. No one would dare harm David. Father would see to that."

"But you don't have to be ashamed of what you are now. You are a very rich young woman, April. You can have whatever you wish, within reason, of course," she added, thinking of David. "If you are unhappy in San Francisco, we'll live somewhere else, wherever you say."

"China," April insisted.

Lydia's patience flew away. "Really April, you are acting like a spoiled brat. You cannot live in China. Regardless of who your father is, it would not be a safe place for you. You're an American so far as the Chinese are concerned. They would not let you forget that, believe me." She got up and went to the door. "Now I would suggest you get undressed and climb into bed. We both could use a good night's sleep."

As she went down the stairs to her own suite of rooms she knew nothing had been settled between them. It would take time and a lot of diligence to keep April from making a serious mistake. How she was going to keep her and David apart was a complete mystery. There was no way that she could think of to keep the two young lovers from making the fatal mistake of marrying and sailing to China, if they were determined to do so.

The front door bell rang just as she was turning down the gas lamps in the hall. The silhouette on the other side of the glass door panel was familiar.

"I must speak with you, Lydia," Peter said when she opened the door a crack. "I saw your lights. It's important, I think, for both our peace of minds."

"It's very late."

"I won't keep you long and what I have to say may give you a more comfortable night's sleep."

She opened the door wider and went on into the small parlor under the stairs, listening to Peter's footsteps directly behind her. The heavy manliness of his stride stirred her.

When she reached the marble topped lamp table in the center of the parlor she turned to face him. "Well?"

He smiled sheepishly. "I see you've changed your dress."

"As you know perfectly well, the other was torn," she said acidly.

"I'm sorry. You must let me buy you another."

Lydia drummed her fingers on the marble. "Please say what you came to say, Peter."

He took a step closer, pausing when Lydia retreated slightly. "I am sending David to Lorna's relatives in New York," he said.

Lydia found herself releasing the breath she'd been holding. She wondered if he expected her to thank him. She couldn't bring herself to let him see how relieved she was for fear he'd take that as encouragement. Instead she said, "Once again you've taken command, without consulting me."

His eyes grew angry. "I thought you'd be pleased."

She let her shoulders droop. "Oh, I am, Peter. I'm sorry. It's been a very hectic evening." She moved away from the table.

Why did she feel this terrible need to hurt him? "Would you care for a drink?"

"Yes, thank you."

As she splashed some scotch into a glass she said, "When will David be leaving?"

"First thing in the morning." He took the glass from her, gave her a little salute with it and drained it.

Lydia took it from him and refilled it.

"Lorna's standing guard over him tonight," he said with a grin.

"Your wife is very much in love with you, and you treated her shamelessly this evening."

"I treated her no differently from any other woman whom I care nothing about." His eyes fixed themselves on Lydia and she saw his meaning all too clearly. She handed him the glass of scotch and when his fingers touched hers, she pulled back sharply, almost letting the glass fall to the carpet.

He smiled his devilish smile and emptied the glass again. "You're afraid of me," he said matter-of-factly.

Turning quickly away she bumped the table, sending the prisms on the lamp shade jangling. "I have no reason to be afraid of you, do I?" She wouldn't let him see that he was right.

She could sense the heat of him as he came up behind her. When she felt his arms go about her, a tremor went through her. He cupped her breasts in his massive hands. She gave a little groan of protest and started to pull away but he held her captive.

"Don't do this, Peter," she moaned, knowing she did not have the strength to fight him off after all that had happened this evening, after all he'd done to help her.

"Don't talk," Peter said. He spoke low in his throat, reassuringly, as he caressed her lovely breasts.

"Peter, you mustn't...."

"Quiet. Quiet," he murmured. He turned her easily and felt the trembling of her body as he swept her up in his arms and carried her into her downstairs bedroom.

Hard as she tried to resist him she knew she could not. She

let him undress her and watched, fascinated as always as he stripped himself slowly, deliberately, as in an erotic dream, until he stood before her completely naked.

With some hypnotic power he held her gaze until, like the cobra's prey, she found herself incapable of moving away from him. He lowered himself on top of her, kissing and sucking the pouting nipples of her breasts. She wasn't conscious of the low, long moans that came from deep inside her...the cravings of some savage animal that Peter had awakened within her.

It was always the same. Why did she fight him when reason told her these were the arms that she wanted to hold her, this was the only man she truly loved and needed. Still, she could never give either of them that satisfaction.

His mouth burned a wet, hot trail down over her throat, igniting again the tips of her breasts until flames leapt up deep within her, searing everything they touched.

Lydia cried aloud, writhing, twisting, squirming under his manipulations, oblivious to the world, to everything except the sensations of his mouth and his hands and his body. The ecstasy of it was almost too much for her to bear as she thrashed about, thrusting herself up hard against his touch.

He entered her slowly, smoothly, forcefully. Wave after delicious wave of scorching pleasure splashed over her sending her from one peak of sensual delirium to another. She thrilled to the feel of him deep, deep inside her. She welcomed every move, every thrust of his magnificent body. She enveloped him, clinging wetly, refusing to let him draw back, sobbing helplessly as new waves of ecstasy swept over her, making her body jerk and arch, and thrust. Her senses spun like insane tops in the throes of what might have been her last breath, or her first breath; only dimly was she conscious of his final brutal, jabbing thrusts, the jolting of his hard, manly body, the crushing of his muscular hairy chest on her breasts.

* * * * * * *

Lydia was the first to wake. She lay beside him, drifting happily on a rolling wave of remembered pleasure, delighting in the feeling of loving him, of his loving her. She glanced at his nakedness in the dawning light coming in through the windows. She enjoyed admiring his strong body and thrilled at recalling how carefully he kept a tight rein on its powerful strength so that, forceful and brutal though his assault on her had been, she was never hurt. She cherished, the marks he'd left on her skin like souvenirs of a wonderful experience.

One moment she was reveling in the delicious ecstasy of what had happened, the next moment a surge of disgust and annoyance began to creep up inside her. The man lying naked beside her was the man she hated most in the world. He was the one who'd used her so cruelly, had abused her and cheated her.

She yanked the coverlet he was lying on, jostling him awake.

"You've got to go," she said coolly.

He smiled and reached for her.

Pulling the sheet quickly up around her, Lydia got out of bed, tripping over the clothes that lay in a heap on the floor. "It's morning," she said over her shoulder.

"Come back to bed," he said.

Without a backward glance she moved toward the closet and pulled on a robe. "You must leave," she said as she left the room and went into her dressing area.

She was sitting at her dressing table a few minutes later when Peter came in to stand behind her, fully dressed. He touched the red-gold hair that fell in cascades about her face and shoulders and smiled sweetly into the mirror, fastening his gaze on her dark, green-jade eyes.

"I love you, Lydia," he said simply.

She was angry, more at herself than at him. How could she have been so weak as to give herself to this monster, this conceited bully. "You love what I have to offer," she said. She got up from the mirror and walked to a safer distance.

Peter felt a stab at his heart and straightened his spine. "You're a fool," he said.

"After what I permitted last night, I agree with you. I am a fool. But you may rest assured, I will never make a fool of myself again. Now please leave."

He hesitated. One part of him said to grab her in his arms, rip off her robe and throw her on the bed and brutalize her sexually. Yet another part of him cautioned him to be rational, that the slightest display of harshness would chase her away from him forever. There would be other times, times like last night when she'd be vulnerable.

He could wait. He *would* wait. He'd wait forever, if that was how long it took. He only hoped that at the end of forever they would not still find themselves strangers.

"Good morning then," Peter said as he started for the door.

She was careful to keep her back to him and wouldn't trust her voice so she said nothing; she merely stood there holding her breath listening to his heavy footsteps as they crossed the marble floor of the foyer, reached the front door. The door slammed behind him and he was gone.

Only then did she turn and run after him. As she reached the foyer she called his name, knowing he could not possibly hear her.

"He's gone." April looked down from the top of the staircase. Mother and daughter stared at each other, one showing shame, the other bitterness and disgust.

April suddenly was convulsed with tears. With a wailing cry of terrible pain she fled to her bedroom and locked herself in.

* * * * * * *

In his little room above the bakery shop, Kim Lee awoke from his deep, happy dreams. He threw his feet over the side of his pallet and sat up, rubbing his temples. There was something important he had to do this morning, something involving his student, April. He shook his head. He'd forgotten.

"Ah, it could not have been very important after all," he said as he got ready for his day.

CHAPTER EIGHT

It happened at a time when Andrew Carnegie was beginning to make steel in Pennsylvania, the Rockefellers were refining oil in Ohio, and steam-powered ships were beginning to replace sails. Lydia was seated behind her desk checking a manifest on a shipment of exotic plants Raymond had ordered from the Philippine Islands. The prices were exorbitant and the customs duty for importation was even higher.

She was about to ask Evelyn Clary to call him from his chemistry lab when Raymond hurried in wearing a smug smile. He held up a glass vial between thumb and forefinger.

"Your future fortune, Madame," he said with a flourish.

Lydia's breath caught in her throat. She stared at the vial, fighting back a sudden excitement. "You mean...?" she gasped.

Raymond's smug little smile widened into a delighted grin. "Yes. I've finally succeeded," he said. He handed her the vial. *"Nightsong,"* he announced dramatically.

At first she was afraid to touch it for fear it would smash all her hopes and dreams. Carefully she took it in her hand and lifted it to her nostrils.

It was there!

She inhaled all the erotic secrets of the Orient, the heady intoxicating aroma of love and passion, lightness and air. The yellow brilliance of the Empress's silk ceremonial robes, the splashes of chrysanthemums with their fragile petals, the orange blossoms and pomegranates, the majestic peacocks and alabaster palaces. It was all there in this magnificent fragrance, this provocative scent of intrigue and feminine allure.

"My God," she breathed as she inhaled the aroma again. She dabbed a drop on her wrist and smelled the transformation it made of her skin, like bathing in a haunting elixir that made one irresistible.

As if in proof of its power, Raymond took her in his arms and kissed her long and passionately. "Now I have given you what you want."

"Oh yes, Raymond," she gushed. "It's perfect. It is absolutely identical. I can't begin to tell you how much I am indebted to you."

He glanced at the manifest she'd been scanning and said, "You even forgive me for my Philippine extravagances?"

Lydia threw her arms about his neck. "I'll buy you the Philippine Islands if you want them. Anything you want, Raymond, simply name it and I give you my solemn oath that I will not deny it you."

"How about dinner tonight to celebrate? You and me and April, if she wants to come along. We will go to the finest restaurant in San Francisco."

"We'll fly to the moon if you like," Lydia said.

"The moon it is, then," he answered, and again he kissed her on the mouth. He raised her wrist to his nostrils and inhaled the beauty of the fragrance. "Like flowers and moonlight on a garden pond," he said as he touched his lips to it. "We must start making preparations for its distribution. The container must be *très chic,* in the shape of an almond blossom perhaps."

"No, no," Lydia said, reflecting. "The Sung vial in which *Nightsong* came with me to America—we must duplicate it in the finest, loveliest of crystal."

"Of course. Perfect. I know just the man. He is in France but plans soon to come to America...New York, he says, to open his own glass works. Tiffany. Louis Tiffany, he calls himself. He is an extraordinary craftsman, the finest in the world, I think. I will ask him to design the container for *Nightsong.* I will write to him at once." At the door he paused and turned back. "Until tonight, Lydia my sweet," he said.

"Until tonight."

Later, it surprised Lydia when April put up no objections to joining them for dinner.

"Why not?" April sighed. "It will be a welcome change from the inside of this prison."

David was gone and her world was dead. What did it matter now if she ate alone or with the servants or in a fancy restaurant with Lydia and Raymond? There was no way, April found out, that she could communicate with David. If he had written, his letters had undoubtedly been confiscated by Lydia. Certainly she had not seen them, or heard from him since that fateful night. She had even bribed a delivery boy to take a note to his house, but there had been no reply.

Yes, April said to herself as she sighed and threw herself across her bed, life was finished for her. All that was left now was existing until the end came.

Suddenly an idea struck her. Why hadn't she thought of it before this, she asked her reflection as she glanced over at the mirror of her dressing table. She hopped off the bed and astonished herself by giggling. Why not? If her mother could flirt there was no reason she couldn't. It might be fun to see if she could vamp Raymond Andrieux. She knew her mother wasn't in love with him, but she certainly enjoyed his attentions, and thinking that he loved her.

Suddenly the entire evening that lay ahead took on an entirely different color. April flung open her closet door and started searching through her dresses. She chose her favorite yellow silk with the wide sash that tucked in her tiny waist and accentuated her lovely young breasts. Where her mother would dress with sophistication, April decided to emphasize the one thing Lydia did not have: Youth. She pulled a long yellow hair ribbon from the satin box and threw it on the bed beside the yellow silk gown. Lemon silk pumps and a long filmy cape completed the ensemble to her liking.

April looked ravishing, Lydia thought as the girl came into

the drawing room. Raymond was having a cocktail and Lydia sat sipping sherry.

" *Très, très belle,*" Raymond gushed. *"Exquisite,"* he added, kissing the tips of his fingers. "I am the most fortunate of men tonight." He offered April a sherry, which she accepted. "Your mother has told you the good news, I assume...about *Nightsong?"*

"Yes, she mentioned it. I don't pay much attention to my mother's affairs I'm afraid. But congratulations," she said, raising her wine glass.

Lydia ignored the barb and said, "It will mean a great deal of money. I'm toying with the idea of expansion all over the country."

"The world," Raymond corrected.

"New York perhaps," April suggested with a complacent smirk.

"Of course," Raymond was quick to say. "New York first of all."

April sipped the wine as she watched her mother. "I don't suppose we will be moving there."

Lydia was uncomfortable under April's cool, steady eyes. "I think that unlikely," she said, brightening as she added, "but Paris would be a lovely place to live, I think."

"You would adore it," Raymond said, taking her hand.

And while he was rhapsodizing about his favorite city April's mind began to race. If she could get Raymond to take her to New York she'd surely be able to track down David MacNair. The only problem with that was, how did she get Raymond to take her to New York?

"We should be going," Lydia commented, noting the time. "But excuse me for a moment. I've forgotten to tuck a handkerchief into my bag. I'll only be a moment."

The wiry little Chinese ducked behind the screen just as Lydia came back into her bedroom. She went directly to the chest of drawers and took a handkerchief from the sachet scented box. She had turned and started back toward the drawing room when suddenly a hand was pressed over her mouth, stifling her scream.

In the drawing room Raymond thought he heard something smash. It had come from Lydia's suite he was sure. He frowned at April. "I heard your mother drop something, I think."

"While we're waiting," April said as she stood up, ignoring his remark, "I'll ask Nellie to find us a carriage."

Alone, Raymond finished the rest of his cocktail. Just as he placed the glass on the small drum table beside his chair he heard another thump, as though something had been overturned.

The door to Lydia's suite of rooms was open. Raymond stepped inside, walking through the sitting room toward the bedroom. He froze when he saw the silhouette of a short, muscular man struggling with Lydia. The windows had been latched back, letting in the light from the street and the man was dragging Lydia's resisting body toward the windows. One hand was pressed tightly over her mouth, the other was locked around her, pinning her arms to her side. A small lamp stand had been knocked over and an unlit lamp lay shattered on the oriental rug, its thick oil soaking into the delicate weave.

Raymond sprang, surprising himself at the quickness of his response and with the almost forgotten reflex of his years at the military school where he was supposed to learn discipline. His left fist crashed down on the back of the man's neck. One blow was enough to weaken the assassin's hold on Lydia. The man's grip fell away and Lydia toppled free.

As if in a dream, one moment the assailant was there under his grip, and the next, Raymond was somersaulted over the Chinese's shoulder and was flat on the floor watching through a daze as the wiry little man vaulted over the sill and out onto the street beyond. By the time Raymond regained his full senses, the man was gone.

"What happened?" April asked as she hurried into the room. She saw Raymond peering out the window and her mother gasping for breath on the floor.

"A burglar," Raymond said. "Your mother obviously surprised him when she came back for her handkerchief." He went quickly toward Lydia and helped her up.

To her own surprise, April found herself fetching a glass of water and some spirits of ammonia. Lydia saw the concern on April's face and her heart began to thump in her breast. If it took dying at the hands of an assassin to cause her daughter to look at her like that, it would be worth it, Lydia told herself. She took the water and inhaled the ammonia April held beneath her nostrils.

"He was no burglar, Raymond," Lydia said as she felt her composure return. "I warned you earlier about the dangers we would encounter from the Dowager Empress. That was one of her hired assassins. I've met with others of his kind. I had hoped that old woman would have forgotten by now, but I should have known better. Like the elephant, she will never forget an injury."

"You're over-reacting, Mother," April said, her usual coolness returning. "I'm sure Raymond is right, that it was just a burglar."

"No," Lydia insisted. "I know better than that."

Raymond said, "Put it out of your mind." He righted the overturned table and began collecting pieces of the shattered oil lamp.

"Leave it, Raymond, Nellie will clean up. I'll go and fetch her. She's still outside searching for a cab," April said.

"Perhaps we should postpone the little celebration we planned," Raymond suggested.

"Nonsense. I think it will do me good to get out of the house, away from the reminders," Lydia insisted.

* * * * * * *

The restaurant was new and glittered with Victorian splendor. Their table was set with vermeil service; an enormous silver and crystal epergne containing fresh fruit dominated the center. Overhead a lovely Baccarat lamp hung from the ceiling on a velvet cord. The walls of the room were covered with watered silk in a deep rust-beige that matched the velvet seats of the

Queen Anne chairs. The whole room was a bravura gesture of Victorian excess but it all blended into a stunning experience.

"It's magnificent," April gushed as they settled around their table in the alcove to the accompaniment of glances—some appreciative, some hostile—from the other diners in the room.

"I am very pleased you like it," Raymond said. "The proprietor is from Paris and the cuisine, I assure you, is as fine as the decor."

Lydia slowly pulled off her gloves and felt the coldness of her hands. She could still feel the pressure of those strong, deadly fingers at her throat.

"You're quite pale," April said to her mother.

Again Lydia's heart raced at this demonstration of her daughter's concern. After all the hostility she had shown of late, it renewed Lydia's hopes that one day April would grow to realize that everything she had been made to suffer had been for her own good. "Perhaps some wine will calm you," Raymond suggested. He motioned to the sommelier. "Champagne. Laurent Perrier."

Forcing herself to smile, Lydia said, "Let's forget the burglar and remember that we are here to celebrate."

She glanced in April's direction in time to see a sudden transformation. A minute before, April had looked tender, almost affectionate; now, unaware that her mother's eyes were on her, she had again retreated behind a facade of disapproval and resentment.

Lydia felt a stab of disappointment, but she carefully rearranged her own mask, and made a pretense of enjoying herself.

Raymond, at least, seemed to be having a grand time. He was raving to April about his great success.

"But how can you be sure *Nightsong* will be such a success?" April asked him.

"Because," Raymond boasted, "it is the most beautiful perfume I have ever created, perhaps the most beautiful in the world. Of course, we must not forget that the Empress of China played a part in its creation as well." He gave a begrudging smile.

A shiver went up Lydia's spine, so abruptly that she turned to see if a window had been opened.

Raymond raised his glass. "However," he said, "as much as we are indebted to that powerful lady, we cannot give her all of the credit. Nature had much more to do with it than anyone. So here is to nature." He toasted.

Lydia frowned, her contribution to the accomplishment seemed to have been quite forgotten.

They sipped the excellent champagne. As the evening passed, Lydia noticed that Raymond was getting a little drunk, not only on the champagne but on his own loquacity. He was painting an altogether different picture of himself than the one she knew. To listen to him speak to April, one would take him to be a meek, retiring young man, a shy European completely at the mercy of the brash American world. His life had been one of endless struggle and privations, leaving him vulnerable to the unscrupulous of the world. Lydia wondered if he was including her among the unscrupulous.

But April was amused and it was good to hear her laugh and to watch the way the candlelight made her lovely eyes twinkle with delight. She was seeing in Raymond what she wished to see in him. To Lydia it was girlishly innocent and charming to watch.

The food was as good as Raymond had predicted and with it he'd insisted upon more champagne, which Lydia could see he did not need, but did not deny him. He'd gotten a little louder, but certainly not to the noticeable stage. Even when drunk, Lydia doubted if Raymond Andreiux ever lost sight of the high esteem in which he held himself.

It was April Lydia was becoming a little concerned about. She had tried, tactfully, to remind April that she was on her third glass of champagne, only to be met with April's belligerence.

"Oh, let her be," Raymond said, patting Lydia's hand. "It isn't every night I get to enjoy her company."

Nevertheless, Lydia was glad when coffee and dessert were

served. Listening to Raymond's endless chatter and to April's giggling, she realized that it really hadn't been much of a celebration for her. In fact, the entire evening had been a disaster from start to finish.

She said as much to Raymond after April had brazenly kissed him goodnight and skipped off to her room.

"It was that nasty business with the burglar," Raymond said as he helped himself to a nightcap. "I suppose I should have put you to bed rather than take you out to dinner."

It hadn't been entirely the fault of that attempt on her life, Lydia thought, though she supposed that had a good deal to do with her mood at dinner. Mainly, she felt, she'd been an outsider all evening. And the fact that an assailant had attacked her earlier made her feel that Raymond should have paid attention to her rather than April the whole of the evening.

"And I don't think you should encourage April," she said aloud. "Especially just now when she is so very vulnerable"

"Oh that broken romance business you mentioned to me." He sipped his drink and eyed her questioningly. "April didn't seem particularly brokenhearted tonight. In fact, I find it hard to believe all you've told me. She hasn't behaved as I imagined a jilted lover would behave."

"She wasn't jilted. The boy's father simply thought it best that they be separated. We both agreed that they are much too young to be thinking of marriage."

Raymond let a slight frown crease his handsome brow. "Too young? I disagree. In Paris, April would be looked upon as an old maid in a few more years."

"We do not live in Paris."

Raymond ignored the remark and seated himself beside Lydia on the velvet loveseat. He took her hand in his and said, "*Nightsong* will go into production very soon now and we haven't agreed upon the price you offered me."

"You have but to name it."

Raymond hesitated as he looked deep into the green-jade of her eyes. "I want a wife," he said softly.

She leaned toward him as a sign of her resignation, her submission to his desires. "There are barriers to my marrying," she reminded him gently. "But I have no objections to any other arrangement."

Lydia closed her eyes as Raymond tilted her face up to his. He touched his lips lightly to hers and waited until she opened her eyes again.

"I want April," he told her firmly.

CHAPTER NINE

Lydia was astonished and yet somehow relieved. As she paced back and forth across her bedroom she tried to think how she was going to approach April. There was no way she could renege on the promise she'd made to Raymond, though in truth she had expected an entirely different demand for payment: Herself.

And were it not for her Mandarin husband in China, she would have married Raymond without hesitation, if for no other reason than to be married and not alone and susceptible to Peter's attentions.

Looking at her reflection in the glass she saw the threatening lines and shadows of age, the results of the rigors she'd been forced to endure. She wondered, not for the first time, whether her hasty marriage along a roadside in China would be upheld in an American court of law. After arriving in San Francisco she remembered her near marriage to Walter Hanover, the man who'd rescued her when she and April had arrived here penniless, the man who'd financed the first Empress Cosmetics company, the man whose mother had destroyed the proposed marriage and the earlier cosmetic company when she announced Lydia already had a husband in China.

Lydia bit down on her lower lip. Perhaps she should have brazened out Walter Hanover's mother's threats and found out whether her Chinese marriage to Prince Ke Loo was valid under American laws.

No, she said, shaking her head at her image, if she had

done that and had been successful she would now be married to Walter Hanover, a man who'd almost ruined her, a man she would prefer to forget together with his domineering mother and Kathy, his rude, incorrigible daughter.

The problem at the moment had nothing to do with any of that, Lydia told herself; it was with April. Assuring Raymond that she would keep her promise was one thing; getting April to agree to marry the man was another. Somehow she had to convince April that her love for David was utterly futile. Even then, would April do something to please her mother, Lydia asked herself? It was unlikely, but Lydia had no other choice than to give it a try.

She sat thinking of her dilemma and strangely enough it occurred to her that the only person in all of the city who could help her was her sworn enemy. It wasn't Peter MacNair who could help; it was a greater enemy, a woman she disliked as much as Lorna MacNair disliked her.

* * * * * * *

Dogs were barking as Lydia walked up to the MacNair mansion. Peter wouldn't be home, she knew. The dogs unnerved her, their barks sounding like harbingers of some impending terror. She remembered the barking of a circle of dogs preparing to devour a Chinese girl infant left to die, long ago in China. It was the customary way of disposing of girl children the peasants could not afford to raise, and for her it had always symbolized the horror and brutality of China.

She shivered as she walked on. From far back in the recesses of her memories she saw the long, pointing finger of the Dowager Empress with its exaggerated, lacquered nail guarded by a jade and silver sheath, singling out the condemned.

"You?" Lorna said frostily after the maid announced Lydia and she was shown into the bright, plant-filled solarium. It was a room that suited Lorna; everything was arranged in perfect symmetry, nothing casual or informal. Each plant was neatly trimmed, each perfectly distanced from the others. The wicker furniture was white and sterile, reflecting dully in the highly polished onyx of the floor.

The room was obviously Lorna MacNair's; Lydia couldn't imagine Peter in it.

Lorna laid aside her pruning shears and removed her gardening gloves; they were spotless, Lydia noticed.

"Now that the situation between David and your daughter has been resolved to everyone's satisfaction, I do not see what you and I have to say to one another, Mrs. Nightsong," Lorna said.

Lydia stood in the doorway, fighting down the urge to turn and leave. "I need your help," she said bluntly.

It was the last thing Lorna expected to hear. Her brows lifted. "My help?" She looked at Lydia for a moment then laughed a harsh, cheerless laugh. "Surely you can't be serious."

"It concerns David."

Lorna's eyes narrowed as she took a wary step toward Lydia. "What about David? He's safely out of your girl's clutches and he'll stay there."

"I am just as opposed to April's affair with David as you," Lydia said.

"Affair?" Her brows arched haughtily. "You refer to it as if it were one of those sordid things you involve yourself in. David is not so easily corrupted, hard as your girl may have tried."

Lydia wanted to slap the contemptuous smirk off her face. She pulled herself back and clasped her hands in front of her. "I did not come to trade insults, Mrs. MacNair," she said, forcing herself to remain, civil. "I ask your help...for both our sakes."

"I will do nothing to help you."

"It will help you more than it will me."

"Oh?"

"It will insure that David and April never resume their relationship."

"I will insure that, without any interference from you or your daughter," Lorna MacNair assured her.

"You are deceiving yourself if you think you can keep those two young people apart. If David is anything like...." She stammered and caught herself before she said, *anything like his father;* instead she said, "...anything like April, he will find a way to get back to her. April may even find a way to get to him in New York."

"How do you know David is in New York."

"Your husband told me," Lydia replied.

Lydia saw the stab of pain in Lorna's face. Cruel as it was, she felt a surge or pleasure well up in herself. "April has tried everything to find him and I've already intercepted David's letters to her," she went on, without waiting for Lorna's reply. "In time one will get through. So you can't be so blind as not to see that the more we force them apart the more their love for one another will keep them together."

"Love? Don't use that word. David doesn't love your daughter," Lorna sneered. "He merely found her...different. It is only a boyish infatuation."

"Perhaps that is true. Even so, that infatuation, as you call it, may become an obsession."

Lorna hesitated. The odious woman was right, of course, she told herself, though she hated admitting it. "And how do you suggest killing this attraction before it becomes more dangerous?"

"With your help."

Mrs. MacNair turned toward a tall, graceful rubber plant and tested its broad green leaves for evidence of dust. "Very well," she said after careful reflection. "What kind of help do you need from me?" She raised a finger. "Mind you, I am not saying I will give it; I only want to hear what it is you want."

"You have very influential friends in the newspaper business, I understand."

Lorna nodded. "I know the Hearst family, who own the San Francisco *Examiner*. Phoebe and George are very close friends. Young William is running the *Examiner* now."

"And they would place an announcement for you in the

society column if you asked?"

With an arrogant tilt of her head Lorna said, "Anyone in San Francisco society can make an announcement in the newspaper. But I suppose you aren't aware of the privileges of society."

"I was referring to a false announcement," Lydia said, ignoring the insult.

"My dear Mrs. Nightsong, I am not accustomed to lying and would certainly not consider doing so publicly."

"Not even to save your son from the clutches of my half-Chinese daughter?"

Again the eyes narrowed and the flinty expression chiseled her features. "Kindly explain."

"I have a gentleman who has asked for April's hand in marriage. I doubt very much if April will accept the gentleman's proposal in view of her love for your son. But if David were to marry, she might be more disposed to accept Monsieur Andrieux's offer of marriage."

Lorna put her finger against her cheek and strolled toward the wicker chaise. She turned back. "And by the time David hears—if he ever does—about the fraudulent wedding announcement, your daughter will be married and out of harm's way."

"That is as I hope it will work out."

Lorna MacNair thought quickly. Of course she knew Lydia was her husband's mistress, or had been, according to Mr. Ramsey's detective report. Her first impression had been that this was a trick of some sort—but she could see the wisdom of the scheme.

"Very well," Lorna said finally. "I'll arrange for an engagement announcement to appear in tomorrow's newspaper."

"It must be a wedding announcement. April must be made to believe that David is completely lost to her."

"I see." She thought for another moment. "All right. I suppose I will be able to explain it all to our friends." She looked down her perfect, regal nose and said, "It is unlikely that your daughter will hear of the charade from any of my circle. She doesn't belong to their class."

Again Lydia took the slap without comment. Lorna MacNair could say whatever she wished just so long as she did what Lydia wanted her to do.

"A wedding announcement for little David," Lorna mused, clasping her hands and laughing. "Oh, I'll have great fun telling my friends all about this little joke."

"Then I have your solemn promise?"

Lorna breathed an impatient sigh. "I said I would do my part in this hoax. You may be assured that I will."

"Thank you." Lydia turned and started to leave.

"I would prefer your assurance that your daughter will marry this suitor."

"Of course I can give no guarantee of that, but if you assure her that David has married another, I have a feeling that April will follow suit."

"You are a devious woman, Mrs. Nightsong. I wonder why men make such fools of themselves over women like you?"

Lydia replied, without hesitation, "I have never thought of your husband as a fool, Mrs. MacNair. Good day."

She felt the bristling at her back as she walked slowly toward the door, any minute expecting a vase or a potted plant to come smashing into the back of her head.

The maid stood with the door open. Lydia left the way she had entered, with shoulders square, chin firm, head high.

As she walked home, Lydia wondered if she had made a fatal mistake by losing control of her composure. Lorna might take the insult too much to heart and renege on her agreement to publish the wedding announcement.

No, Lydia told herself as she let herself in. Lorna MacNair was too shrewd to ignore the opportunity of being rid of the threat of April Nightsong once and for all. The wedding announcement would appear.

* * * * * * *

It was on the front page of the society section with a large picture of Lorna and Peter smiling at the readers.

"Eldest son marries New York debutante."

Lydia found she could not watch April's face as she read hurriedly through the short article. The girl's eyes darted from word to word as if searching for something that said it was all a lie.

Slowly, only by the sheerest effort of will, April raised her eyes and let the paper fall into her lap. She sat as immobile as a granite statue, then gradually her fingers curled around the paper, tightening, tightening until she'd crumpled it into a ball. She shoved back her chair, toppling it over backward, and dashed from the breakfast room and up the stairs to her bedroom.

The crumpled newspaper lay within reach. Lydia carefully unraveled it and stared at Peter's face. The stinging behind her eyes came quickly. Then, as if a barrier had collapsed inside her, she buried her face on her arm and gave vent to her pain.

"Beg pardon, Mrs. Nightsong," Nellie, the housekeeper said. Lydia raised her head and wiped her eyes. "Mr. Andrieux is here. I put him in the back parlor."

"Very well, Nellie," Lydia said, dabbing at her eyes. "Thank you."

It took all her courage to get up from her chair and not tell Raymond Andrieux to go to blazes, that she had given her permission for April to marry young David MacNair, that she personally was taking the girl East to find him. But she knew what she had to do and with a heavy sigh she stood and went toward the parlor.

"Good morning, Raymond," she said, forcing herself to sound bright and carefree.

"You spoke to April?" he asked.

"No, not yet." She saw his immediate annoyance. "Be patient. I am certain April will accept you if your proposal is handled properly."

"You are her mother. In France a girl does what her parents tell her to do."

"It is something like that here too, Raymond, but April has always been rather independent and headstrong. She does not take well to dictates."

Nellie came in wheeling a Hepplewhite serving cart with coffee and breakfast pastries.

"Just have a little patience with her," Lydia said, fixing him a cup of coffee and waiting for Nellie to leave the room. "And I think it would be better if you proposed to April directly."

Raymond looked astonished. "Would she accept me without your telling her to?"

"Yes, I believe she would. Give her a little time. You may be surprised at how quickly she says yes to you."

Raymond looked unconvinced. "Just remember," he said, "I will not reproduce the first quantities of *Nightsong* until after April and I are married."

"I understand."

It didn't take much time for April to come around. When Lydia came home that evening April was curled up in the window seat of the downstairs sitting room reading a book. She was wearing a lovely pink chiffon dress with matching ribbons at her wrists and throat. The pink of the gown was an exquisite complement to her China doll complexion and long, black shining hair.

She looked up from her book. It gave Lydia a stab of pain to see the terrible hurt in her eyes.

April said, "I assume you know what upset me this morning?"

Lydia walked over to the table beside the fireplace and began to rearrange the three jade figures which sat on it. "Yes, I read the announcement."

When April spoke, it was in anger. "How could David be so weak, Mother?" she demanded. "I know he was forced into marrying that debutante, but still that isn't any excuse. Was he always weak? Did I just never notice?"

Lydia could not reply. After a moment, April answered her own question. "He was terribly spoiled by his mother, I know, and he didn't seem to care about anyone but himself. But I was sure he cared about me. He always did whatever I wanted him to do. He never argued with me. I thought it was because he loved me so much, but now I see he was just a jelly fish."

Guilt wouldn't permit Lydia to let April destroy her memories completely. She sat beside her daughter, took the book away and held her hand.

"I don't think David is a jelly fish, darling" she said gently. "Men just don't put importance on things the way we women do." She thought of Peter and said, "Marriage doesn't mean as much to them. Try not to be too hard on David, April. His parents are strong-minded people. It must have been difficult for David to stand up to them under pressure."

"But he isn't like that. He wouldn't collapse under pressure from his family. He always did exactly what he wanted."

"You and I have not been very close of late, April. I've been too busy trying to make a comfortable life for us. I'm sorry I was so unreasonable about your relationship with David. I should have been more tactful in my objections to him, but he was never for you, darling. His mother would have made your lives miserable and you could never transplant him or yourself successfully to China and be happy. In time David would miss everything he knew and so would you."

She kissed April's forehead and ran her hand lovingly down the long cascade of black hair. "People can be cruel wherever one goes, my dear, even when they do not intend to be. Even mothers."

In her urgency to undo some of the terrible hurt she'd caused, Lydia impulsively said, "Perhaps all of this news about David is some kind of mistake. We could go to New York, you and I, and...."

"No," April said sharply, jumping up. "I'm sure it is all true. Besides, the last thing David would want is to see me now that he has a wife. There's nothing to be gained by making myself look more ridiculous, or by creating some kind of scandal." She gave her mother a slow smile that started in her dark, sad eyes and moved by degrees to her lovely mouth.

The smile was so painful it only made Lydia's heart ache all the more for the child's unhappiness. Yet for all her shame for what she'd done, Lydia could not bring herself to tell April the truth.

Besides, what would it accomplish if she did, she asked herself, watching April move slowly toward the arched windows overlooking the side garden. She'd run to David, they'd marry and be off to China which would be more monstrous than her inflicting April with this momentary pain. What she had done was for April's own good and Lydia reminded herself that she had to keep her resolve firmly fixed.

April turned back. "I haven't quite convinced myself that what happened was for the best but I will, in time."

* * * * * * *

That evening, when April joined Lydia and Raymond for dinner, she was again wearing the gay little mask of affability to hide her broken heart. She talked incessantly, saying nothing, filling in every second with words that would keep unpleasant thoughts and memories at bay.

Raymond said, "Rather than answer all the questions you ask about Paris, perhaps I could take you there."

"Oh," April gushed, exaggerating her enthusiasm. "I'd adore it. I wish we could go right now, this very instant."

Lydia smiled conspiratorially at Raymond and said to April, "Perhaps a cruise might be the very thing you need to get your mind off things."

"Yes, a cruise. That would be wonderful," April said. Then her heart sank when she thought that sailing to Europe meant going to New York. She wasn't sure her fortitude was strong enough yet for that difficult a test. Being in the same city with David and his wife would be very hard. "Of course," she said hesitantly, "there would be many things I'd have to get before thinking of making such a trip."

"Paris is the capital of fashion, little one. I will buy you the city if you would permit me."

April heard a strange passion in his voice and looked at him, frowning. There was something in his expression that confused her, as if he were looking at her suddenly with different eyes. Her face went blank as she fixed her gaze on her plate. She didn't like the way they were both watching her. She touched the front of her dress to be sure it wasn't undone.

Nellie relieved April's discomfort by coming in with the strawberry dessert.

"Let's have it in the drawing room," Lydia suggested as she got out of her chair. She searched for some logical excuse to leave Raymond and April alone but could not think of one.

She found her excuse when Nellie announced that Evelyn Clary was at the door. "Something about a shipment that the railroad lost."

"Oh dear. Show her into my study, Nellie." Lydia hurriedly excused herself, giving Raymond a knowing look and telling him to entertain April until she returned.

"Your mother is a very talented business woman," Raymond commented when they were alone. "I'm surprised you haven't taken more of an interest in what we do at Empress Cosmetics."

April shrugged. "I never thought about it." She could not dispel the uneasiness that was crawling up and down her spine. As long as she'd known Raymond Andrieux she'd always thought him a suave, yet brash man, full of his own self-importance. Now he was suddenly so serious, almost shy.

She cocked her head as a thought occurred to her. "Are you planning on marrying Lydia?" she asked boldly.

Raymond put back his head and laughed; the laughter relieved some of the heavy foreboding that hung over April's head. "You are enchanting," Raymond said. He paused, looking fondly at her beautiful face. "Surely you must know that it is you I want to marry."

"What!" she managed to gasp.

"Didn't you know that I am in love with you, April?"

"Me?" she answered, stupefied. "I thought...." She motioned

in the direction in which Lydia had gone.

"Your mother is well aware of how I feel, April. She warned me of my stiff competition. David? Isn't that his name?"

It was as if a bullet pierced her heart. She lay her hand quickly over the pain. "Yes." She let her hand fall into her lap. "He isn't competition anymore."

"I see." Renewed courage took hold of him. "Then perhaps I could hope that you might consider me as a suitor?"

Her heart began to beat a little more quickly. "I suppose I could."

"I fell in love with you the very first time I saw you. I wanted to ask you to marry me then." He said nothing more, only watched her sitting passively on the settee, toying with a ribbon on her dress.

"I don't really know you," April said finally. She did not look at him but she was conscious of his extreme good looks, his maturity, his generosity. Lydia had told her that he was rich; he could give her the world if she asked for it. She would never be able to return the obviously devastating passion that was in his heart but perhaps he would, in time, make her forget David MacNair and her Chinese homeland. Perhaps this handsome Frenchman was the remedy for her broken heart, her disillusionment.

Raymond gave her a look and she felt her eyes drawn to his. She saw a hardness there, a hardness she interpreted as determination. "You can get to know me well enough on our trip to Paris," he said.

She was not the least bit in love with this man, but there were so many things about his proposal that would solve her problems. Going to New York as Mrs. Raymond Andrieux would remove all temptations of wanting to see David or his wanting to see her. They would travel to Europe, stay for a very long time, and when they returned she would have left David MacNair somewhere in the excitement of Paris, the color of Italy, the freedom of Spain. Raymond would show her all of it and rid her of David for always.

"If I did agree to marry you, when would it be?"

His smile was brilliant. "Whenever you wish. Tomorrow, if you like...or next year. I will wait."

In a flash she saw in her mind's eye a similar announcement to the one she'd read in the San Francisco *Examiner,* adding that the happy couple would be returning to the bridegroom's estate in Paris for an extended honeymoon. She'd insist upon a big wedding, something to show the world how much disdain she had for it, and also that a half-Chinese girl was not, after all, someone to be looked down upon.

April stretched out her hand. "I believe I could become very fond of you, Raymond, if you will give me time."

"Then you are accepting my proposal?"

"Yes, I suppose I am," April answered.

There was a quiet celebration when Lydia and Evelyn Clary finished their business and Raymond told them the happy news. When he was busy opening the champagne and April had gone to tell Nellie the news, Evelyn leaned close to Lydia and said, "You could have knocked me over with a feather. I thought you were the one who would be the happy bride."

Lydia shrugged. "Raymond had his choice. I lost, that's all."

Her flippancy changed to dejection when she found herself alone in bed. She did not exactly resent Raymond's choosing April, but she did not enjoy the outlook that lay ahead for her. April would be gone out of her life just as totally as if she'd married David and had run off to China. She had, of course, saved April from that horrible mistake, but it nonetheless did not alleviate her melancholy.

All she'd worked to attain she'd attained, but now there was no one with whom to share any of it. Once she had had a dream of creating a dynasty, like the Manchus of China, with dozens of heirs, children laughing and racing through every corner of the house.

Her eyes opened wide as she remembered the son she'd been forced to abandon so many years ago. She suddenly wanted to know what he looked like now. He'd be a few years younger than April, just a teen-aged boy. Perhaps someday, through some miracle of chance, he would be her hope for a dynasty.

CHAPTER TEN

It was with a great many misgivings that Lydia agreed to April's demands for a big, elaborate wedding. Far back in her mind she recalled the humiliation she'd been forced to suffer when her own wedding to the prominent Walter Hanover was announced and Peter MacNair had revealed to the world that the future Mrs. Hanover already had a husband in China, a Mandarin prince. The scandal was long since dead but the disgrace was still with her. Peter denied it, naturally, but he was responsible for the story being printed. Lydia had no doubt of that, which was just another reason for her to despise him.

Of course she could understand why April wanted a splashy wedding, and deep in her heart she felt she owed it to her. She'd made her daughter suffer too many indignities as it was; it was only fair that she be allowed to try and make a place for herself in society. The Nightsongs were, after all, wealthy now and Raymond came from a fine old French family. So why shouldn't April have all the same privileges as the daughters of all of the other Nob Hill families?

Unfortunately, Lydia had to face the fact that they had very few friends in San Francisco society. Everyone attending the ceremony and reception would be either business acquaintances or employees, which started Lydia thinking.

Why couldn't she become just as important a socialite as the other Nob Hill families? Her parents had been respectable and she was certainly rich enough, even well known. She contributed generously to all the local charities. And for the few in high

San Francisco society who spurned her—Lorna MacNair and the Walter Hanovers—there were twenty times as many who welcomed her generosity and, therefore, should be willing to welcome her socially as well.

With a new determination she rang for Evelyn Clary.

When Evelyn came in Lydia said, "April has decided on a late September wedding."

"I know. I've already lined up a caterer, a minister and a decorator for the house."

"Good. Now about the invitations...."

"The printer is coming over for the copy this afternoon." Evelyn handed her several pieces of paper. "I made some drafts for you to choose from."

"How many were on that list of guests which I gave you?"

"Sixty-two."

"I'm changing all that," Lydia told her. "If April wants a first class wedding then she's going to have first class guests. I'm inviting every socialite and every prominent name in San Francisco, in the State of California for that matter."

Evelyn stared at her.

"Get me a list of all the charities we contribute generously to every year and then find out the names of the ladies or gentlemen who head those drives and organizations. I want to talk to each one of them personally. You've heard, of course, about buying your way into society; well, that's exactly what I intend doing. It's time I got some use out of the people I support, and that goes for the mayor, the governor and anyone else of importance who benefits from Empress Cosmetics and Lydia Nightsong. We are becoming a very prestigious firm, Evelyn, and when *Nightsong* goes on the market we will gain even more prestige. It's about time I cashed in on it, for April's sake," she added almost as an aside. "It's the least I can do for her."

Over the following days and weeks Lydia spent all of her time promising financial support to every worthwhile charity in the city and at the same time making friends with the prominent citizens involved. She never failed to mention April's forthcoming wedding and the great disappointment Lydia would feel if they did not attend.

She promised several thousand dollars to the Steinharts for their proposed addition to the aquarium, like amounts to the Morrisons and to the deYoungs, contributions to the museum and to the new planetarium, reminders to Governor Stoneman of the substantial amounts paid into his political campaign, reminders to the Huntingtons with laughing references to the exorbitant sums paid by Lydia's company for use of their rail lines. She held similar conversations with the Stanfords and the Crockers, bankers, builders, shippers, sellers. She applied pressure on all of them. The wives were indignant; the husbands admired Lydia for her business acumen and the wives, in the end, did what their husbands told them to do.

Evelyn Clary's eyes widened in surprise one morning when she saw a name that Lydia had asked her to add to the invitational list. "Are you sure, Lydia?" she asked. "Walter Hanover, his daughter and his mother? You know what a rotter he was, and his mother absolutely loathes you. And you've never liked that snobbish little daughter of his."

"Invite them. They're high society. I can't afford to snub them. The same goes for the Hearsts and the MacNairs."

Lydia's heart gave a little tug. She was certain Lorna MacNair would be furious at receiving a wedding invitation but she had a suspicion that Peter would attend. As for the Hearsts, young William Randolph was a fire-brand. His parents were rather superior but Lydia had liked the young son and he'd promised her he'd attend when she promised him her large advertising program in his newspapers.

April's photograph appeared on the first page of the society section of the *Examiner*. The wedding was scheduled for September twenty eighth. The ceremony and reception would be held at the Nightsong Nob Hill mansion. The couple would leave immediately for an extended honeymoon at the groom's family residence in Paris.

April wanted to leave as soon as possible. She had her heart set only on getting married and starting to rebuild the life David MacNair had destroyed.

April did not delude herself as to why she was marrying Raymond. It was her punishment for having been so happy. She thought often of something Kim Lee had once said to her: "In nature there are neither rewards nor punishments, there are only consequences."

And this, April thought as she looked at the large diamond engagement ring on her finger, was the consequence for having loved.

As the day of the wedding grew nearer, the acknowledgements began pouring in and Lydia was overjoyed to see more acceptances than regrets. Lorna MacNair, she noticed, had not even deigned to reply. The Walter Hanovers would be unable to attend, Lydia noted and smiled at the hastily written note Walter had included.

"I'll be in Europe with Mother and Kathy. Perhaps you would permit me to call and pay my respects when we return."

* * * * * * *

Evelyn Clary came into the private office carrying another stack of replies. "And it is doing wonders for business," she said as she showed Lydia another of the society editor's updates on the forthcoming ceremony, which Lydia was amused to notice was now being referred to as the "wedding of the season" or the "most fashionable wedding of the year." She had been promoted from the owner of Empress Cosmetics to "the queen of the cosmetic industry," "Countess of Fashion," "Baroness of *Haut Monde*." Of course Raymond's being French helped a great deal in establishing the whole new image that was being created for her. San Francisco's upper crust were mostly *nouveau riche* and insecure in their positions. They were intimidated by his lineage and old wealth.

Evelyn handed her a stack of letters. "Empress Cosmetics is now being asked for by the middle classes," she said with pride.

"We're inching into P.M.'s territory according to these recent requests we've received. Kress and Company doesn't want our top-priced products but have asked if we could make a less expensive product for them with the Kress logo on it."

Lydia shook her head. "Nothing goes out of my company with any logo other than Empress Cosmetics." She put aside the Kress request. "But invite the Kress family to the wedding. Now, how is Marketing coming along with that container Raymond's friend, designed for *Nightsong*?"

"Already in the works, only there's one very major problem."

"Such as?"

"No *Nightsong* perfume to put into the *Nightsong* bottle."

"The first quantities of *Nightsong* perfume will be given us on September twenty-ninth," Lydia said. "I've already alerted Manufacturing."

Lydia saw Evelyn's mind at work. April's wedding was the twenty-eighth of September.

"Men," Evelyn said as she sat down at her desk and rolled a piece of letterhead into her typewriter. "They always go for the pretty goldfish when a marlin could keep them in food for a lifetime."

CHAPTER ELEVEN

In New York David found an entirely different world from the one he and April had shared. The people he met on the east coast didn't seem to hate the Chinese as much as they did in California, partly, perhaps, because there were fewer Chinese in evidence.

After the first weeks of living with his mother's family in the Fifth Avenue townhouse, David was determined to marry April and bring her here where she would be admired rather than chastised.

He liked New York and was glad now that his father planned to open an eastern branch of P.M. Cosmetics here. Everything was working out just fine, he told himself as he thought of today's letter that he had just posted to April. He couldn't understand why she hadn't replied to his earlier letters and was terribly impatient for her reaction to his proposal that they live here.

The newsstand on Forty-third Street and Broadway was the only place he could buy the San Francisco *Examiner* and even then it was sometimes weeks old by the time it reached New York. Scanning the pages his heart jumped when he saw April's picture on the front of the society section. Slowly he forced himself to read the article. A pain began at the back of his eyes and the words began to blur together. Again and again he tried to piece the message together with the picture, frowning at April, telling himself it wasn't really her face, it wasn't her wedding they were talking about.

"Raymond Andrieux," David said, making a passerby turn

and frown at him. He had heard April mention the name; but he was the man who worked for her mother.

A shot of hope leapt up inside him as again he gazed at April's photograph, thinking that the paper had made a mistake and had published April's picture instead of her mother's. Perhaps the man was to marry Mrs. Nightsong. But no, the announcement made it quite clear that it was April's marriage that would take place. It said quite plainly, "April Nightsong, daughter of Lydia Nightsong."

His first reaction was that he had to save her from making this dreadful mistake. Hadn't she gotten his letters? Didn't she know that this forced separation was only temporary? Surely she didn't think so lowly of him that she could believe he'd abandoned her?

He had to get home. He had to reach San Francisco before— he checked the newspaper article—before September twenty-eighth.

"Good Lord," he breathed, asking without a thought for who was to answer, "what's today's date?"

The *Examiner* was dated September second, but that was weeks old.

"September sixteenth," the news seller told him, giving him a wary look.

He had less than two weeks to get back to California.

David reached San Francisco on the morning of September twenty-eighth, not knowing whether the planned wedding was to be held in the morning or when. In front of the Nightsong mansion was a line of every type conveyance of quality that could be imagined, with all the drivers in livery. He saw guests walking up the stairs to the house and knew he was in time. The men were in formal morning clothes, the women in flowing silk, wide flopping brimmed hats and long ribbons. The day was warm, almost hot, and he felt uncomfortable in his East Coast fall clothing.

David jumped the fancy wrought iron fence and hurried toward the service entrance at the back. The kitchen was a swarm of activity, maids in crisp white and black scurrying about like queens in their own domain. Dodging his way between trays of champagne and caviar, platters of canapés and pates, he found himself in the back hall where a stairway started up to the second level.

"What are you doing here?" Lydia demanded harshly just as David started to climb.

He'd never seen a more beautiful woman, or an angrier one. The white trail of silk with its overlay of white satin roses embroidered down the front, gave her the look of an empress.

Slowly she raised a white gloved arm and pointed to the door. "Get out!"

David stood firm, his chin jutted out. "I didn't travel thousands of miles just to turn around and go away. I intend seeing April."

"Why?"

"She can't marry this man. I won't let her."

"And what do you propose to offer her as a substitute, yourself?"

"Yes."

Lydia noticed a few wandering guests moving closer to listen. She grabbed David's arm and drew him into the back parlor, closing the sliding doors. She whirled on him and said, "And what can you give her that will make her happy? Your family? Your mother despises her. April is being married to a very respectable man from a highly revered family. He can give her the world."

"Father is planning on opening a P.M. plant in New York. I'll take April back with me. I can make a life for her there."

"Be sensible, David," Lydia said as her anger began to grow. "If you marry April just how long do you think your parents will permit you to remain a part of their family? You'll be kicked out into the streets without a cent. I will not permit you to drag my daughter down into the gutter with you."

"We'll find a way," David said.

"Young people always say that," Lydia argued, more gently

but no less firmly. "But just think—she would never be happy with you in New York, even if your father permitted you to remain with the firm, which he wouldn't. You could hardly live here, with the prejudice against her, and against your marriage. Could you really be happy living with her in China?"

David shifted his weight from one foot to the other.

He did have reservations about journeying to China, though he had been reluctant to voice them to April. "I can't give her up," he said helplessly.

"She already thinks you have. I've kept your letters from her—oh, I know, that was cruel and unfair, but mothers are never fair where their daughters are concerned. The point is, you've nothing to blame yourself for, it was my doing, but she has finally begun to get over the hurt. She is trying to build a new life for herself, and David, if you love her, you can see it's a better life than you can give her. Raymond is mature, well-to-do, a man of the world—and a foreigner himself. I know it sounds foolish, but people will resent her marrying him less than if she married you."

"I'll never marry anyone else," he said. Tears had begun to fill his eyes, and now they rolled unchecked down his cheeks.

"Do this for her, if you really love her," Lydia urged.

David opened his mouth to speak but could not find his voice. With a helpless shrug, he turned slowly and walked out of the house.

Lydia went to the window and saw him start up the hill toward his home. The air was suddenly cool, heralding the coming of autumn and another season. High in the sky, white, puffy clouds sailed slowly across the deep blue of the sky. She watched as David held himself very straight, and she found the slight tilt of his head very gallant. He was a trim, handsome figure, so like his father.

David disappeared around the corner of the street, and was gone.

CHAPTER TWELVE

April's marriage to Raymond went badly from the start. The love she felt for David never left her for a moment; it was an effort to allow Raymond to touch her. As for Raymond, the pride he'd taken in April's exotic features, her almond eyes, the porcelain skin, slowly turned to resentment every time a maitre d' raised a questioning eyebrow or guests ignored them at parties. In Europe the resentment hadn't been so pronounced, but April hadn't much cared for Europe and their honeymoon was cut short.

Back home, the long-seeded prejudice against Orientals came home to him in all its ugliness, and by the time they reached their third month anniversary Raymond knew he'd made a mistake in his choice of wives, though his vanity prevented him from admitting it. If only he could have April as a mistress rather than a wife, all would be perfect.

Nightsong was a raging success, however. Lydia found herself flooded with orders from all over the country, orders she could not possibly fill even when Raymond cut short his honeymoon and returned to working a full schedule perfecting batch after glorious batch of the intoxicating perfume. The Christmas deliveries sold out in five short days and by the end of January of the New Year the demands for *Nightsong* were overwhelming.

"Of course we must discontinue shipping," Raymond suggested.

"Discontinue?" Lydia gasped.

Evelyn Clary gaped at him. "You've got to be crazy," she

said, rifling through a stack of new orders.

"We ship nothing. We work on stockpiling and then, say in February or March, we begin advertising in the fashion periodicals. We then notify all those who have ordered shipments of *Nightsong* that the price is...let's say twice what it was, maybe even three times."

"You're mad. We'll never get it," Evelyn objected.

Lydia nodded thoughtfully. "I believe we will, Evelyn," she said. "Raymond's right. Supply and demand. If we inundate the market with *Nightsong* it will become too popular. When something becomes too commonplace people stop buying it."

"Bon!" Raymond said. "We will make *Nightsong* the most exclusive perfume ever produced." He smiled impishly and added, "Of course that way I will not have to work so hard."

They laughed. Unfortunately, when Raymond left Lydia's office his good mood dissolved. The challenge had been found and met and he was back feeling at odds with life, restless and bored. The money he was making was a source of solace, but money meant little to him. Any clever man could make money; that in itself was part of the challenge of living.

Raymond left his laboratory office and went to find someplace as depressing as his mood. The Red Plume on the Barbary Coast seemed to suit him as he sidled up to the oak and mirror bar and ordered a whiskey. The prostitutes smiled at him and it pleased him to flirt back. He was in a jubilant mood after the third round of drinks until he reached again for his billfold only to find an empty pocket.

He made a terrible row which ended in his being thrown out of the place. By the time he reached the fashionable apartment overlooking the park he was in a vile state.

April was her usual cool, indifferent self, which only infuriated him all the more. He saw the yellow silk Mandarin robe with its embroidery of pussywillow blossoms. "Why in blazes can't you at least dress like an American woman?"

"Because I am Chinese," April said simply as she bent closer to her sewing hoop.

"Damn Chink," he said as he staggered over to the cabinet and fixed himself a drink.

She raised her eyes to him, then lowered them again as she bit off the thread and made a neat knot at the end of the stitch. "Before you allow yourself to become too drunk, there is something you should know," April said calmly.

"*Dieu!* Now what?"

"I am going to have a child."

The decanter froze in midair as Raymond stopped and looked at her. "A baby? *Mon Dieu!* That is all I need. A damned brat squalling around the place."

"How unselfish of you," she said sarcastically. "I am just as unhappy with the news as you obviously are, but there isn't much either of us can do about it."

"I suppose this will only give you all the more reason not to give me what is a husband's right?" he said.

April had realized that first terrible night the extent of her mistake. The feel of Raymond's body proved odious to her. Though he was trim and firm and muscular, he didn't have that feel or glow of youth which she found in David whenever she touched him, kissed him, looked deep into his eyes. Raymond was a mature man; all of his virgin youth had long since been lost and April felt cheated and deceived.

"You know I do not enjoy that sort of thing," she replied coolly.

"Sex, damn it. It's called *sex,* or don't Chinese princesses know about things like that?"

At first he had liked to hear her talk about her Mandarin father and her princely little brother, but when it interfered with the basics of what he'd expected in a marriage, he began to see how foolishly fake she was, how she deceived herself. He had tried to make a woman out of her but his brute force had only brought hate into her eyes.

"Please don't start, Raymond."

With a sudden burst of temper he smashed the crystal decanter against the marble facing of the fireplace and grabbed her wrist. He pulled her out of her chair and crushed her against him, inhaling the scent of *Nightsong* that clung to her, overpowering his senses, sending a sudden lust for her rushing through his veins.

"No, Raymond," April said, refusing to struggle, knowing any resistance would only increase his desire for her. "No."

He looked down into her face, his eyes blurred from drink. "The hell you say." He tightened his arm around her. "If you're going to have *l'enfant,* this may be the last time you will want to give me what I need."

"Stop it, Raymond," she said as he began to kiss her throat, her hair. His hands moved to grope at her breasts. April pulled herself out of his arms and slapped his face. "I said stop it!"

The sting on his cheek infuriated him. "You prissy little bitch!" he swore. He grabbed at her with both hands, rage mingling with blind lust, and ripped her Mandarin robe open from collar to waist.

April tried to push him away but the liquor gave him an animal strength. He cupped her naked breasts in his hands and began to squeeze. April winced with pain. He squeezed harder until the pain was unbearable, until she was certain the full brown nipples would burst apart. She raised her knee and brought it up hard between his thighs.

Raymond screamed in pain and toppled to the floor, writhing in agony and clutching himself.

April quickly pulled her torn robe over her nakedness and ran into the bedroom, locking herself in.

When the white hot pain began to subside Raymond got unsteadily to his feet. He saw the closed door to the bedroom and staggered over to it and tried the knob.

"Open the goddamn door, April." He began pounding on it with his fists. When he realized she had no intention of obeying him he took a step back, raised his foot and kicked the door from its hinges.

April was standing near the foot of the bed with a long, sharp fingernail file pointed threateningly at Raymond's stomach.

He advanced toward her, slapping her hard across the face and breaking the nail file easily between his fingers.

She struggled against him but he pulled her forcibly into his arms and began to tear the rest of her clothes from her body. When she was completely naked he picked her up and threw her on the over-sized bed.

"Raymond, no, please," she cried as he fell on top of her. She tried desperately to scramble out from under him. The smell of his breath, the feel of his coarseness, the heat of him repelled her, made her stomach retch.

April cried out with pain as his hands dug into her breasts again, kneading, pinching, hurting. In a clumsy fury he forced himself between her legs and when she tried to clamp shut her thighs he hit her again, harder.

They were both breathing heavily; April was close to exhaustion, Raymond far gone toward lust. When she went still in his arms he took her stillness for surrender. As he smiled victoriously down into her face April drew back her head and spat into his face.

His right hand lashed out like a whip. He slapped her across the face and wiped off the spittle on the back of his hand.

"Damn you, Chink, you can't do that to me," he swore. He grabbed her by the shoulders and began shaking her, not caring about the ugly bruises he was leaving on her flesh.

"Now you'd better start giving me what is rightfully mine if you know what's good for you, you slanty-eyed bitch," he said through his drunken lust.

She knew it was senseless to refuse him unless she wanted to be brutalized further, possibly killed by this drunken beast.

When it was finished and Raymond snored contentedly beside her, she moved away from him in utter disgust. "Never again," she swore. Somehow she had to be rid of this horrible man.

She had never gone to her mother with her problems, not since she had been a little girl. Now, however, there was no one else to whom she could turn.

* * * * * * *

Lydia listened quietly, trying to hide the pangs of guilt that April's story caused her. She, after all, had influenced April to marry Raymond, though the decision had been entirely April's.

Or had it? Lydia pressed a hand to one temple. Raymond was so important to them just now. And every couple had their quarrels, especially when starting out. April was so headstrong, and a man would resent that in a bride, especially a man like Raymond.

"I won't go back to him," April said when she had finished her story.

It was hard for Lydia to believe that the man April described was the same Raymond Lydia herself had known sexually. He had been virile, demanding, but certainly never violent.

No, April's heart was still with David. She had locked herself and her feelings behind a door; Raymond could hardly be blamed for trying to force that door open.

"You must think of your child," Lydia advised. "A baby very often makes a big difference in a marriage. I know it did in mine," she said laying her hand gently over April's. "You married a man you did not love, but there is no reason why you can't learn to love Raymond. He can give you a wonderful life, if you'll let him."

"If he doesn't kill me first. Oh, mother, you just don't realize." Suddenly she undid the top buttons of her dress and pulled aside the neckline, revealing the ugly marks on her skin. "Look how he's hurt me."

Although the bruises were shocking, Lydia recalled all too clearly her Mandarin husband and his cat-o-nine tails. "Men are not as capable of self-control as women are, April."

April looked hurt. "Why do you take his part and not mine?"

"I don't take his part over yours, darling. But Raymond is a man. He knows the world you are just starting to learn about. Be patient both with him and with yourself," she said kindly.

"I won't go back to him," April insisted stubbornly.

"You must, if not for yourself and your baby, then do it for me."

"For you?"

"Surely you know how important Raymond is to Empress Cosmetics."

"Why is he still important? He copied the Dowager Empress's perfume. He knows the formula, which I am sure he gave you or would sell to you."

"There is no formula for a perfume as rare and as fine as *Nightsong.* Each individual batch must be inspected by Raymond personally. Only a *Nez* can tell when the individual batch of perfume is an exact reproduction of the original. It is all inside Raymond's head, his talent for detecting scents, his uncanny sense of smell. No two batches of *Nightsong* are alike until Raymond makes whatever alterations are required; only then is the batch sent to the bottlers and sent out to our customers. Have you not wondered why the more exotic perfumes are always so expensive? It is because they cannot be mass produced from a formula; each must be duplicated exactly from the original."

April dropped back into the soft cushioned settee.

"The ingredients for concocting *Nightsong* are inside your husband's head and he alone can continue to reproduce it. If he loses that talent, that special knack, then *Nightsong* will cease to exist unless we find another *Nez.*" Lydia patted April's hand. "So be patient and try to understand, my darling, that we both need Raymond far more than he needs us."

It was with a heavy heart and heavy footsteps that April returned, retracing her path back to her richly furnished apartment overlooking the park. She would have Raymond's child but she vowed that she would never give herself willingly to him again.

* * * * * *

Lydia heard the bell and, thinking April had forgotten something, went to answer it herself. She was dumbfounded to find herself facing someone she'd thought never to meet again.

"Walter Hanover," she exclaimed.

He smiled meekly. "Have I caught you at an inconvenient time? I know I should have called," he said, speaking quickly, "but, well, things have been quite muddled of late. I thought talking to you would help me."

For a moment Lydia felt all the old resentments. But the moment vanished and she smiled at the man who'd been so kind to her when she first arrived in the city. She'd almost forgotten how he'd misused her, the terrible scandal his mother had caused.

"Please Lydia, I must talk to you," Walter said. "There is so much I should explain."

Her first impulse was to slam the door in his face, the way his mother had done to her. "There isn't very much more that needs to be said, Walter, but if you feel you must speak with me, then come in. There's no point in our remaining enemies, I suppose, when we can be friends."

They settled themselves in the sumptuous drawing room. Walter looked about and said, "This is a far, far cry from Van Ness Street, or that hideous tailor shop in Chinatown."

"Yes."

His eyes went sad. "Mother died, you know."

"I'm sorry. No, I didn't know, but then I don't have time for much else but business. I hardly ever read a newspaper."

"We were in Europe when she suffered a heart attack."

"I'm sorry," Lydia said again, feeling guilty that she really didn't care.

"Kathy took it rather hard."

Lydia remembered his daughter as a selfish little thing who was incapable of feeling sad about anyone else. She watched Walter's gentle eyes cloud with tears he fought hard to hold back. Still the same meek Walter, not quite as tall as she, with the same dark hair flecked with grey at the temples, the neatly trimmed moustache that hid an almost womanish face.

"I've sent her to stay with her Aunt Augusta," he added.

Lydia could not help wondering why he had suddenly come to see her after all this time; they only lived several blocks apart. She passed the Hanover mansion every time she turned up Taylor Street. Never had she caught a single glimpse of any of them. She had decided years ago that they had moved; but there was always the occasional mention in a society article, and then Walter's hasty note that came in reply to the wedding invitation she'd reluctantly mailed.

"So you're alone," Lydia said pointedly.

He was quick to catch the innuendo. "Oh, I would have liked so much to have come before this. I went to your old house on Van Ness but you'd moved. It wasn't until we received your invitation to April's wedding that I learned we were actually neighbors."

He looked at her but then, as if his courage failed him, he let his eyes drop. After a moment he said, "Lydia...."

"There really isn't very much you can say, Walter, to ever make things right between us. Your mother saw to that with Peter MacNair's help."

"Peter MacNair? What does he have to do with anything?"

"Please don't insult me further by pretending you don't know," she fumed. "When the announcement was made that you and I were to marry, there was only one person in San Francisco who knew April was my daughter through a Chinese marriage. Only Peter MacNair could have supplied your mother with that information."

"But you're wrong, Lydia. It was Lorna, his wife, who told Mother. She had your past traced by a detective, a Mr. Ramsey. I saw his report. Lorna showed it to Mother before she gave the story to the newspapers."

"Lorna," Lydia breathed.

Again she felt a terrible sense of loss. All these years she'd hated Peter for wrongs which hadn't been his doing. All her life she'd blamed him, driven him farther and farther away from her. But she reminded herself that it had never been her that he'd desired; it was *Nightsong* he wanted to possess.

"Regardless," Lydia said, feeling her resentment of Peter returning. "It was the MacNairs that almost destroyed me in this city. Peter was as guilty as his wife."

"You've hardly been destroyed by all that old gossip," he said looking around at the expensive drawing room. "You've become an extremely rich woman, Lydia."

And it had all started with him, she was quick to remind herself. If it hadn't been for Walter Hanover, God only knew where she and April would be today. Some of her old resentment of him fell away and she felt her old gratitude return.

"Thanks to you, Walter." She hesitated a moment then said, "And your mother. It was she who first gave me hope for the success of *Nightsong*."

"I remember. She raved about its scent for weeks." He lowered his head. "Too bad...." His voice broke.

Lydia shifted uncomfortably. "So," she said brightly, "what business venture are you involved in nowadays?"

They began to talk easily, just as they once had years before. The shadows had crept well across the carpet before either of them realized the afternoon was almost evening. Lydia heard the clock in the foyer strike four. "My, I had no idea it was so late."

"Have dinner with me," Walter suggested. When he saw her hesitate he added, "There's something I wish to talk over with you—a business matter, to be perfectly honest. Please say you will. It's important to me, Lydia."

"Very well," she said, seeing how serious he'd grown. There was almost a frantic look about him she thought.

"Good. I'll call for you at seven."

CHAPTER THIRTEEN

Peter MacNair saw Lydia and Walter Hanover get into the carriage and drive away. Immediately his suspicions flared to life. He had heard that Hanover was back from Europe; he had also heard that his mother's estate was being settled and from business gossip there were an awful lot of creditors waiting with their hands out. From what Peter's friends had told him, Walter Hanover was over his head in debts and even his mother's vast estate wouldn't cover all of them.

Why, Peter wondered, was he suddenly paying court again to Lydia?

For a moment he was tempted to follow the carriage but Lorna entered the parlor and called his attention away from the window. Peter bit down on his lower lip. He'd give half his fortune to know what Walter and Lydia were talking about right now.

* * * * * *

"Nightsong," Walter said as the carriage moved down the hill toward the Palm Court. "I hear women raving about it everywhere I. go. You really must begin distributing in Europe, Lydia."

She smiled, pleased as always to hear plaudits for the scent on which she'd gambled so much.

"Mother would have been so pleased that it was she who'd first recognized the perfume's potential." He looked at her out of the corners of his eyes.

"It all seems so very long ago," Lydia said. She found herself thinking that what he'd said wasn't quite true. She herself had always recognized the perfume's potential. And before that, even, it was Peter McNair who had first told her about it. The truth was, if she owed anyone but herself for her success with Nightsong, it was Peter, though she would never tell him that.

Walter gave a tight little laugh. "If I had followed my instincts and ignored the horrible slander, you and I would be partners today."

"But the slander was true."

He let his eyes slide forward. "And what of your husband in China?" he ventured.

"Under Chinese law I am still married, I suppose. However, I am not in China."

"I see."

Lydia was not quite sure how she should interpret the way his lips were pursed together, the nervous little drumming of his fingers on the tip of his walking stick. He was angling for something, she decided. She knew him well enough to know he was a snob, like his mother and daughter. He couldn't possibly still want to marry her.

But he did, Lydia found out as they were having coffee and dessert.

"I have never changed in my feelings toward you, Lydia, hard as that may be for you to believe," he said abruptly.

He had rhapsodized too much about the success she'd made of Empress Cosmetics for her to believe him. She decided to toy with him.

"Surely you haven't forgotten my Mandarin husband and my half-Chinese daughter," she said, in a teasing manner. She couldn't help but smile at the way he tried to hide his discomfort.

"April is married now," he hedged.

"And expecting a child."

"Excellent." He swallowed some coffee and tapped on the

table with his fingertips. He cleared his throat and said, "If mother hadn't had that first attack when the news of your husband was published, I would still have insisted you keep your promise to marry me."

Hiding the shadow of a smile, Lydia arched her brows and said, "Ask me to commit bigamy, Walter?"

"I am certain all of that could have been cleared up with the help of a good attorney. I'm surprised that you yourself haven't taken steps to free yourself from the Chinaman."

Lydia shrugged as she ate the Bavarian cream. "I had no reason to."

"Then there is no other man in your life, I take it?"

Without a pause Lydia asked, *"Other* man? There is no man, period." She saw his disappointment at her firmness.

"I still love you, Lydia," he said, his voice flat.

When he reached for her hand Lydia picked up her napkin and blotted the corners of her mouth. "Exactly what do you want, Walter?" She leveled her eyes firmly on his.

"You, of course," he said a little too enthusiastically. He grabbed her hand, this time trapping it.

"Walter," she said patiently, "We have known each other a long time and I pride myself at being rather good at spotting trouble. To me you look like a man in trouble."

He gradually shrank back into his chair, letting her hand slip out of his.

"You once helped me from the very doorstep of destitution, Walter. I owe you a great deal," she went on, but more kindly. What Empress Cosmetics was today was because of her own money and her own labors, but it had been Walter Hanover who had come to her rescue that day she and April were forced to leave the ship with only the clothes on their backs. "If there is anything I can do to repay your kindnesses to us, Walter, I will be more than happy to do it." '

"Marry me."

Lydia laughed as the waiter in the white linen jacket refilled their coffee cups and took away the dessert plates. "Is it as bad as all that?" she asked, still smiling.

Walter looked confused. "I beg your pardon?"

"You must be in very deep trouble if it takes marrying the mother of a half-Chinese girl to get you out of it."

How different their conversation was now. Back then it had been Walter in control. He had led and she had followed. There was something pathetic about the switch in roles, she found.

"Please, Lydia, don't refuse me. If you recall, I refused you nothing once."

The reminder angered her. He had refused her nothing, true, but he'd made sure she'd signed for every penny he'd advanced to her enterprise and when he walked away, humiliated by the scandal she'd caused, it had taken years for her to pay off the debt to him and the others left in his wake. Now he was making himself sound so noble, so righteous.

"Just tell me what you want, Walter."

He fidgeted uncomfortably. "April aside, I would still consider marrying you, Lydia."

"But I would not consider marrying you," she said firmly.

"I see." He drummed the tabletop and thought for a moment. Lydia sat watching his rather weak, dull face suddenly grow dark and spiteful. "I had hoped you'd still feel the same about me, but I see I was wrong."

"Oh, Walter, you know perfectly well that marriage between us would be a disaster. Back then it would have been a business arrangement, nothing more; that was the only reason I'd agreed. You must know that to be true."

"That is exactly what I am offering you now."

Lydia failed to see the connection. "But there is no reason for us to marry for business reasons, Walter. We aren't connected in any way."

"But we are." He reached into the inside pocket of his dinner jacket and drew out a legal looking document. "Do you recognize this?"

Lydia frowned at the Agreement. It was the note she'd signed when Walter advanced the initial monies to put Empress

Cosmetics into operation. "Yes, of course. But I've repaid every cent of your money, plus interest."

"I feel that Empress Cosmetics is still fifty percent mine."

Lydia stared at him as he smugly took back the Agreement and replaced it in his inside pocket. "You're mad!" she cried. "The Empress Cosmetic facility you and I formed folded long ago, leaving me terribly in debt. The company I own today has nothing to do with that earlier one."

"A court of law may decide otherwise. Believe it or not, Lydia, I was sincere in my offer to marry you. I continue to find you an extremely beautiful woman, one of the most beautiful women I have ever seen. April need not be a part of our life. We could hide her somewhere, the way you palmed her off once as your maid."

Lydia's cheeks were burning with rage. "How dare you," she snarled.

"Fifty percent of Empress Cosmetics," Walter repeated. "Either I get it by way of a marriage license or by a court order. That is for you to decide."

Lydia got angrily to her feet and slammed her napkin down on the table, rattling her cup and saucer. "You'll never touch a penny of Empress Cosmetics. Do what you think you must, Walter, but I will see you in hell before I turn over any part of what is mine."

It was as if someone had held a mirror up to time as she remembered another flight, years before, when she'd dashed blindly away from Peter MacNair and ran headlong into the arms of Walter Hanover. This time it was exactly in reverse.

"Lydia," Peter said as she bolted out of the door, almost knocking aside the doorman in uniform when he tried to open the door for her. Peter saw the tears streaming down her cheeks and the fact that she had forgotten her evening wrap convinced him something was dreadfully wrong.

"Here," he said, opening the door to his carriage. "Get in out of this night air." He put his coat around her and helped her into the carriage.

The moment he was seated beside her she collapsed against his chest and began to sob. She wasn't conscious of the way his heart was pounding against her ear or the feel of his hands soothing her body. The feel of him was hard and solid and dependable. Even the smell of him gave off strength and stability. She took the handkerchief from his breast pocket and held it to her eyes, soaking it with her tears.

The carriage began to move over the cobblestones, but if Peter MacNair were taking her into bondage she wouldn't have cared. How long they drove through the streets she had no idea, nor did she care. She was aware, however, that he hadn't taken her home.

"Do you want to tell me about it, Lydia?" he asked softly as she raised her lovely face up to his. His heart began to beat a little faster. She was the loveliest creature in all the world.

"Walter Hanover," she said, her voice choking.

"The bastard! I'll kill him," he swore.

She felt his anger and put her cheek against his chest again and listened to his heart. "No, Peter. That wouldn't solve anything." She burst into tears again and Peter let her cry as his brain seethed and his blood boiled.

"What does that bastard want?" Peter asked after a while.

"Fifty percent of Empress Cosmetics," she managed to say as she forced back the tears and wiped her eyes. She sat up and for the first time was conscious of how freely she'd been acting. Her cheeks began to get hot, and she was glad that the darkness of the carriage hid her embarrassment.

"What?" Peter gave a laugh. "He must be insane. I've heard the man is in a very bad financial state, but surely he can't be serious about this?"

"I'm afraid he is dead serious." She slowly told him the whole of the conversation.

"He's bluffing," Peter said when she'd finished. "There isn't a court in the country that would acknowledge his claim."

"I wonder," Lydia said twisting the handkerchief nervously in her hands. "If nothing else, he could get an injunction against my firm, stop all production until his suit is decided. A stop-order like that could drag on indefinitely and eventually eat up every cent I have. I've invested a lot of my profits in the success and future of *Nightsong*. All I have is tied up in it."

She suddenly realized the confession she'd made and turned sharply. Even in the dark she could see the glint in his eyes, hear his mind clicking along. If Empress Cosmetics went under he'd profit handsomely not only from the loss of its stiff competition but he might even be able to finally get his greedy hands on *Nightsong*.

The old saw about half a pie being better than no pie at all came back to her. At least with Walter Hanover she'd still have some part of *Nightsong*. She clenched her fists until the nails hurt her palms, cursing herself for telling a man as unscrupulous as Peter how vulnerable she was.

She gathered her skirts closer about her and sat straighter on the seat, refolding Peter's handkerchief. She calmly handed it back to him and said, "Of course, perhaps it wouldn't be so terrible to have Walter Hanover as a partner."

She heard his quick intake of breath. "Do you mean marry him?"

"No, of course not." A little shiver of pleasure ran through her when she heard the jealousy in his voice. "As a business partner."

"Hanover would have you bankrupted in six months. From what I understand there are creditors from here to London waiting to be paid."

"That's what unsettled me. I thought the Hanovers were one of the wealthiest families in the country."

"Walter goes through money like water. You above all others should know how generous he is."

She heard the veiled accusation and stiffened. Naturally, he was right. Walter had always spent money as if there was no end to its supply. "Still," she said, "I would at least be able to look out for fifty percent of my company."

Peter crossed his legs and told the driver to take them to

Lydia's house. "You'd be a fool to have anything to do with that vulture. But you've always been a bit of a fool about a lot of things."

"Not as much a fool as you'd like to think," she snapped. "I suppose you think I'd be better off dividing Empress Cosmetics and *Nightsong* with you?"

"Not dividing," he said evenly, "combining. I told you a long time ago, Lydia, rather than fighting one another we should be...." He cut himself off, afraid she'd again kick his heart into bits.

"Should be what, Peter? Making love? Is that what you were going to say?"

He felt the kick and turned aside. "Let it alone, Lydia. I'm sorry I said anything at all."

She hadn't wanted to hurt him; she'd just had the need to lash out at someone and relieve some of the terrible turmoil seething about inside her. "You never wanted me, Peter, so please don't play the injured puppy. *Nightsong*. That's all you've ever cared about."

"I said leave it alone, Lydia."

"Nightsong," she cried again. "Once you'd gotten your hands on it you'd sell me again to the first bidder."

"I said leave it!" he shouted. He turned furiously toward her and froze when he saw the defiance in her eyes. For a moment they sat staring at each other; a second later Peter pulled her into his arms. She struggled against him, pounding him with her fists, trying to claw his face with her nails, but he pinned her arms behind her back and kissed her passionately on the mouth.

"Damn it, Lydia, don't you know I love you?"

When he kissed her again she sank her teeth into his lip, drawing blood. He gave a yelp of pain and shoved her hard against the side cushion.

They rode the rest of the way to Lydia's home in silence, each licking their private wounds. Lydia thought of what Walter had told her about Peter not being responsible for the scandal that had almost ruined her. She wanted to tell him now how sorry she was for having blamed him, misjudged him all these years, but she could not bring herself to again display a weakness he'd only be too quick to take advantage of.

Peter dabbed at the cut on his mouth and wondered how he would ever convince her of how much he loved her, how much he wanted her to be his forever, but he said nothing. She spoke the truth when she accused him of wanting *Nightsong*. Perhaps she was right. He'd give his soul for that exotic perfume. If he didn't know himself, how could he convince her of which he wanted most?

When the carriage stopped before her door Peter got down to help her out. "May I come in?" he asked.

She gave him a withering look. "You must indeed think me a fool." She slipped his coat from her shoulders. "Goodnight, Peter." She hesitated a moment and with her head lowered said, "Thank you."

He took it as encouragement. As she started up the stone steps he spoke her name in such a provocative way that Lydia felt herself melting. She turned slowly and saw the desire in his eyes. She steeled herself against her own need. "Goodnight, Peter," she said again, then turned and ran into the house.

Peter wanted to run after her, to sweep her into his arms and feel her resist him, excited by the feel of her kicking and pounding. In contrast to Lorna's submissiveness, her begging and groveling, making love to Lydia was the most fantastic experience in his life. Too many times, after Lorna's shameless pleadings, had he dressed and sought out one of those houses on Barbary Coast where the women prided themselves for what they were and not for what a man made of them.

He didn't want to think of Lorna as he glanced up the hill to his mansion and got back into his carriage. And he didn't want a woman from the Barbary Coast. He wanted Lydia and as he gave directions to his driver he didn't give a damn what it cost him to have her...and *Nightsong*.

Walter Hanover was just getting out of the hackney cab when Peter's carriage pulled up behind him. Walter frowned and searched for the pistol he carried in his cloak. There were stories lately about Chinese heathens terrorizing the rich people on the Hill.

"Mr. Hanover," Peter called as he saw the flash of steel in Walter's hand. The pistol disappeared back into the folds of the cloak as Walter recognized him.

"Mr. MacNair."

"I'd appreciate a moment or two of your time, sir," Peter said, walking up to Walter. "Could we go inside?"

"Of course, of course." Walter reached inside the hackney to retrieve something from the seat. Peter noticed that it was Lydia's evening wrap, the one she'd left behind when she fled from the Palm Court.

The anger Walter felt at the evening's disaster was now under control. In its place he displayed a hearty cordiality as he draped the evening wrap over his arm and went up the steps to the mansion.

"The servants are off, unfortunately, Mr. MacNair," he apologized, unlocking the front door himself.

Off indeed, Peter mused. He'd heard they'd all had to leave for want of back wages. The lack of them was evidenced by the ill-kempt parlor and its month-old layer of dust.

"We've been in Europe and mother...." Walter turned up an oil lamp and the dirty room became even more shabby. "Brandy, Mr. MacNair?" He brandished an almost empty decanter.

"Thank you, no."

"Well," Walter said a little unsteadily. "And what is it you wanted to talk to me about at this hour, Mr. MacNair."

"Nightsong," Peter said bluntly.

He saw Walter's eyes dart, then suddenly go blank as if he didn't understand. *"Nightsong?"* His frown deepened as he digested the word. He brightened. "Oh, yes, the Empress Cosmetic fragrance all the ladies are so keen on."

"I'll come right to the point, Mr. Hanover. Lydia told me about your unsupported claim to fifty percent ownership of *Nightsong.*"

Walter's eyes narrowed. "I see." He leaned back. "Well, I wouldn't exactly call my claim unsupported, Mr. MacNair." He watched his guest carefully. Peter MacNair was an extremely clever man, he knew. And dangerous, if even half what he'd heard was true.

"It's unsupported until a court of law says otherwise. That may take a very long time."

"I am a patient man," Walter said, sipping his brandy.

"But are your creditors?"

The brandy snifter almost slipped from Walter's fingers. He glowered at Peter and said, "Just exactly what is it you want, Mr. MacNair?"

"I am not a man who beats around the proverbial bush, Mr. Hanover. For instance, I know for a fact that you are heavily into debt, that this house and everything you own has been mortgaged. The only thing I don't know is the precise amount you will need to get out of debt and back on your feet."

"Why do you need to know that?"

"Because I am prepared to give you whatever amount you need. In cash. Tomorrow morning."

Walter did not move, didn't risk even the flicker of an eye for fear he'd miss something fast Peter MacNair was trying to pull. "And what is it you want in exchange?"

"Your so-called claim on *Nightsong.*"

"But you yourself said it is an unsupported claim."

"Let's just say I am a gambling man, Mr. Hanover." He let a sly smile curl his lips. "And I can afford to wait for a court decision."

"And you think I cannot?"

"I *know* you can't."

Peter saw the trapped look and knew he'd won. All that was left for him to do was sit quietly and wait for Walter to calculate his debts then double or triple the figure. Whatever, Peter was prepared to pay it.

"One million dollars," Walter said, pronouncing each word with precise exactitude.

Peter stuck out his hand. "Done," he exclaimed.

Walter hesitated as he looked up at Peter. Then after a moment he reached for Peter's hand, cursing himself for not having asked for more.

CHAPTER FOURTEEN

Lydia spent a restless night trying to decide on what she should do, only to find she was no farther ahead with her problem than when she'd brought it to bed. And it wasn't only Walter's threat that was upsetting her; April's unhappiness weighed heavily on her conscience. She had actually sold her daughter into a marriage which was making the child miserable.

It was with a sense of resignation that she decided she had no other recourse so far as Walter Hanover was concerned, but to marry him. She'd given it a lot of thought and it was the best way out of the dilemma. She was still young enough to have children and Walter would father the dynasty she longed to build. Besides, being Lydia Hanover would open still more doors into society. Walter was an odious snob, she reminded herself, but had Ke Loo been any better? And she'd survived that ordeal. It was a decision she did not look forward to, but she resigned herself to it.

That evening at dinner, Walter beamed at her across the table when she told him she had decided to accept his proposal of marriage. Earlier, when she had telephoned him and asked him to join her at her home, Walter had been reluctant. When she gave no hint that Peter MacNair had talked to her, however, he accepted the dinner invitation, just as he was accepting now her promise to be his wife.

"You've made me deliriously happy, Lydia," he said, picking up her hand and kissing it. "When will it be?"

"As soon as you like. And as soon as the legal problems can

be resolved. I'd prefer a small, simple affair. After what I went through for April and Raymond, I don't think I want to face a large wedding for quite a while." She noticed the way his expression changed at the mention of April's name.

"You need not concern yourself about April," she told him. "I've been planning on expanding my...*our* operation to Europe. I intend asking Raymond to open the offices in Paris. April will accompany him, naturally."

Walter was beside himself with joy. Not only had he gotten a million dollars for an unsubstantiated claim on *Nightsong,* he'd gotten *Nightsong* as well. All he needed to do was keep the news of their engagement secret; he couldn't chance Peter MacNair's finding out and botching things up. "I agree we should be married as soon as practical and I too dislike displays," he agreed. "Big splashes are fine for young couples but when mature people marry I think it's vulgar to make a gaudy show of it." He kissed her hand again, lifting one eyebrow slightly. "Even the wedding announcement should come after the ceremony, I believe. It's in much better taste, don't you agree?"

"Whatever you say, Walter. You're far more familiar with social etiquette than I."

"I'll begin the arrangements tomorrow. If all is in order, and I see no reason for it not to be, we shall be husband and wife by the weekend. Now," he said feeling a bit giddy, "where shall we honeymoon? Monte Carlo, Rio, the Swiss Alps?"

Lydia shook her head firmly. "I'm afraid I can't possible leave the office now. We're launching a new advertising campaign for *Nightsong.*"

"But you must begin delegating your authority, my dear. It would be unthinkable for Mrs. Walter Hanover to work at a position."

"I'm sorry, Walter, I'll agree to be your wife, but I will not agree to give up my work at Empress Cosmetics." She saw that he was going to argue the point and put her hand firmly down on the table. "That is final, Walter. If it is not to your liking I can easily withdraw my acceptance of your proposal."

Walter visibly shrank into his chair. "Very well," he said in a meek voice. "If you insist."

"I do. I've worked far too hard to put my products on the market and make a success of them to turn it all over to someone else now that the hard part has been accomplished."

Seeing how adamant she was, Walter decided to change the subject. "Peter MacNair is opening his New York plant next week, I understand. It surprises me that he would quit San Francisco."

"Oh?" Lydia said as her pulse quickened. "He said nothing to me about that."

"You saw Mr. MacNair?" Walter paled slightly.

"Yes. Yesterday."

"You haven't spoken to him today, have you?"

"No. Why?"

Of course she hadn't spoken to him today or she wouldn't be accepting your proposal of marriage, he told himself. Everything was going well at last. It was about time his luck took a turn for the better. A million dollars had been put into his account this morning and this evening he'd just gotten engaged to a cosmetic factory worth millions more, and he was getting a beautiful wife in the bargain. His future was absolutely secure.

Walter lingered quite late. Lydia knew why; his innuendos were plain enough and the lust in his eyes couldn't be mistaken for anything else. That was going to be the difficult part of the bargain, she reminded herself, thinking back to the time Walter had forced himself on her. Then too it had been when she'd agreed to marry him; she did not intend to repeat the mistake. Sex would come as part of her marriage contract and not before, she resolved.

For all his need for secrecy, Walter Hanover was not the type of man who could keep from bragging about good fortune, especially when it was better than anyone else's. It gave him a sense of superiority over his fellow man, particularly the less affluent and principally those who were once on the same social level as himself and hadn't fared as well. One of his biggest joys in life was seeing envy in men's eyes.

He had to celebrate his good fortune. Going home to an empty house was a depressing thought. It was unthinkable when he felt so marvelous. He chose the new Stanford Club. He wasn't a member but what did that matter? His name was sufficient to gain him admittance. The bar was crowded with members whom Walter thought he'd easily impress. By the time he'd treated the room to a second round of drinks he was feeling far too exuberant not to toast his forthcoming marriage to a cosmetic empire.

* * * * * * *

Peter MacNair heard the news when he was cleaning up the last few matters on his desk. He'd planned on catching the three o'clock train east until Lorna came in carrying his briefcase.

"You forgot this at the house," she said.

He was always annoyed by the way she tried to anticipate him, especially since she was always wrong. "I didn't forget it, Lorna. Susan was supposed to take it to the bank for me. I wanted the papers inside to go into my vault. I've told the bank president to watch out for her." He took the case from her and glanced at the clock on the wall. "But I'll have time to take care of it myself I see."

"Will you have time for lunch?"

"Sorry. I have too much to do."

"When do you intend sending for us, Peter?" Lorna asked.

"I've told you a dozen times, Lorna, that when I've found a house and can give you an address to ship everything to, I'll send for you. Your mother's written you, I know, about the list of prospects."

"I still think I should come with you now."

"Impossible. You can't yank Efrem and Susan out of school now, especially with Susan in her last year."

Lorna sighed. "I suppose not." She pulled on her gloves and turned toward the door. "Incidentally, Phoebe Hearst told me an interesting bit of gossip this morning." She saw he was paying her no mind. "About Lydia Nightsong. She's going to marry Walter Hanover, of all people. Clara would turn over in her grave if she knew and her poor body is scarcely cold in the ground." She clucked her tongue and watched him carefully.

Peter didn't dare look at her for fear she'd see how disconcerted he was. Lydia marrying Hanover? his mind kept repeating. It couldn't be true.

Lorna said, "I thought you might be upset that your little friend was finally going to make herself respectable." She made a face. "I wonder what she intends doing about her Chinese husband?"

"Please, Lorna, I am far too busy to listen to your prattle. Now if you will kindly excuse me I must finish this work. I'll see you at home when I come for my luggage."

The moment she was out the door Peter unstrapped the leather briefcase she'd left on his desk. He took out Hanover's assignment of his claim to *Nightsong* together with the original Agreement Lydia had signed. He hadn't intended telling Lydia he had bought the proposed claim and if she admitted to him that she was marrying Hanover because she wanted to marry him and not because she was forced to, she'd never learn that he had these papers.

He tucked the documents into his pocket and swept the remaining papers on his desk into an untidy stack which he handed to Miss Adams on his way out.

His offices weren't far from the offices of Empress Cosmetics, but Lydia was not at her office. She was at home, Evelyn Clary told him. "She sounded awfully strange when she rang me up earlier, like she had a cold," Evelyn said. She knew Mrs. Nightsong disapproved of Mr. MacNair, but she couldn't understand why. He was such a nice man—and so obviously in love.

Peter caught a hackney on the corner of Sutter and Mason and gave him Lydia's address.

"What in hell's this business about you marrying Walter Hanover?" Peter demanded when Nellie showed him into the back parlor.

"I shall marry whomsoever I choose," Lydia said, giving him an arrogant look. The mere sight of him made her go weak. How could she love him so and hate him so at the same time? And why did the hate overpower the love she wondered as she gazed at his handsome face, his superb, masculine body.

"Why Walter Hanover?"

"Why not? I told you last night of his offer and of his purported claim. I decided simply that I might just as well have a partner who is also my husband, rather than give fifty percent of *Nightsong* to an outsider."

"Then it is more or less a business proposition?"

Lydia walked slowly toward the fireplace. Half way across the room she stopped and turned back to him. "I have always prided myself on being a practical woman."

Peter took the documents out of his pocket and threw them on the table beside her. "I hadn't intended showing you these but under the circumstances they might change your mind about marrying."

Lydia looked down at the papers and for a moment couldn't bring herself to touch them. Some inner force was holding her back. A little voice inside her head was reminding her that whatever came from Peter MacNair's hands meant disaster.

Carefully she unfolded the documents and began reading. "But this...." She looked up sharply after recognizing the Agreement she'd signed with Walter years before.

"Read the other," Peter said.

Warily she moved her eyes to the second document. The first few lines made no sense. She went back and read them again until the meaning of the message started to become clear and its force struck her full on the brain.

"Walter sold what?" she demanded glaring up at him, the documents feeling like molten lead in her hands.

"His fifty percent claim on *Nightsong*," Peter said without moving a muscle.

"How dare you!" She could feel the fury gathering, like gale winds beginning to swarm, whipping up angry waves, twirling them into hurricane force. "How dare you!" she repeated as she crumpled the papers in her fist and took a step closer to him.

"Because if anyone is going to stake a claim to any part of *Nightsong,* it will be me."

"You? You are entitled to nothing of mine."

Peter shrugged. "I don't see it that way. The entire idea was mine originally. But as I said, I only show you these papers because I had a feeling Hanover had no intention of mentioning them to you. I paid one million dollars for them in case you're interested."

"Then I'll pay you back your million dollars."

"I don't want it," Peter said. He stepped forward, picked up her arm and pried the documents out of her fist, replacing them in his pocket. "Whether you like it or not, Lydia, you and I are finally going to be partners."

"Not until you have your claim verified by a court of law."

Peter smiled. "I doubt if I'll ever do that, unless, of course, I'm forced into it. Just make certain you don't give me too much competition, Lydia. You know how badly I react when I'm put up against a wall." As he looked at her he felt the same old feelings creep over him. Despite the angry cloud over her brows she completely mesmerized him with her beauty. Her red-gold hair sparked in the sunlight from the window, igniting the fire in his loins. The deep green of her eyes made him begin to stiffen.

"You're the most ravishing woman I've ever seen," he breathed.

"Get out, Peter. I never want to see you again."

He gave her a slow smile. Watching him, she could see the direction his thoughts were taking.

"Get out," she said again, but a little less forcefully. She turned her back to him.

"I'm leaving for New York this afternoon. If all goes as well as I predict, it might be that you will have your wish, that you will never see me again."

Her heart plummeted. Keeping her back stiff, her shoulders straight, she raised her hands to her mouth and bit into her knuckles to keep back her despair. Behind her she could feel the heat of his body, even seem to hear the pounding of his heart as he came closer. When his hands touched her waist she thought the floor had been pulled away. She felt herself falling and could do nothing about it.

Peter leaned her back flat against him, knowing she must realize his need for her. He couldn't let them part like this. He wanted her one last time; he wanted her more desperately than he wanted life.

"Lydia," he breathed into her hair.

"Oh, please, Peter, get out. Go to New York. Leave me alone."

"Promise me you won't marry Hanover. Promise me," he urged as he put his arms around her and inhaled the intoxicating scent of her hair.

Some strange, disconnected voice took possession of her. "I promise." The words sounded so unnatural, so far away she couldn't be sure it was she who'd promised.

"I want you, Lydia," he said, cupping her breasts and burying his face in her hair. He pulled aside the red-gold cascade that fell over her shoulders and began kissing her neck.

Tiny shivers rushed through every part of her. "Don't, please, Peter," she moaned.

"I must have you, Lydia. I must."

"No."

"You can't deny me. I won't let you."

"I must. I...." She stopped, reminding herself why she hadn't felt well when she awoke this morning, why she hadn't been able to go into the office.

"I can't leave you like this."

"No, Peter," she said a little more firmly. "You must. Please go."

He pushed her away so hard she almost fell forward. "Go to your damned Walter Hanover. Go to hell for all I care!" he stormed as he snatched up his hat from the table near the door and marched toward the foyer.

"Peter, wait!"

He stopped and came back, scowling like an angry bull. "Wait for what? So you can tantalize me some more? Until you have me completely out of my head? Goddamn it, Lydia, can't you see how you torment me?"

"I don't mean to cause you such discomfort, Peter. It's just that...."

He saw her weaken but when he walked back and tried to take her in his arms she pushed him away. He stood glowering at her, then on impulse he reached inside his coat and threw the two documents at her feet. "Give me what I want and I'll give you these."

Lydia turned. She saw the papers lying so pristine and innocent on the rug. She looked into Peter's face and knew he wasn't playing a game.

"Well?" he demanded.

"I...."

"The documents for one hour in bed with you." He stood with feet planted firmly.

She felt the tears stinging her eyes. She was only barely aware that she nodded her head. A moment later she felt herself being lifted in his arms and carried toward the bedroom.

Peter laid her on the bed, but before getting out of his clothes he went back into the parlor and picked up the documents. He placed them carefully on the marble topped stand beside her bed and put his stick pin and signet ring on top of them.

She loved to watch him undress, which he did with the professional ease and grace of an athlete.

Naked he lay down beside her and began removing her clothes as he kissed her. He felt her trembling with desire as he took her into his arms, relishing the feel of her skin against his own, her full firm breasts pressed tightly against his hairy chest. The smell of her aroused his passions still farther, flooding his senses with the sweet clearness of a summer day after a shower.

Lydia let her inhibitions fall away as she admitted to herself that this was what she wanted because afterward he would be gone from her forever. Brazenly she let her hands rove over his hard, strong body as she buried her face in the crook of his shoulder and kissed his bare skin. She felt the smooth rounded strength of his buttocks as her lips played freely with the muscles of his neck, delighting in the way the cords stood out so prominently, the way the veins pulsed and throbbed.

He moved easily, gently over her, until he found himself in control, then gradually he became more forceful in seeking out his goal. He felt her arms tighten round him and as she clung to his body he increased the tempo of his thrusts.

"I adore you," he breathed.

Lydia kissed his mouth, blotting out the lies she knew he was telling. But she wanted to believe him. And for the moment she did as wave after wave of searing passion raked her body. Tomorrow would never come, she kept telling herself as Peter moved more desperately, more urgently. There was nothing for them but here and now.

"Peter," she moaned softly as she felt herself falling over the edge of the deep, dark chasm. "Peter," she called weakly as every ounce of strength poured out of her and she felt herself floating, floating in a billowy abyss where she knew she was trapped forever-more.

Peter felt the last of his strength leave him, pangs of sheer ecstasy throbbed throughout his body.

"Lydia," he said softly, touching his lips lightly to hers.

He looked at her through his lowered lids, smiling as he noticed the vein at her throat pulsing dully. She lay asleep, dreaming delightedly of the pleasure he had given her. His smile broadened as he rolled from on top of her, draped the coverlet over her nakedness and got out of bed.

She wasn't conscious of how long she'd slept and for a moment or two she couldn't remember when she'd undressed and had gotten into bed. The long lingering shadows of the late afternoon drooped over the bedroom like warning fingers. Lydia's eyes suddenly flashed open as she remembered what had happened.

"Peter!" she cried as she sat bolt upright in bed and looked around the empty room.

A heavy heart beat sadly in her breast as she faced the fact that he was gone. She glanced at the clock on the nightstand and saw that it was almost five. His train, she recalled him saying, had left at three. He was on his way to New York and it was unlikely that she'd ever see him again—certainly not in the immediate future.

For a long time she lay in bed reliving the passion he'd made her experience and only when Nellie tapped on the door and asked about dinner did Lydia finally stir.

She felt miserable and wonderful all at the same time and as she soaked in her warm bath she tingled at the remembrance of his powerful body and how it excited her to the point of madness.

Wrapping herself in thick, soft towels warmed by the fire, she went back into the bedroom and started to dress, still going backward over the afternoon.

Suddenly she remembered the bargain, the papers he'd offered her for one last hour of passion. She smiled, knowing she would have given him herself without the need of bargaining. Still, it had been a good bargain, she told herself as she went over to the table where Peter had left the two documents.

They were gone, as was everything else that would remind her of him.

PART TWO

CHAPTER FIFTEEN

Far in the distance was a jagged silhouette of a mountain, darkly outlined against the China sky. Ke Loo's cold eyes stared straight ahead as his bearers carried his chair toward *Tien An Men* gate, the gateway of Heavenly Peace, the entrance to the Imperial Palace where *Tz'u-Hsi*, the all powerful Dowager Empress, had summoned him.

It had been a long time since last he'd visited the Forbidden City, as her palace was called, a place, like China itself, of brooding mystery and exotic intrigue.

White fluffy clouds sat on the horizon like the white jade leopards of *Shih Huang Ti*, first emperor of Imperial China, fabled leopards that had guarded him from all evil and had made him immortal. As Ke Loo looked at the clouds he wondered again why he'd been summoned and whether his ancestor's lion dogs would protect him as well. Then, thinking of his cousin, the Dragon Empress, he knew nothing could save anyone if she chose to do them harm. She was the great Manchu Empress, more powerful than all the gods, more powerful than the greatest emperors who'd gone before her.

The beating of gongs and blaring of trumpets announced his imperial presence outside the walls. Most likely it was the recent unrest that was slowly spreading from province to province that had caused the Empress to order him here, but surely the peasant rebellion was not serious enough to summon him all the way from his palace in Kalgan. Besides, his cousin, the Dragon Empress, did not waste her attention on peasant unrest.

Ke Loo was borne through the magnificent gates and into the Forbidden City itself, where bronze lions guarded broad courtyards filled with dwarf trees and ornamental pools ringed with drooping willows whose branches dipped into the surface of the water. The dreamlike city stretched out before him with its rose red walls, its yellow roofs of tile and gold, its glistening lacquers and magnificent trappings. One courtyard led to another and still to another, all protected by marble tigers and dotted with lily-covered ponds and cooing doves and endless doll-like palaces where the Emperor's concubines lived.

Ke Loo's chair was set down at the top of a long flight of stairs and he got to his feet. He stood and surveyed the grandeur below him as white doves fluttered over his head and the cool scent of almond blossoms soothed his senses. Then, he turned and made his stately entrance into the palace as eunuchs bowed in obeisance to his royal personage, his princely right as an heir, however distant, to the throne of China.

Ke Loo was bowed into the vast interior, through the two main halls into the Chambers of Great Light, the throne room of the Dowager Empress, the dragon ruler of China. The vaulted ceiling—almost two hundred feet above his head—was encrusted with gems and precious metals and the inlaid ivory, alabaster and gold floor stretched over two hundred feet in one direction and one hundred and twenty-five in the other. The whole room was surrounded by a marble veranda of white and beige and bronze with marble staircases, one on each side, which led from floor to veranda to throne dais.

A great golden gong was sounded and huge double doors of red and gold lacquer swung easily on silver hinges as a train of powerful eunuchs, fifty to a man, entered the throne room bearing their imperial lady on her luxurious sedan chair.

Ke Loo prostrated himself before this square little figure of a woman dressed in her stiff yellow silk robes, elaborately embroidered with fire-breathing dragons and bursting chrysanthemums. Her mouth was set in a perpetually unsmiling line and her eyes were bright penetrating slits of ebony. Her black slick hair was pulled tight into a bun on the top of her head, held rigidly in place by long pins of jade and ivory.

Her divan was carried to the throne dais and she adjusted herself on her seat of imperial yellow silk, her unbound feet encased in painted square-toed shoes which barely touched the marble floor.

She spoke his name and gave permission for him to stand. "You are well, cousin?"

"Very well, Imperial One," Ke Loo answered with a courtly bow.

"And Li Ahn, your son?"

"In the very best of health, my majestic cousin. He and his train are a day behind me, as you directed."

"Good. I have business with you first before I turn my attentions to Li Ahn." Her black glinting eyes bore into him as she leaned slightly forward. "You have another daughter whom you have permitted to live, I am told."

"A wish of her mother's and a whim of mine," Ke Loo answered.

"It is your royal privilege. And what do you call this girl child?"

"Mei Fei."

The Empress bobbed her head, approving. She thought for a moment, aligning her thoughts into precise order. "Your American wife, she must be brought here to China."

Ke Loo stared up at her. "Lydia? But why, cousin? I thought we were pleased to be rid of the woman."

"But we are not rid of her. If your poison had accomplished its purpose I would not be constantly nettled by that foreign woman and her female brat. Too many of my efforts to be rid of the mother have been thwarted. It is becoming more and more difficult for my subjects in America to accomplish anything. Every crime committed is blamed upon my citizens. I want that woman dead. I will not be at peace until it is accomplished. I have decided that in view of the trouble and expense she has caused me, it would please me to see that she die here before my very eyes."

Ke Loo saw that she was adamant. "As you wish, of course, cousin," he answered obediently. "If you are still distressed because...."

"Whatever my reasons for being distressed, they are no business of yours, Ke Loo. I am distressed. That is all you need concern yourself with."

Ke Loo bowed subserviently before her anger. "I thought perhaps if it was the royal scent which...."

The Dragon Empress raised her threatening hand with its seven inch painted, pointed nails encased in silver sheathes. "The royal scent is where it belongs, safe in my vaults. That which was taken from this city is certainly not a royal scent and all records of it, as well as its concoctors, have been destroyed."

Again Ke Loo bowed low.

"All that remains to remove the memory of that scent is to be rid of the thief who contaminated this palace. She will be brought here and beheaded beneath my windows."

"As you wish, cousin, so it will be." He knelt and touched his forehead to the marble and alabaster floor. When he raised himself and again looked up at his cousin he saw that her anger had passed.

"Now, of Li Ahn. His studies are progressing satisfactorily?"

With a sad shake of his head Ke Loo said, "He is an extremely bright boy, cousin, but he is easily distracted. He seems to have no head for his duties. I constantly remind him that he may one day sit on your throne...." He realized his mistake but too late.

"Silence!" she roared.

Ke Loo prostrated himself immediately.

"How dare you? I am immortal! Is that what you are filling the boy's head with, promises of my throne?"

"No, Imperial One."

"Silence!" She stood over him like a raging flame. "Or is it that you are teaching him patience, that he must wait until he succeeds your ascension to my throne? Is that what you are plotting, Ke Loo?"

Ke Loo lay trembling under her wrath.

"Answer me!"

"No, Imperial One," he repeated.

"Mark me, Ke Loo. I have been aware of your ambitions in my direction for some time now. I have had you watched very closely and if I hadn't had need of your services my executioner's blade would have fed on your neck long before this. Curb your ambitions, Ke Loo, or I will curb them for you."

"Yes, Imperial One," he stammered, quaking in his robes.

They were plotting against her, she decided. Ke Loo and his house had always been a greedy lot, she reminded herself, but they kept the peace in her northern provinces and she needed them for that. And she had a plan to keep Ke Loo from feeding his ambitions.

Ke Loo had only one son, whom he prized highly. If she were to place Li Ahn somewhere out of his father's reach but within her own, she could force Ke Loo to behave at the cost of losing his only son and heir. By making a hostage of the son, the father could easily be kept in line.

The Empress said, "We spoke earlier of bringing your American wife back to China."

Ke Loo still lay flat before her.

"Get up, get up," she ordered impatiently, "I have decided that you will send your son, Li Ahn, to America to induce the American woman to return."

"If it will please your Imperial Highness, so be it."

"It will please me," she said flatly. "I will instruct the boy myself when he arrives here tomorrow. Now," she said as she switched subjects, "I understand there was a small uprising near Kalgan recently."

"There are always a few malcontents in every province, cousin," he said, his voice still trembling slightly. He fought to control it.

"From what I am told, it is not a simple matter of a few malcontents, Ke Loo. Rebellion against the foreign devils is one thing I highly condone; however, these recent uprisings are Chinese against Chinese. Over twenty years ago similar uprisings occurred as well you know and our majestic Manchu dynasty was almost overthrown. We managed to put down that rebellion; unfortunately, it was with the help of some westerners, which I fear was a major mistake on our part, one which we will someday regret."

"Our dynasty will live forever," Ke Loo assured her.

She made a derisive sound deep in her throat. "Dreamer," she muttered. "Tell that to the Hsins and to the Mings and the Sungs, the Chous, the Ch'ins. What the Mongols once accomplished from outside our walls, our own people can accomplish from within them. Do not think these outbreaks are simply restless peasants dissatisfied with their yearly yields. I have had terrible dreams, Ke Loo. We must be alert to every danger. We have been too easy with the foreigner's interventions in our land."

"I am ready to do what you ask of me."

"We must prove to our people that the Manchus do not want the foreigners' help or interference. We will rid China of all white devils once and for all. We will convince our subjects that what we do for China we do for them."

"But the opium trades?" Ke Loo argued. "We need the western revenues to support our economy, Highness. And we cannot violate the existing trade agreements already established by the Treaty of Nanking."

"This is my nation," the Empress fumed. "There will be no treaty recognized. We will close all ports to every outsider. The opium trade can continue," she said with a conspiratorial glint in her black eyes. "The revenues need not be cut off. I am sure you, Ke Loo, can arrange for these secrecies without the populace being aware of the royal arrangements."

"Yes, of course."

"Now," she said, "I am tired. I will retire." With a wave of her imperial hand the entire room came alive as she was borne away on the shoulders of the army of eunuchs.

Ke Loo stood in the empty chamber and breathed a sigh of relief. Glowering at the doors that closed behind his cousin, he began to seethe with indignation, remembering how she'd made him grovel. Perhaps he should encourage these rebels in Kalgan, these Boxers as they called themselves. Perhaps he should help them turn against this female dragon and put him on the throne in her place.

A sly smile crept across his mouth as he turned to leave the imperial chamber. This was not the first time such a thought had crossed his mind.

As for his son, Li Ahn, the boy needed discipline, not freedom to travel to America, a release from his duties and his studies. The old dragon had spoken and there was little he could do to change her decree, but there was still time for him to act.

When Li Ahn returned with the American woman, they would complete the plans to unseat his royal cousin.

CHAPTER SIXTEEN

Lydia had slept badly again. She had dreamed the same terrible dream, of seeing a lovely head impaled on the stake in the courtyard under the Dowager Empress's bedroom windows. With everything at Empress Cosmetics going so magnificently well, why should she have these recurring nightmares? It was as if some distant hand from far across the Pacific was snatching at her with poisoned-tipped talons.

What did any of it mean she asked herself as she pushed herself away from the breakfast table and rang for Nellie to bring hot coffee to the back parlor? When did these awful nightly ordeals start? She tried to recall.

The day Peter MacNair went away, a voice reminded her. Four months of being afraid to close her eyes for fear the hand of death would catch her. Four months of wondering when and if Peter would lay claim to fifty percent of everything she had.

When Nellie brought the coffee she found she didn't want it and sent it away. Although she didn't feel much like it, Lydia forced herself to dress and go into the office.

"You look like the devil," Raymond Andrieux said when he walked into her office a few hours later.

"I feel like the devil," she admitted.

"Bad night?" He winked at her.

"Not the kind you think. I haven't been sleeping very well the past several months."

"You shouldn't have sent the Hanover guy packing. A husband is always the best medicine for a good night's sleep."

Lydia thought of how unhappy April was with this husband she had turned out of her bed before little Caroline was born.

Lydia asked, "How is the new batch of *Nightsong* coming along?"

"Fine. I will be able to stockpile enough for about a year while I get on with the business in Paris. You know," Raymond said, "you should give yourself a vacation and come with me on my next trip."

"Wouldn't it look better if you traveled with your wife rather than your mother-in-law?"

Raymond shrugged. "April doesn't want to do anything, especially with me."

"How is she feeling?"

"Like any new mother, I should think. Very bossy, very protective." He screwed up his face. "No, she really isn't all that protective, now that I think about it. I can't put my finger on it, but there are times when I see April and the baby together and she looks like she hates the little bugger."

"Raymond!"

"It's true." He let the darkness leave his face. "Well, perhaps it isn't hatred, more like resentment, as if she didn't want it to be a part of me. Little Caroline looks a lot like me, you know," he said proudly.

Lydia didn't agree. Caroline looked more like her grand-mother, she thought, except for the dark hair. She said, "April had a very difficult delivery. Such things sometimes affect the mother. April will get over it."

Raymond slumped into a chair. "I thought you told me the baby would help patch things up between April and me."

"Give it time, Raymond. Caroline isn't a month old yet."

"And April gets more distant every day." He eyed her admir-ingly. "I should have known better than to marry the daughter when I could have had the mother."

It always infuriated her when Raymond made such a callous reference to how he came to marry. It was as if Lydia had purposely placed herself and April on an auction block. It had been Raymond's demand; but she had willingly offered him anything and he had chosen. Oddly enough, even though she had never loved him, she truly believed she could have made him happy; and perhaps even herself as well...as happy as she could have been with any man, she told herself, purposely excluding Peter MacNair from her list.

"You made your choice, Raymond."

He got out of his chair and came over to her. "I still think of you more than I care to admit."

"Then stop thinking of me, Raymond," she said.

"I can't help it, Lydia. You're one of the most exciting women I've ever been to bed with."

"I forbid you to think of it, Raymond."

"Why? Does it make you all jittery inside? The same way it makes me?" He laughed and reached for her again but Lydia slapped his hands away.

"When do you leave for Paris?" she asked, skirting the table and placing herself in a clear line of escape to the door.

He saw the futility of his pursuit and sat back down in the chair. "Next week. The office furniture should be in but the factory supplies will take a few weeks more."

"And next year's exposition? Do you still think we should wait that long to introduce *Nightsong* to the European market?"

Raymond nodded. "It's not so far in the future. This year is almost over, remember. Besides, we are just establishing a very solid reputation here. By the time we introduce it at the Paris Exposition people will be tearing their hair out for it. Mrs. Astor, I hear, caused a sensation at the Paris Opera opening when she wore *Nightsong*."

He looked at her and his eyes pleaded. "Come to Paris with me, Lydia. You will have the time of your life. I will personally see to it."

"I can't, Raymond. There is too much to be done here."

He looked up encouragingly. "Well, at least you did not say you would not go. Think about it. I won't stop asking you."

He was almost out of the room when he paused. "I almost

forgot," he said. "Evelyn is looking for you. A young Chinese is upstairs asking to see you. Very polished, she says."

Lydia frowned. She had no dealings with any Chinese distributors nor were there any in her future prospects.

She didn't recognize the young man who sat so relaxed in the deep leather chair outside her office door. He was no more than a boy, she noticed, no more than fifteen and a handsome lad. He stood up and bowed his respects. His dark, limpid eyes looked at her with intense interest, as though she were a curiosity he found fascinating.

"Mrs. Nightsong," he said with a heavy accent.

"Yes?"

"It would please me if we could speak in private." He saw her hesitation and added, "I believe you will have wished it when you know why I am here."

Over his shoulder Lydia saw Evelyn Clary raise her eyebrows and shrug. More than once she had been accosted by thugs sent by the Dragon Empress to punish her for stealing *Nightsong;* but this young man seemed different.

"I assure you, I mean you no harm," he said.

She saw the delicate hands, the innocent expression, the slight, boyish body—and something more, something she couldn't name, but that was vaguely familiar.

"No, I don't believe you do," she said. "Come with me."

She led the way into her private office. When they were alone, he grinned at her and said, "I did not know whether your people here in America knew that you had a Chinese son."

Lydia felt the blood drain from her face. "How do you know that?" she asked. "Who are you?"

He smiled, seemingly unperturbed by the underlying note of anger in her voice.

"It is a long time since you have seen your son," he said, "so long, his face is unknown to you."

She continued to stare. "Li Ahn?" she said, comprehension slowly dawning, the disturbing familiarity coming into focus. "Is it really you?"

She came quickly around the desk, which she had deliberately used to keep him at a distance.

"Yes, I am Li Ahn, son of Ke Loo," he said, beaming, "and of Lydia Holt."

For a second she was unable to move or speak. Then, tears suddenly streaming down her cheeks, she embraced him. It was a moment before she became aware of his stiff response to her hug, and remembered that his manners were those of the Chinese aristocracy.

"Forgive me," she said, stepping back and making a futile attempt to dry her tears. "It's been so long...."

She gave him the formal bow, and said, in Mandarin, "You are very welcome, Li Ahn, son of Ke Loo."

He returned the greeting, looking far more pleased than he had a moment before.

She could not help staring. How handsome he was! April's brother, the son she thought she would never see again. She had been unable to bring him with her when she had fled China.

"Oh, Li Ahn, I am sorry," she said, still unable to hold back the tears. "You can't imagine how happy I am to see you. You were so very little when your father took you back to Kalgan."

"My sister, she is well?"

"Yes. She recently had a daughter of her own."

She saw his look of displeasure and smiled. "It is not shameful here to bear a female child. All children are highly cherished."

"Ah, yes." He paused and then said, "I suppose you are wondering why I am here."

"Well, yes," Lydia said a bit self-consciously, "Though you need no reason, you know. Why you've come makes no difference. I am only pleased that you are here. I am your mother, after all; that should be reason enough."

"Of course," he admitted with another respectful bow. He looked at her with what might have been admiration or deference, it was difficult to decide. "There is more of your blood flowing in my veins than my cousin, the Empress, suspects," he said.

Lydia raised her eyebrows. "Oh?"

"I have come to ask you to return to China with me. Ke Loo, your husband, my father, commands it." He spoke with his eyes straight ahead, his voice cold and formal as though he were reciting a carefully practiced piece.

He moved his eyes to hers. "I will be beheaded if I return without you," he said.

CHAPTER SEVENTEEN

Li Ahn walked across the intersection and started along Powell Street, walking at a slow, deliberate pace, ignoring the stares and the sneers. He glanced with interest at the furniture in the store window, strange looking pieces, bulky and formless. Here and there a clothing shop with western suits hanging on racks caught his notice. He paused before the bakery, smelling the fresh bread and the little bookseller next door reminded him that he did not live on bread alone.

He turned right at the first corner and followed the straight, unswept street to the little park across from which his sister, April, lived with the foreign husband and the beautiful girl baby. He liked coming to visit with his lovely sister, especially when her husband was away, which seemed often. Two days he had been staying at his mother's home, and already he had begun feeling that his days were not complete unless he saw April and little Caroline.

She told him much about this hate-filled city and how she longed to return to Kalgan to their father's house. He would gladly have taken her if he could, but he knew that a wife must follow the dictates of her husband, not the selfish desires of her brother or of her own heart. He was careful not to remind her of that too often, however, because it always made her cry.

Li Ahn liked some things about the city, but not the steep hills which one was forced to climb. Of course, one could choose to risk life and limb on one of those clanging wagons that were pulled by invisible cables. Still, there was an excitement here that bristled like cat fur and which he found much to his liking. There were so many amusements, so much noise and movement. He found he secretly wanted to stay a part of it. Lydia was always quick to remind him that he carried her blood in his veins and it was only natural that he should be excited by America.

He liked his mother. She was so different from other Chinese mothers, who seldom laughed and were always quick to scold and to correct.

Strolling across the neatly groomed park, Li Ahn remembered a similar little square in Kalgan where his tutor was wont to take him on hot summer days and where he'd fidget through his lessons. He knew he was a bright boy because everyone was quick to tell him so. He didn't let them know that the lessons always came easy to him, even the difficult English he'd learned without much struggle.

Of his mother he remembered very little except almost forgotten glimpses of her in the palace garden playing games under the pear trees with his older sister. And he remembered seeing her when she was summoned before the Dowager Empress, looking very beautiful in a kimono the color of lilacs with lavender peonies and wearing a strand of gleaming gray pearls.

He thought then that she was the most beautiful woman in all the kingdom and could not understand, if she was his mother, why he was not permitted to be with her as April had been.

Despite his strict education and the constant reminders of his father that he was an heir to the throne, albeit a distant heir who would succeed only after his father, Li Ahn still felt unfulfilled. He sometimes compared himself to the *yuan*, a silver coin stamped on one side with its value and purpose, but the other side clear and without designation waiting for a different imprint, a different future.

He'd spoken of these strange inner feelings to his father once, only to be reprimanded and then punished. The switches with which he'd been thrashed had opened the skin and afterward he'd been bled of half the blood in his body. He recalled little of that time, only the stream of physicians, the amahs who nursed him gradually back to health.

Ke Loo had explained that he'd carried foreign devil blood in his veins and it had to be drained away, but Li Ahn knew now as he walked up the steps to April's apartment that all of the foreign blood hadn't been taken out of him or he wouldn't be feeling suddenly so divided in his loyalties.

April hugged him and took his hand. "I have decided," she told her brother. "With or without my husband, I will come back to China with you."

Li Ahn smiled patiently. "It cannot be, April. To leave one's husband is punishable by death. It would be the Empress's duty to behead you for bringing disgrace to the family. You are your father's daughter. You are a Manchu, like our cousin the Empress."

"But I am her kin," April argued. "She would do me no harm."

"All the more reason for a severe punishment. It is said that she had her own sister boiled alive for a less serious transgression."

"I will come to China," April said stubbornly.

"I only wish it could be in my company, but it cannot." He squeezed her hand. "But when you come, you will always be welcome in your home in Kalgan. Sometimes the eyes of the old Empress are too weak to see that far," he added with an encouraging smile.

"When do you leave, Li Ahn?"

"Our mother has not told me. It will be soon, I trust."

Little Caroline began crying in the next room and April went to pick her up.

"Where is the amah?"

"In America, servants are given time off for themselves," she explained. She quieted Caroline and said, "Is mother in danger if she returns?"

"No," he replied.

"Then I wonder why father wants her back?"

"Perhaps it is love," he answered, grinning. "Our mother is an extraordinarily beautiful woman. When I saw her I could understand why father chose her for his wife and now wants her to return."

"There is more to it than that, Li Ahn," April said as she walked back and forth, patting Caroline's tiny back. "Something just isn't right about them sending you here to get her. And that business about their cutting off your head if you come back without her...." She shuddered. "Will the Empress really cut off your head?"

Li Ahn shrugged. "Perhaps," he said, in a matter-of-fact tone. "The Heavenly Empress does not like disappointment."

"I still don't think Mother should go. She stole from the Empress. My old tutor tells me the punishment is having the hands cut off if the object stolen was of importance, the fingers in whatever number and degree commensurate with the value of the stolen article."

Li Ahn frowned. "You really believe our father and the Empress mean to harm her?"

When Li Ahn was told by his father and the Empress that he was to travel to America he had not been given any reason for the journey except that he would be escorting his mother back to where she rightfully belonged.

He thought it odd that his mother was wanted or needed after so long, but he did not believe she would be harmed in any way. Now, April was planting seeds of doubt which were making him uncomfortable. Ke Loo had said the woman might refuse to come to China and had directed him to invent something to force her to accede to his wishes.

"She is an American woman," Ke Loo had reminded him. "And American women are headstrong and independent. They think of themselves of having minds of their own. Therefore, you must frighten, threaten or even resort to force if necessary to teach them their duty of obedience."

"Our mother stole from the Empress?"

April laid Caroline back into her cradle and began rocking it. She told him about what had happened after Ke Loo left them in the Forbidden City and had returned to Kalgan with Li Ahn and his new mother.

Li Ahn was horrorstruck. "But no one is permitted to use the Empress's scents. It is *death*!" His eyes went wide as he put his hand over his mouth and stared at April.

She nodded slowly.

"What can I do?" Li Ahn asked, knowing now that he would be taking his mother back to certain execution. He felt a chill as he thought of what he'd said to force her to obey. "What will I do, April?" he repeated.

"I don't know, Li Ahn." After reflecting she said, "Perhaps we are all meant to pay the price for our mother's sin."

* * * * * * *

Lydia knew what awaited her in China; the only question was how to save herself and Li Ahn as well. Somehow she must induce the boy to stay here, never to return to China; but that was impractical and probably impossible. When Li Ahn did not return, armies of the Empress's assassins would be dispatched if needed and there would be no half-hearted efforts such as those made previously. These assassins would not fail.

She thought of the last attempt on her life, the assassin who'd lain in wait for her in her bedroom, and now that she thought of it more rationally she wondered why the man hadn't killed her instead of trying to carry her off. She mulled it over in her mind and came to the only conclusion she could think of—the old dragon wanted her dead but she wanted it done in her royal presence where she could see for herself that proper punishment had been dispensed, with Lydia's head on a stake for all her subjects to see.

Li Ahn would die if she did not return, Lydia told herself. And she would most assuredly die if she returned with him. It was a problem that had to have a solution.

She was staring off into space, deep in thought, and did not hear the front door open and close, or Li Ahn's footsteps as he came into the room. When his shadow fell across her she gave a strangled cry and looked up sharply. Seeing him she breathed easier and smiled at him. But there was something very different about him, she noticed. His young face had a troubled look about it.

"Li Ahn, what is wrong?" she asked in Mandarin.

He looked at her a long time as if memorizing her face. When he'd satisfied himself he said, "I return home tomorrow. You will stay here."

Lydia got up and put her hand on his sleeve. "No, I will come with you," she said. "But as I told you, I have work that must be attended to before we go. It will only take a few days more."

"I spoke with April," he said. "She told me about *Nightsong*. You will die if you return to China with me, I know that now." She saw genuine concern in his eyes and her heart swelled in her breast as her eyes grew cloudy with tears. She kissed his cheek.

"But you can't return without me. Your cousin will see to it that you die in my place."

"I know that now, but I believe my father will intercede on my behalf. I will go directly to Kalgan, to somewhere where I have people who will hide me."

Lydia shook her head. "There is nowhere anyone can hide from the Dowager Empress. You know that better than I, Li Ahn. Her subjects are everywhere; you know what I say is true."

He turned abruptly, his fists clenched, his young eager mind racing. "There are those who are against the Empress, those who want to see China as a republic. I will go to them in Wuhan where even the Dowager Empress's fingers will not be able to point me out. In Hanchow there are new revolutionaries who are gathering into an army to overthrow the Manchus."

Lydia put her hand gently against his cheek. She saw his stubborn boyish pride shining in his eyes. "You are a Manchu, Li Ahn. They would not question your loyalties; they would destroy you first. You know what I say is the truth. You cannot deceive me into thinking you would be safe. I have lived too long among your people. I know how they think and what they believe."

She took his hand and led him to the settee where they sat close together. "We must think of some way to out-fox the Dragon Empress."

"No one can, as you say, *out-fox* my imperial cousin. She is far too wise."

"Perhaps for a man, but you must remember that I am a woman and women very often think alike. I'll think of something. In the meantime, where would you like to go for dinner tonight?"

She was surprised to find that Li Ahn particularly relished French fried potatoes, frankfurters and salted pretzels.

"The waterfront restaurant April told me about where the shrimp are a foot long and the lobsters as big as Caroline."

Lydia laughed. "Well, April may have exaggerated a little." She got up. "Why don't I ring her on the telephone and see if she and Raymond can join us? Would you like that?"

He nodded eagerly and watched her speak into the brown box that had a wire connected to it. It seemed unnatural for someone to talk to a brown box and answer a voice he couldn't hear.

When she turned back to him she said, "Everything is arranged. Now you'll have to excuse me, Li Ahn. I have a rather urgent appointment on Taylor Street in half an hour but I will be back in plenty of time for dinner."

"It will be no trouble amusing myself," he assured her. "I have much thinking to do."

She knew his troubled thoughts, but she had troubled thoughts of her own which were more pressing.

* * * * * * *

The doctor's office was halfway down Taylor Street, part of an old clapboard house sandwiched between two new commercial buildings, tall and cold looking. It would only be a matter of time, Lydia knew as she went up the walk, before this house too would be torn down by those city improvers who wanted to expand San Francisco's business district.

Lydia was positive she knew what was wrong with her and she knew she'd been running away from the truth, hoping for some miracle.

When she saw the doctor, he said without preamble, "Surely you know you are pregnant, Mrs. Nightsong,"

Her heart fell like a stone. She sat perfectly still with her hands folded demurely in her lap, her face deadly pale. The miracle she'd been praying for hadn't happened. For a moment she thought she was going to faint.

Dr. Carrol saw her sway and quickly got out of his chair but Lydia raised a hand to him then touched it to her forehead. "I'll be all right," she managed to say. "It's just that...." She couldn't hold them back; her tears came as she buried her face in her hands.

The doctor filled a glass from the water carafe and gave it to her. He had little patience for these modern, high-fashion ladies who believed pregnancies happened only to the more plain women.

"Surely you knew, Mrs. Nightsong, or at least surmised," Dr. Carrol said. "According to your file, this is not your first pregnancy."

Lydia made a gesture that meant nothing, helplessness perhaps, and searched for a handkerchief. "It's just a surprise," she finally managed to say. "I thought I was past the age."

The old doctor removed his glasses and rubbed his eyes. "Thirty-four is hardly being past the age, Mrs. Nightsong," he said patiently. "You are still a young woman and healthy enough to have a dozen more."

"Heaven forbid," she said, drying her eyes.

"Some women do, you know."

It was Peter's child, of course, Lydia told herself— had been telling herself ever since she first suspected. The future suddenly didn't seem as bright as before, clouded now by a scandal that would surely endanger her reputation even more, to say nothing of what it would mean for Empress Cosmetics. Peter already had a claim to fifty percent of *Nightsong* and his child would certainly entitle him to a measure of control.

He must never know, she decided as she climbed back into the carriage and started for home. Somehow it must be kept a secret. But how?

That was a question she had no answer to until she was with Li Ahn, April and Raymond at the noisy waterfront restaurant. There were several couples with children and lots of laughing, especially on the part of April, who found everything Li Ahn said enchanting or amusing.

It was when April spoke of little Caroline that Lydia conceived the notion. April said, "Caroline has stopped being so peevish. Actually she is hardly a bother anymore. It is like someone replaced her and gave me a new baby."

"Perhaps we should think about that," Raymond said good-naturedly.

Lydia saw the revulsion in April's eyes though she quickly covered it with an indulgent smile.

"Hardly," April said.

Raymond shrugged self-consciously. "Only a thought," he said and gave Lydia one of his looks that showed how deeply he wanted her understanding and compassion.

All that night Lydia wrestled with her problem. If she returned to China with Li Ahn there would cease to be any problem. That was one thing in death's favor; it erased pain and misery in one fell swoop. But somehow she had to convince Li Ahn to stay in America with her. In that event, however, she was still stuck with her present predicament and the only way out of it was, perhaps, through April.

Before going into her office she stopped at April's apartment. She lost no time in getting to the point. "I hate to put it this way, April, but I desperately need help and you are the only one I can think of to give it to me."

April stopped bouncing Caroline and cradled her to her breast. She saw her mother's worried look and said, "If it's about returning to China with Li Ahn, I don't think you should."

A warm feeling flowed over Lydia. "Thank you for that, darling. I know what is waiting for me in China when I return but perhaps after you learn of my trouble you'll have second thoughts about your advice."

"What is it?"

The nurse came in and they both fell silent until she'd taken Caroline from her mother and left the room.

"I am going to have a child," Lydia said, keeping her eyes lowered.

"You are *what!*"

Lydia looked hurriedly around and held up her hands. "Please," she begged. "No one must know."

"You are going to have a baby?" April asked in a hushed voice. To Lydia's surprise her daughter threw back her head and started to laugh.

"I fail to see the humor in it," Lydia said.

April had a difficult time controlling herself. "But it is quite funny, Mother. Justice and retribution and all that sort of thing. Surely, in view of all your activities you must have known it would happen sooner or later."

With an angry flounce of her skirts Lydia got to her feet. "You are being insulting."

"I don't mean to be," April said still chuckling. "Merely realistic. You can't honestly stand there and feel that you are exactly faultless?"

"Faultless, no, but you make it sound as if I were a common strumpet."

April refused to be contrite. "Well, after all, Mother, you must admit there have been a goodly number of gentlemen friends in your life. Who's the father, may I ask?"

"Peter MacNair," she answered without hesitating, almost as if she were proud of it. And she felt the need to hurt April for having laughed at her.

If April were hurt she didn't show it. "At least it isn't that dreadful Walter Hanover or one of those other men you were so eager to entertain."

"What I did...."

"I know," April interrupted. "You did it all for me."

"As you would do it for Caroline," Lydia said, pointing to the nursery.

April was unmoved. She sat like a stone, staring at her mother with cold, indifferent eyes. "No, you're wrong," she said. "If David MacNair walked through that door this instant I'd be gone with him regardless of what I would be forced to leave behind. You forget, Mother, that I carry my father's blood in my veins."

"Difficult as it may be for you to admit it, April, you also carry mine. Someday you will realize that as you will also realize what it means to sacrifice everything for your child."

"Tell me, Mother, if everything you've done was for me, did you also get pregnant for me?"

Lydia's cheeks flamed. She glared at April, then with an indignant toss of her head she started out of the room.

"Wait!" April called. There was an apologetic tone to her voice. "You said you need my help. What is it you want?"

Lydia's heaved a deep sigh and slowly turned around.

It took a few minutes before she had the courage to raise her eyes to April. When she did she said, "I am going to do everything I can to induce Li Ahn to remain here in San Francisco with us. In that event, if I am successful, I would want you to take my baby."

CHAPTER EIGHTEEN

April sat for a long time staring out of the window at the tidy park across the street. She wasn't thinking of her mother; her thoughts were, as always, on David MacNair. Through some perverse kind of reasoning she told herself she was right in taking Lydia's child, especially since it would be part MacNair, which indirectly would be part David. If she could not have David at least she would have a part of his bloodline, a half-brother.

Her mother's plan kept running through her head and the more she went over it the more she felt that at last she was being given an opportunity to break out and at least try to resolve her present circumstances. Marriage to Raymond was impossible. He was inconsiderate, vain, arrogant, selfish and on occasion cruel. She refused to allow him to touch her. His initial anger had given way to indifference. He easily found lots of women for that purpose, she'd learned.

April thought at first that Raymond might have been the father of Lydia's expected child, and that was why Lydia had come to her. It was the straight-out kind of thing her mother would do, never realizing that April would flatly refuse her and wind up hating her all the more both for her transgression and her honesty.

She wondered idly if Raymond had ever been one of her mother's lovers. The thought disgusted her and she quickly shrugged it off. No, she was almost positive that the relationship between them had always been purely business and nothing more. If she ever found to the contrary she could never bear to look at either of them again.

And Lydia's plan suited her like a glove—a plan contingent upon Li Ahn remaining in America. They would travel first to New York and then to Paris to await the birth of the baby there.

"First to New York," April repeated. She would refuse to take the nurse, which would give her the excuse of taking Caroline out every day of their visit. "David lives in New York," she told herself with a smile. It wasn't impossible that they might meet. And if not in New York then in Paris, perhaps. It was well advertised that Empress Cosmetics was introducing *Nightsong* to Europe at the Paris Exposition. Peter MacNair would surely be there and he might have his son with him as well if David were now working for P.M. Cosmetics.

At least that was in her prayers as she knelt beside her bed that night, her eyes shut, her lips moving softly as she intoned the help of her patroness, the divine Dowager Empress of all China.

In her oriental way of thinking, it hadn't been right for her to interfere with David's marriage when she herself was unwed. Now that they both had a spouse to shed it put them on a par and it didn't seem so wrong for her to try and find him and win back his love.

* * * * * * *

Li Ahn watched Morris carefully mix the contents of the two beakers. It reminded him of watching as a very small boy when his father's brother mixed the powders that exploded when touched with a flame.

"It's called chemistry," Morris explained as the two fluids congealed into a thick mass and began to change color.

"Yes, my uncle has a laboratory in Peking, but it is not as large as this one. He would let me watch him combine the different portions of sulphur and charcoal and another powder."

"Potassium nitrate, we call it," Morris clarified.

"He filled little paper casings and connected them on a string; then they were exploded whenever there was a festival or some other celebration."

"Gunpowder," Morris said. "Your ancestors were the first to learn how to make it." He gave a wry smile and added, almost to himself, "And they never learned to use it as such."

"And cosmetics?" Li Ahn asked as he picked up a cream base Morris was perfecting. "Did my ancestors discover this as well?"

"Probably. History gives credit to the early Egyptians and Ancient Greeks but I wouldn't be surprised if the Chinese weren't using them long before that." Morris blended a small amount of glycerine and a perfume into the cream base and held it up for Li Ahn to smell. "What do you think?"

"Very nice. What is it?"

"A new lotion for cleansing the skin. It moisturizes as well as cleanses."

Li Ahn rubbed some of the lotion between his thumb and forefinger and was amazed when it disappeared, leaving his fingertips soft. "Could I learn to make such things, Morris?" He looked suddenly embarrassed. "In China, only women make such things, but I must say I always liked to watch them though it was forbidden and far beneath my dignity."

"Of course you can learn to make such things, Li Ahn. All it takes is a little knowledge and a great deal of dedication and interest."

"I have always been a very quick learner and I find myself fascinated by the way things change completely when mixed or boiled or baked."

Morris chuckled. "I'm afraid you are destined for far more important things in life than being a chemist, Li Ahn. Your father is a Mandarin prince, is he not? Which means you are an heir to the Chinese throne."

Li Ahn's look grew sad. It had been almost two weeks since he'd arrived in this fantastic city with its cars that moved all by themselves on steel wheels, where people laughed and everyone lived in peace and no one was tortured or put to death. In fact, he had seen no evidence of death here in this strange and beautiful country. Death was unknown.

Now that he had found something with which to compare his earlier life, it was as if he had been walking along a path where he did not belong, a path that he'd been forced to take, a path that secretly frightened him—which he never admitted to anyone, especially not to his royal father. It wasn't that he feared death or pain or even the displeasure of the gods, which bothered him more than he liked to admit. Still, those fierce gods that breathed fire and demanded such obedience seemed so far away now, too far to reach him here in America where they didn't have any place. He found comfort in being so far away from their wrath.

"I don't want to be an heir to the Chinese throne," he found himself saying. "I never want to go back. I want to stay here."

"You can't mean that you like it here in San Francisco?"

"I do."

"Your sister wouldn't agree with you from the way she speaks about the place."

"April is a girl," he said as if that excused everything. "She dreams too much." His whole face lit up. "San Francisco is the only city I've ever seen where there is so much activity, even the air is purer. I've been reading books about America. Democracy is a wonderful thing, Morris."

"Unless you have too much of it," Morris cautioned, trying to temper Li Ahn's boyish enthusiasm.

"Freedom is all that really matters. Now that I have tasted it I loathe the thought of going back to China."

"All the same, you have little choice now, do you?"

At dinner with Lydia that evening Li Ahn posed the question.

"But we both have to return, don't we?" Lydia asked.

The color rose in his cheeks. He shoveled another spoonful of ice cream into his mouth. "I would like to stay here forever. I feel as if I belong here, Mother."

He looked wistful. "I know my father expects me to be like

him, a Mandarin prince, an heir to the throne, but I'm afraid."

"Afraid of what, Li Ahn?" she asked, laying her hand on his.

"I think the Dowager Empress hates me. It is the way she looks at me, as if I were a threat to her throne. I know I am far down a long line of princes but Father does not see so long a line. He imagines himself next emperor of China. I feel I am being disrespectful to my father but I fear for his ambition."

He looked at Lydia with wide, frightened eyes. "I have never said these things to anyone before, not even to my amah or to my tutor. But you are not one of them. I don't want to go back, Mother. I am not suited to be a prince. I don't care a thing about ruling, or government, or all that pomp and ceremony. I would make a terrible emperor."

"But you can't change your birthright, my son," she said, trying to keep her heart from bursting with pride and joy for this wonderful son.

"I could if I stayed here with you. It wasn't until I came here that I knew I had never been my real self. I like Kalgan and all the palaces and the luxuries but all the same I always felt as if I didn't really belong there."

"Of course you belonged."

He shook his head slowly. "I played a part because I knew it was what father wanted, but there was always something inside me that wasn't satisfied. Every time we moved from one palace to another I felt that we were interlopers and one day the real owners of the palace would come back and we would be evicted."

Lydia listened, wondering how much his sudden disdain for China had been clouded by the release from responsibilities which he'd found here. "You do not have to return if you don't want to," she said.

She knew the Empress would never leave them in peace but she could find places for Li Ahn to hide until her threats were finished. From all evidences of events in China, it was only a matter of time before the entire country closed itself off from the rest of the world or the world opened it up like a clam and routed the evil woman from her throne.

"No one can force you to do anything you do not wish to do, Li Ahn. I *am* your mother so the law cannot deport you. You can apply for citizenship if you are sure you truly want to stay here with me; that way the laws of America will always protect you from any possible harm that may be directed at you from China."

There would be trouble, she knew. Ke Loo would not give up his son without a battle but, as she told Li Ahn, there were laws to protect him. "You are welcome to stay here with me for as long as you wish."

Li Ahn beamed as he attacked the rest of the ice cream in the dish and Lydia asked Nellie to bring him another serving.

"You realize, Li Ahn, that your decision might break your father's heart?"

"It is his heart or mine," the boy said and Lydia was quick to see the duality of his personality. His strict upbringing with its emphasis on self-importance would never be erased no matter how long he remained outside his homeland. He would go back one day; she felt it in her bones.

Li Ahn softened his voice and looked at his mother pleadingly. "Why can't father just let me stay here in peace? He is next in line to the throne, he tells everyone. He will live forever. He does not need me. He can sire another son. My stepmother was heavy with child again when we left Kalgan. It will be a boy this time, my amah says. And he will be *all* Chinese, not only a part of him, like me. He would make a much more suitable successor."

"If it is what you want, Li Ahn, then I will do whatever I can. But you must remember that being a Chinese is not particularly good here in San Francisco."

Li Ahn shrugged. "I will cease being Chinese. Today I bought a western suit of clothes." He winked. "From a Chinese tailor. I intend being more American than you Americans."

"Well, after all, half of you already is."

"Then tomorrow I will make the change complete. I will get

a western haircut," he said, laughing as he touched the queue that hung down his back. "I have been taught that this is the symbol of true China."

CHAPTER NINETEEN

It was several days before April told Raymond about Lydia's baby and he was not pleased with her decision to take the child. "Why in hell can't you have my baby? Why take Lydia's?" he demanded.

She leveled her eyes on him as if he didn't exist. "You'll never touch me again, Raymond. I know all about your other women so I feel no wifely obligations. You're free to visit them as often as you wish just so long as you leave me alone."

"But why take Lydia's bastard?"

She lowered her eyes to her sewing. "Why does that bother you? It isn't half yours is it?"

"Don't be disgusting. You know there has never been anything between Lydia and me," he lied.

"That surprises me, but my mother told me who the father is and I believe her."

"Who?"

"That is something we've agreed never to reveal."

She laid aside her sewing and went toward the nursery. "As far as anyone is concerned, the baby is ours, yours and mine. That should be sufficient to soothe your male French vanity."

It wasn't, and Raymond began thinking of ways of spiting April...perhaps through Lydia. The three of them would be in Paris together. The baby would be born in five months and they would be staying for the Paris Exposition which opened a month later.

His conceit was too great to even consider the possibility of failing to lure Lydia back into bed with him after the baby was born. That would show April that he was just as independent of their marriage vows as she was. And what greater insult could a husband give an uncaring wife than for her to learn that he preferred her mother to her?

* * * * * * *

After tucking Li Ahn safely away in a private school in an exclusive section of Santa Barbara with Evelyn Clary's and Morris's assurances that they'd see to his every need, including companionship, Lydia started across country with Raymond, April and little Caroline. It was at April's insistence that the child's nurse be left behind for the sake of secrecy, April said, assuring Lydia that between them Caroline would be well looked after.

The Huntingtons had graciously loaned them their private rail car, the epitome of luxury and comfort. The car had its own kitchen, a dining room that could seat twelve, and three bedrooms, each with its own bath; and of course, a sitting room with an observation deck off of it. In exchange for the use of the car, Lydia promised Arabella a life-long supply of *Nightsong,* a scent she too had adopted as her own.

"That's the hidden magic in *Nightsong,"* Raymond explained as they jostled their way over the rails that crossed the plains of Kansas. "It changes with every woman who wears it, accentuating all her personal loveliness, bringing out the hidden beauty that lies deep inside her. No two women could ever recognize the same scent when worn by another. *Nightsong* is a mystery. Even I don't understand how its chemistry changes when it comes in contact with its wearer's body chemistry. It's truly fabulous."

In New York they rested for a week at the Fifth Avenue Hotel, where they discovered, to Raymond's discomfiture, that they were the only occupants of a suite without personal servants.

April was adamant: No nurse, no maid.

Lydia found New York stimulating, staring enthralled at

the heights of the buildings, the awesomeness of the private mansions that lined the park. Everywhere they went they were met with much ceremony and dignity. Eastern decor was much fussier than San Francisco's. Here every room was crowded with tall palm trees and fat green pots of flowers. Red damask and marble walls were very much in vogue and every room reeked of cigars and cigarette smoke and of burning anthracite coal.

April, she noticed, spent all of her time with Caroline, either basking in the sun of the park or strolling the Avenue looking into the store windows. Lydia held her breathe every time April left the suite—which seemed constantly—in fear that by some fluke of fate she'd meet David MacNair.

In Madison Square Lydia's heart gave a tug when she saw a sign advertising P.M. Cosmetics. Peter MacNair was in the city too, as she well knew. Just knowing he was somewhere near made her anxious to be away to Paris, while at the same time another part of her wanted to see him.

She was glad when the day came for them to leave New York. Raymond had obtained first class passage for them on the return-portion of the maiden voyage of *The City of Paris*.

"A steel ship?" April gasped when their victoria pulled up at the custom's shed. "And it has no sails."

"The first of its kind," he explained. "But there is absolutely nothing to be nervous about."

"But how does it move through the water?" Lydia asked.

"By steam engines and twin propellers that push it along. Come," he urged. "It's very luxurious, they tell me."

The crossing was fast and much smoother than what Lydia or April remembered from their crossing from Shanghai to San Francisco. And by the time they reached France it was difficult for them to imagine that they'd been on water for so many days, except it did feel odd walking on land again after so long.

Paris was the most romantic city Lydia had ever seen. Everywhere there was glitter and music and lovers walking hand-in-hand beneath the trees bordering the Seine. April too seemed to come out of herself, making a daily routine of wheeling Caroline along the cafe-lined boulevards with their rows of little outside tables nudging the passers-by.

Like New York, people hurried regardless of the time of day, but unlike New York, there was a camaraderie among the Parisians, who nodded and smiled as they went along. They seemed intent upon preserving their individuality, but at the same time they were friendly.

Raymond found a doctor who spoke fluent English and his offices were on the Champs Elysees, just around the corner from their luxury hotel. Lydia was beginning to show, even under her voluminous drapes of satin, and her back ached constantly.

It surprised Lydia that they all got along as well as they did. She felt closer to April than ever before. Yet for all April's display of friendship, Lydia got the impression that the real April was hiding behind a mask...waiting. Waiting for what, Lydia had no idea.

The city was a jumble of excitement and activity as the preparations for the Exposition began to key up. The Empress Cosmetic exhibit was built in the shape of a royal crown with its windows in various hues and patterns to resemble cut gems. Lovely young French girls in white silk and paste-diamond tiaras would act as hostesses to the public. Everything was moving in perfect precision; the offices were now operating under Raymond's strict control and the promotion campaign was ready to bombard the European market when the Exposition was officially opened.

Raymond had arranged a surprise for Lydia and April, a surprise that horrified April.

"Do you mean you want us to get into one of those wire cages and go to the top of that steel tower? You must be mad to even consider such a thing and particularly with mother expecting any day now."

Lydia laughed. "Oh, April, it might be fun."

"Fun? You're as mad as he is. Why the tower hasn't even been christened yet. Besides, it's a monstrosity; everyone is laughing at it. I doubt if they've even tested it to see if it's safe."

"Of course it's safe. Mr. Eiffel is no imbecile. His tower will last forever and one day it will symbolize Paris if not all of France. It is a great honor that we have been invited to this private affair hosted by the President."

April huffed out of the room when Caroline started to cry. "Kill yourselves if you like, but count me out of your suicide party."

"Perhaps I too should wait until after the baby comes, Raymond. It wouldn't do if he decided to be born with me nine hundred feet up in the air."

It proved a wise decision on Lydia's part. It was on the night of the Eiffel Tower dedication party that Lydia went into labor and was rushed to *Hôtel Dieu*, which Lydia thought was another hotel but turned out to be Paris's oldest and finest hospital.

Marcus was born at exactly ten o'clock on May twenty-ninth, 1889, one month from the date the Paris Exposition would officially open. Lydia chose the name Marcus for no particular reason; she could hardly name him for his father, and in any event the child's name would be Marcus Andrieux.

April really didn't care what they named the baby. Marcus was as good as any other name for a boy. She was too preoccupied with strolling the Quays, the Tuileries, the Place Vendome, all the places she knew David might stroll. She took long rides in the quaint fiacres, scanning the faces of the people she passed as Caroline gurgled with delight at the cloppity-clop of the horses and the pretty blossoms on the trees.

"You spend too much of your time alone with Caroline," Raymond objected. "I don't understand why you refuse to let me take on a nursemaid. You will surely need one when Lydia is released from the hospital."

April saw the sense of that and decided to agree as she recalled her confinement after Caroline was born. She didn't want to go through that restriction again, especially with David surely in the city somewhere, or soon to be.

"Very well, Raymond, hire your nursemaid," April told him.

"Good. And you would do me a large favor if you would go

to St. Honoré or to the Place de l'Opéra and shop for something suitable to wear to the Empress exhibit opening. Something in white."

"Yellow," April insisted. "But I haven't decided if I will attend." Of course she intended to be at the opening but it pleased her to toy with Raymond.

"I insist that you be there. Lydia may not feel well enough and I must have a hostess."

April shrugged. She would be there because she knew that if David were in Paris he would come to the Empress Cosmetic exhibit, if for no other reason than to check out the family firm's competition.

Over the next several days, shopping for just the right gown consumed every minute of April's time.

And when you meet him? she asked herself. The question stopped her dead in front of the Gautier Salon on Avenue Georges Cinq. "What do I say to him?" she asked her reflection in the window backed by Austrian fringed drapes.

She told herself not to worry. They still loved each other. His love hadn't been so shallow as to evaporate simply at the insistence of his parents. Of course he still loved her; she was convinced of that. And if she could leave Raymond, David would willingly leave the wife who'd been forced on him. They were no longer two innocents who had to be watched over like naughty children. She'd find him and this time they would make good their escape to China. Paris to Kalgan was half-way around the world, yet somehow she knew instinctively that their likelihood of succeeding was assured.

And what of Caroline and Marcus? She would take them or leave them. David would advise her. The children were minor details. Once she found David again everything would fall into place.

But suppose he refused to leave his wife?

April looked at the yellow gown draped on the floor mannequin. It was the most exquisite thing she'd ever seen. Dressed in that, she knew she could gaurantee any man's love.

* * * * * * *

Lydia slept late and when she awoke to the brilliant spring noon she stretched her hands over her head and luxuriated in the softness of the elegant bed.

A son, she told herself as she ran her hands over the flatness of her stomach. She had another heir to add to the Nightsong dynasty. She knew she should feel contrite about giving up her son—Peter's son—but it wasn't as if the boy were being adopted by strangers. It couldn't be helped, anyway. She forced herself to think of other things.

Today the Exposition opened and this evening would launch the European debut of *Nightsong.* "*Nightsong* will capture the fancy of every woman of taste in the world," Raymond assured her, adding with a smile, "That is, every woman of taste and money."

Lydia didn't feel like going to the exhibit. Down deep she knew Peter MacNair would be there. She felt his presence all around her. He was here in Paris, she was sure of it. She prayed that his magnetism wouldn't prove too strong for her to repel.

Exercise, the doctor had recommended, and that was what she would do. She would keep her mind occupied by things moving about her. As she swung herself out of the Louis Quatorze bed she decided she'd do some more sightseeing—alone—and possibly shop for one of those new wide brimmed hats which seemed so terribly in fashion here in Paris.

The noise of the trams and the people and carriages enveloped her the moment she stepped from the hotel and trundled off through the gay little streets. She crossed over the Pont Neuf and along the narrow ways of the Île de la Cité.

A gendarme saluted and smiled as he passed, scanning the crowds, reminding Lydia that fairs meant throngs and throngs meant pickpockets. She took a firmer grip on her bag but refused to let anything spoil her glorious mood. Little Marcus was sound and healthy and seemed to be in love with this new world she'd brought him into. Even April took to the baby at first sight; it had been as if April saw something in the tiny boy that no one else saw.

The afternoon was full of the newness of spring and the enchantment of the city. She spent several hours visiting the shops, buying whatever pleased her, and when the late afternoon light began to dwindle she still felt surprisingly alive and untired. She made her way along the boulevard after handing her parcels to a fiacre driver and tipping him generously to deliver them to her suite at the hotel.

Up ahead something lit the sky and she walked eagerly toward it. She stared in awe at the arch of glaring electric light that curved over the square. The vivid light was blindingly unflattering, and she fled down a side street. She found herself on another boulevard noisy with yellow trams that crisscrossed in every direction and made her laugh aloud for being so alive.

The light of the day was fading fast as she installed herself at a little table outside one of the numerous sidewalk cafés. The Café de Versailles, the menu proclaimed proudly as she used the little French she knew to try to decipher the listings. She decided on coffee and brioche, reminding herself that she had better let Raymond and April know she intended skipping the opening of the Empress Cosmetic's exhibit. She was too pleased with herself and with Paris to be interested, for once, in business.

She'd send a note, she decided as she looked around, asking herself why she hadn't thought of that when she sent the fiacre driver to the hotel with the packages. Every other table was taken, she saw, curiously studying the people, wondering if she could identify someone who spoke English. In the corner was a family group chattering away in French, and there, near the box hedge, a knot of men in black berets and trim beards nodded solemnly over their *apéritifs.* Closest to her sat two men who looked like artists, with women who looked like models, all paint and poses.

Her heart leapt when she heard Americans loudly arguing about the merits and demerits of the Eiffel Tower.

"If we had it in New York, they'd tear it down."

"It's an engineering marvel."

"It's an eyesore."

"What do you know? You didn't even go up in it. You should have seen Paris from the top."

"You can have it."

Lydia turned to see a trio of teenaged boys gesticulating wildly, each trying to be heard over the others.

When she asked them her favor she noticed that they weren't particularly keen on the idea of interrupting their evening by taking a note to Lydia's hotel but their manners wouldn't permit them to do anything but oblige a compatriot, and especially a lady.

When she'd finished the last of the brioche and coffee and the boys were gone, something they said gripped her fancy. She suddenly had an urge to see Paris from the very top of that crude metal tower that everyone was talking about. And it seemed the perfect night for the adventure. Perhaps these new glaring electric arc lights wouldn't be so unsightly from far up in a dark sky.

The gigantic tower rose into the sky like some huge skeleton, cold and menacing, sitting on legs that flowed in graceful arches. There was a long queue which she skirted and went toward a gendarme standing in front of a side entrance that looked private. She introduced herself and explained to the policeman that she was an exhibitor at the Exposition and had been invited by the President to the inaugural party opening the tower but was indisposed and could not accept the invitation.

"Is there anyone here this evening who would grant me permission to tour the structure, Monsieur?"

He picked up a small telephone which Lydia hadn't noticed and spoke fluidly into the ivory mouthpiece. A moment later he saluted her and pulled open the grilled gate.

"Monsieur Eiffel is hosting a party for some American friends of yours, Madame Nightsong," he said.

"Who, may I ask?"

"Madame and Monsieur Hearst from San Francisco."

Something told her to turn and run away; she wasn't really in the mood for the Hearsts. But she did not want to be rude, either, and by now they knew she was here.

"They insist that you join them, Madame," the gendarme said.

He ushered her toward the lift. "Someone will meet you when you get off the elevator," he said with his thick French accent. "The party is still on the first level."

Her heart began beating rapidly as the steel grilled door clanged shut on the private elevator cage and the operator in his stiff blue and brass uniform waited until she was comfortably seated on one of the velvet couches. He said something in French that she supposed was meant to be reassuring, and threw a mechanism and the cage began to slant upward.

The ground fell away as she was carried up, up, up into the fancy steel patterns of the tower's base. A moment later it came to a jolting stop and before the attendant pulled open the grilled door she recognized Peter MacNair's outline on the other side.

"Lydia," he said.

His voice erased every other thought she'd had. He was dressed in evening clothes which only heightened his good looks. Hard as she tried she couldn't stop looking at him.

Peter held out his hand to her. It took time for her to gather her courage to touch him. She managed to collect herself and said, "Hello, Peter."

"Not surprised?" he asked.

"I rather suspected you'd get around to checking on your fifty percent investment," she said. In fact, she hardly felt surprised at all—the meeting felt inevitable.

He ignored the slur and touched her hands to his lips. "You are more beautiful than the last time I saw you."

"And how is your wife?" she asked tartly.

"Fine, thank you. Lorna didn't come with me this trip," he answered pointedly.

She saw the expression in his eyes and her heart gave a little flutter. But she said nothing and took the arm he offered as he led her toward the edge of the first observation platform. The people below looked thick and crowded together like so many marbles in a circle with only their hats pointed toward them. Lydia found the sight funny.

"You didn't marry Hanover after all, I hear," Peter said.

"I had no reason to after you left. To tell you the truth, I was surprised when I didn't hear from your attorneys regarding your proposed claim."

He laughed as she wanted to laugh at the milling people below. "I know I didn't act as a gentlemen should when I took back those documents. I don't know why I thought I should keep them."

"Because you are an unspeakable, disreputable cad, Peter MacNair. It's as simple as that."

He laughed again, this time more softly and a little self-consciously. "Yes, I suppose it would take one to recognize another."

She turned on him, her amusing smile gone. She opened her mouth to say something but the longing way he was looking at her made her shut it. She swirled her skirt behind her and started back toward the elevator. He grabbed her arm and pulled her against him, covering her mouth with his, holding her tight.

He kissed her hard, meaningfully, and then eased her slightly away. "I love you."

"And I detest you."

"No, you don't. I can tell by the way you pressed against me, the way you look at me. Tell me you love me, Lydia."

"No," she objected when he pulled her into a shadow. The Hearsts and their guests came laughingly around the corner of the observation deck.

"Ah, there you are, Lydia," Phoebe Hearst called as she came forward and embraced her. "You know you are doing a naughty thing by going international with a scent we all believe should be kept strictly American."

Lydia forced a smile. "Good business has no nationality," she answered as she put her hand out to Phoebe's husband. "Isn't that so, George?"

George Hearst stroked his impressive moustache. "You know how I feel about women in business, Lydia, but I must admit I've seen your sales figures and I am deeply impressed." He took her hand and led her away from Peter and began introducing her to the rest of the party.

She wanted to get away. She tried excusing herself, saying she felt out of place in her afternoon dress, that she should get back to the hotel, that she should help Raymond with the opening of the exhibit. None of it would do. They insisted she remain and accompany them on the tour to the top and would take no other answer but yes.

Phoebe Hearst innocently commented, "Lorna isn't here and Peter has been a bear for female companionship. Do be an angel and try to see that he isn't so sulky. Talk to him about San Francisco; I really think he's homesick since he moved to New York."

She was trapped and there was no way for her to break away without being rude to these very influential people.

"So you're stuck with me for at least a part of the evening," Peter said, smiling. "Let's call a truce and try to enjoy ourselves."

Surprisingly enough, as they gradually increased their ascent and the champagne and caviar flowed more freely, Lydia did find herself relaxing and enjoying the conversation. The men spoke of profit margins and marketing percentages, which she understood, and she offered intelligent comments of her own. The women spoke of fashion and travel and family, which she also found interesting and fun. She laughed, drank more champagne, and by the time the lift was taking them up the last leg of their ascent her mood was excellent and the butterfly wings in her stomach had flown off.

Even the creaking and groaning of the steel girders didn't particularly bother her as Peter led her to a corner of the very top level. A wind came up—nothing very severe, but enough to cause the tower to sway. Lydia gave a little gasp and snatched hold of Peter's arm. A moment later his jacket was around her shoulders and his arms were about her waist as she stood with her back to him, leaning against his chest, and the fabulous city of Paris was stretched out at their feet.

"Breathtaking," she murmured as she felt his arms tighten around her and rested her head against his shoulder.

"I feel like Satan all of a sudden."

"Oh?" She turned and frowned up at him.

"Wasn't it Satan who said, 'Cast yourself down and adore me and I will give you all of this?'" He motioned with his hand to include all of the lovely gaslit city, though the electric arch still looked garish even from way up here.

Lydia laughed. "It sounds more like something Peter MacNair would say." Her head felt light from both the altitude and the champagne.

"Why won't you marry me, Lydia?" Peter said after a long moment.

"Because you don't really want me, Peter, you want Empress Cosmetics."

"That isn't exactly true."

She felt the mood leave her and was glad Phoebe Hearst called out that the lift was ready to take them down. As they went back toward the party Peter said, "Why is it so wrong in your eyes for a man to have ambition? I love you, Lydia."

"That's the problem, Peter. I am just not convinced that you do love me."

"Then let me prove it to you."

"How? By making another promise you'll only break? I've been hurt enough, Peter. I don't want you to hurt me anymore."

The party was suddenly all around them again.

"All right everyone. One last toast to the beautiful city of Paris and to Monsieur Eiffel and his magnificent tower," George Hearst called as the attendants refilled the glasses.

"To the Eiffel Tower! To Paris!" they yelled in unison and flung their crystal champagne glasses over the edge of the platform.

CHAPTER TWENTY

The Empress Cosmetic crown shown like a jewel on moss velvet as the torch lights and gas lanterns glowed brightly, inviting everyone into its intoxicating interior of scented air. A trio of harpists sat behind a screen sending muted music through the exquisite exhibit building that throbbed with people. Everyone was in awe of the myriad crystal and glass containers lit from beneath, shimmering on panes of frost, each in soft pastels.

Young girls in paste-diamond tiaras and white satin gowns moved through the milling crowds, offering samples of the creams and lotions, done up in miniature replicas of the products in the display cases.

There was a sudden clamor outside the exhibit which made Raymond look up from the order form he was writing for a London department store buyer. A strange quietness fell over the people, almost a hush as a coach stopped in front of the building.

April stepped out of the carriage and an audible sigh of astonished admiration rose from the crowd. Raymond dropped his pen and stared. She was ravishing. Her long yellow gown trailed behind her like a cascade of saffron and chrysanthemums. The brightness of the lamps made the yellow silk glow with intensity as every other color paled before it. Strands of creamy pearls were entwined in her long black hair, which fell almost to her waist. Her brows were arched and a faint touch of blue-green shaded the lids of her eyes, giving the dark pupils the fire of black onyx. A single diamond and pearl pendant touched the center of her forehead.

April scanned the crowd slowly, carefully, as she made her way into the exhibit. She had dressed only for him; she'd come only to find David. Her heart grew heavy when she did not see his face in the crowd.

Raymond reached for her hand but she tactfully avoided his touch and walked behind one of the glass display counters where she had the advantage of being able to see everyone as they entered the exhibit.

"My wife," Raymond stammered to the buyer he'd been attending.

As he introduced the man, April saw a familiar movement out of the corner of her eye. She turned, knowing he was there.

David MacNair stood just inside the door, his eyes wide, his lips slightly parted. April saw him speak her name. She kept her eyes firmly fixed on him for fear he'd vanish like so many of her earlier dreams and visions. She moved her head in a regal nod of acknowledgement, as though acknowledging a courtier. Then she politely excused herself from her husband and walked toward David. How long she'd waited to hear his voice, to see the way his eyes moved lovingly over her.

"April," he breathed, finding himself incapable of saying anything more. Her beauty was overpowering. "April."

She felt tears threatening her eyes but she held them back, refusing to let him see her vulnerability, her hurt at his desertion.

"Can we talk?" David managed.

She nodded and took his arm as they walked out of the display exhibit. She could feel Raymond's eyes cutting into her back but she didn't care. Her life had started again and no matter for how brief a time, no one was going to interrupt it.

David found he couldn't trust himself to look at her though he knew everyone else who passed them couldn't keep from gazing at this dazzling creature. Somewhere he found his voice and said, "I was hoping you might come to Paris with the *Nightsong* exhibit."

April was tempted to tell him she'd come to Paris to have a baby but couldn't bring herself to spoil the joy of being with him again. She could almost feel the light touch of his lips against hers as they walked slowly through the crowds that parted before them.

David made a sound in his throat. "A far cry from San Francisco, isn't it? They used to curse us back there."

Still she said nothing, wondering when or if he would speak of why he'd let his parents drive him away.

"Are you still living in San Francisco, April? Yes, of course you are. I know. You have an apartment overlooking the park."

"How do you know that?"

"I still have friends there. One of my old school chums who knew you told me about seeing you. He said he often sees you perambulating your daughter in the park."

"And you? Do you have any children?" she forced herself to ask.

"Me? I never married."

The entire world stopped moving. There were suddenly no sensations, no sounds, no motions. Everything was as one would see in a cloudy tintype, immobilized into a blurred mass of shapes and attitudes. April wasn't certain she'd heard him correctly. She turned, feeling a terrible apprehension. "What did you say?"

"I never married. I don't think I ever will."

She only heard the first of it. "You never married?" she asked breathlessly.

"No." He was looking at her horrified expression. "What made you think I would?"

"The announcement. The newspaper," she gasped, feeling as if she were being suffocated. The pressure was becoming unbearable.

"What are you talking about? What newspaper announcement?"

She watched his steady eyes, the anxious line of his mouth. He really didn't know what she was talking about. The oddest feeling came over her. She didn't know whether to scream with rage or laugh with rapturous jubilation. "You aren't married?" she asked again, wanting desperately to hear him say it again.

"No."

A million thoughts crashed around inside her and she found it impossible to concentrate on any one of them. He isn't married! She kept repeating that to herself. He was never married. It had all been a plot, a plan, a cruel joke. They'd tricked her. Lydia had cheated her out of the one thing she'd ever wanted in her life.

With her fists clenched she raised them up to her face and pressed them hard into her temples, trying to stop the clamoring hatred that was seething around inside her head.

"April," David said with concern as she kept beating her fists against her temples. He took her wrists and held them tight. "What is it?"

The clamoring stopped, soothed into quiet by the reassurance of his voice. "Oh, David," she moaned as she put her forehead against his shoulder. "Don't you see how they've tricked us?"

He didn't understand but he began to feel a gnawing anxiety. Something was terribly amiss and he found himself afraid to ask what it was.

"They wanted me to marry Raymond," April blurted out. "They published an announcement in the newspaper, which they made certain I would read."

"What announcement? Who?"

"My mother. Your mother. Obviously they were both in on it. There was an announcement in the San Francisco *Examiner* telling of your marriage to some debutante in New York."

He stared at her. "But that's impossible," he said. "I came to San Francisco to stop your wedding. I even sneaked into the house just before the ceremony but your mother made me see how futile it would be for you and me to marry."

She put her arms around him. "Poor, sweet, lovely David. But it wouldn't be futile. It was only San Francisco that made us look like freaks. Other places aren't like that. You saw your-self only moments ago how people looked at us with admiring smiles."

He eased himself away. "You're a married woman, April," he reminded her.

She frowned at his bowed head. "You've stopped loving me?"

David looked up sharply. "No, never. I could never love anyone but you, April. You know that to be the truth."

"Then let's do what we set out to do."

"China?" he ventured in an unsteady voice.

"China."

His eyes began to move nervously from side to side. "But your husband, your daughter."

April suddenly felt free and very brave. "There is also a son. We'll take them with us or leave them, whichever you like."

His voice deserted him again. He swallowed hard to try and find it. He was more scared than he'd ever been and he couldn't rightly say what he was afraid of. April was different somehow. Harder, he thought.

The night was soft and balmy and behind her the tall steel tower made an awesome pattern against the sky. A cold shiver ran down his back as he peered deep into her eyes.

"You're married," David repeated.

"I was forced into it," she said jutting out her chin. "I don't love him. I love you, David. We must never be separated again." The noise and the sounds of the fair began to filter back into her consciousness, shattering the starry night, their romantic interlude. "Besides," she said harshly, "what does Raymond matter? I despise him."

A look of total confusion came over David. It had all been so much simpler to grieve for an unattainable love. The complications April was now manufacturing befuddled him. Everything had changed much too swiftly. "You must divorce him," he said to her.

"I don't care about a divorce. I want to be with you now. I want to run away from Raymond forever." She saw the way he was looking at her and she grew petulant. "Besides, what will it matter when we are with my father? He will arrange for a royal decree. I am a princess, remember. My father can do anything."

He saw her desperation, her blind defiance, and took her in his arms knowing how it felt to be cornered and threatened. He'd felt the same sense of futility that day when Lydia told him to leave and go back to New York, to forget April. He knew about hopelessness. "It's all right, darling," he said as she trembled in his arms. "We'll work it out." His mind refused to function. "Tomorrow," he said brightly. "When can I see you? We'll talk and plan it all out tomorrow."

"No, David, not tomorrow. Now. We must plan now and not let them interfere again."

He smiled kindly, tolerantly, as one would smile at a precocious child. "Very well. There's a pavilion just ahead where we can have some wine and make our plans."

April fitted naturally against the curve of his body as his arm went around her slender waist. She leaned her head against him and let him lead her to the white-latticed pavilion, unaware that as they entered its raised dais Lydia and Peter got up from a corner table and left through the side archway.

CHAPTER TWENTY-ONE

Lydia couldn't trust herself to let him touch her and when he hailed the fiacre she sat huddled as far away from him as she could get.

"Are you so afraid of me, Lydia?" he asked.

"No. I suppose I'm more afraid of myself." When he reached for her she pulled farther into her corner. "No, Peter. I've told you how I feel. I don't trust you. I don't imagine that I ever will. Kindly respect my feelings."

"I'm a patient man, Lydia, but there is a limit to every man's patience."

"I dearly hope so," she said finally but her heart ached as she said it.

They rode the rest of the way in silence and she discouraged the kiss he attempted when they pulled up under the portico of the hotel. "Goodbye, Peter."

"It isn't goodbye. We both know there will never be a goodbye where you and I are concerned."

She took one long, last lingering look. From somewhere she found the courage to tear her gaze away and fled into the lobby, deafening herself to the way he called to her.

When she reached her suite she ran into the bedroom and threw herself across the bed and burst into tears. She was so alone, so confused. Every thought that came to her contradicted the one before. All she worked for she had achieved, only to find herself alone, isolated from the rest of the world. She'd managed to imprison herself in her own private hell without hope of loving or trusting ever again.

But it was only in her isolation, her loneliness, that she felt safe, even though she knew it meant refusing herself the right to feel the warmth and affection of another human being. She knew she was quarantining herself from the rest of life but there was nothing she could do to stop it.

Her misery only brought more misery; her tears, more fears, as she realized she'd sent away forever the only person in the world who could ever make her happy.

There was a sound in the sitting room that made her sit up, noticing that she'd cried herself to sleep. The marquetry clock on the writing table told her it was well past midnight. The realization made her wonder who could be prowling about her sitting room at this hour.

Raymond was fixing himself a drink when she looked into the room. "Sorry," he said, sounding already drunk. "I ran out of liquor and the service is closed for the night. You don't mind my helping myself?"

"No, of course not. I'll join you, in fact." She tucked up a few stray strands of hair and pushed her combs more securely into the deep waves. "How was the opening?"

When he didn't answer she looked at him more closely. "Is everything all right, Raymond?" She saw his gloom deepen. "Marcus? Caroline? Something's happened to the children," she said as she started toward their adjoining suite.

"No, the children are sleeping and Nurse is with them," he said, stopping her by handing her the balloon of cognac. "It's April."

Her eyes widened. "April? What's wrong?"

"She isn't home yet, that's what's wrong." He took a deep swallow of the liquor and splashed some more into his glass.

"Good heavens. Where is she? Wasn't she with you at the opening?"

"She was...for about three minutes. Young MacNair showed up and she walked out with him."

Lydia's hand flew to her throat. "David? Dear God," she

moaned. "Are you certain?"

"One of the buyers told me that was who she walked out with." Raymond took an unsteady step toward the divan and dropped into the cushions. "She walked away as if she didn't know who I was. The minute she saw him come in she was hypnotized by him. And, God, she was ravishing tonight. So beautiful. Like a vision." He punched the pillows in a suddenly violent gesture.

Lydia was too worried to pay his unhappiness any mind. "We must stop them," she said as she put aside her glass and started for a wrap.

"Stop them?" Raymond said petulantly.

"They're foolish children. They tried to run off once before. I'm afraid they'll be foolish enough to try it again."

Raymond didn't quite comprehend. "Run off? And leave her daughter and Marcus?"

"It's a long story, Raymond. April and David MacNair tried to elope to China just about the time you came into our lives. They were in love."

Raymond remembered the way the two of them had looked at each other at the exhibit. "David MacNair," he said derisively. "So that's who she's been pining over. That's my so-called competition." He suddenly threw back his head and laughed drunkenly. "Well, to the devil with her and her adolescent boyfriend."

Lydia was busily pulling on a cloak.

Raymond ignored her flurry of activity. "I know now I made a mistake, Lydia."

"Please, Raymond, let's not go over that old ground again."

"I should have married you."

There was a sudden sound of a door being unlatched, then softly closed.

"There," Raymond said, motioning to the wall separating their suites. "No need for you to run off into the night looking for the stray cat. She has crawled back to the nest after her night of *amour.*"

Lydia breathed a sigh of relief as she removed her cloak. "Go to bed, Raymond. It's very late."

He poured himself some more cognac. "Another little drink to celebrate the return of the prodigal wife." He raised the glass too quickly and splashed cognac down the front of his evening shirt.

"Here, give me that before you drown yourself," Lydia said. When she reached for the glass Raymond suddenly reached for her and enveloped her in his arms. Reminding herself of how drunk he was she let him hold her for a moment while he swayed unsteadily.

"I really loved making love to you, Lydia," he slurred.

She pushed at his chest and tried to get out of his embrace but he was insistent upon holding her.

"Please go to bed, Raymond. I'm very tired and I have had a very trying night."

"We've both had a very trying night," he said a little more soberly. His voice grew strangely even, deep and comforting.

Lydia found herself relaxing against him, reveling in the feel of a man's strength supporting all her weaknesses. Innocently she let him go on holding her, glad for the protection he represented, however briefly. She could almost imagine it was Peter.

It had been a long time since she'd felt so tired, so depleted. It was as if innocence had been restored to her and she was back in that cluttered shack in China with the exquisite painting of a bird on a plum tree branch, singing to the curved rim of the moon. *Nightsong,* she thought dreamily as she lay her head on Raymond's shoulder and felt the touch of his lips to her hair. How long, long ago it all was.

The connecting door opened and Lydia gave a little start when she saw April glaring at them. It took a few seconds for Lydia to realize the compromising position she'd allowed herself to get into.

"April," she said uncomfortably as she eased away from Raymond. To her horror he grabbed her and pulled her back against him.

"You are trash!" April yelled and slammed the door.

Lydia rushed after her, fighting her way out of Raymond's embrace. She rushed into the adjoining suite. "April," she urged as her daughter went toward her bedroom. Lydia followed close behind her, determined to make her understand. Somewhere behind her she heard Raymond moving in her wake.

"April," she said again, keeping her voice low so as not to awaken the children. "It's not as it appears."

"I really don't care," she answered coolly, seating herself before the dressing table and vigorously brushing her hair.

Raymond stepped forward. He put an angry hand on April's shoulder and spun her around. "Of course you don't care. Why should you after just coming from the arms of your lover?"

"You're right. He is my lover, but not in the disgusting way you both think."

"So what then were you two doing until this hour, holding hands?" Raymond demanded.

"Yes. We aren't animals like you two," April snapped accusingly.

"Listen, you little...." Raymond grabbed her by her shoulders and began shaking her.

Lydia tried to restrain him. "Stop it, Raymond. Control yourselves, both of you."

April whirled on her like a cyclone. "I'm going away with David. And this time no one is going to stop us. I am sick of your trying to ruin my life, Mother. It was you who made me believe that David had abandoned me. You purposely set out to destroy him in my eyes and I almost let you. Well, he's back in my life and not you nor anyone else will keep us apart."

Lydia knew when she'd lost. "And what of Caroline and Marcus?"

"We're taking them with us."

"No you are not!" Lydia said sharply.

April calmly turned back to her mirror. "Of course Marcus is yours. I will take him or leave him as you tell me. David doesn't know. I didn't tell him." She glared up at her mother's stricken expression. "And I did not keep the secret for your sake, Mother, I did it for David. Knowing the father would only hurt him all the more."

Lydia knelt beside the quilted satin bench. "You mustn't do this, April. Stay and think about it. Give it time. Something can be worked out."

"The way you worked things out before?" She resumed brushing her hair. "No."

"But surely you are still not planning on returning to China?"

"It is my home."

"Oh, April, you just don't know. You'll be outcasts, you'll...."

April slammed down the hairbrush. "You have made me well aware of all your objections to my going home to my father but David and I have decided. It is where we want to be."

Raymond stood with his mouth open slightly as he listened, unbelieving that she spoke so casually about their marriage. "And what in hell am I supposed to do while you go traipsing off with your young lover?"

"I don't care what you do."

"I'm your husband, damn it."

April glared at him. "But I've never really been your wife, Raymond. I never will be either, so make up your mind to that. Divorce me. Marry Mother," she threw at them. "You two are perfectly suited."

Lydia said, "I'll speak with David's father. He'll stop this madness." Suddenly, to her horror, she realized that Peter had failed to tell her where he was staying. There'd been some mention of a villa outside Pairs which the Hearsts had leased and where he was a guest, but Lydia did not have the slightest idea of where it was.

"David's father sails tomorrow for New York. Didn't he tell you?" April said smugly.

"No," Lydia said almost to herself. "He didn't."

April saw her mother's hurt and gloated. "Don't fret, Mother. Raymond is still here."

Again Lydia said, "You mustn't do this, April."

"I'm doing it. As soon as David can make the arrangements we will leave."

"And when will that be?" Raymond asked sarcastically.

"When you discover me gone," she answered with brazen defiance.

Lydia felt completely drained. "You will not take the children," she ordered flatly. "I forbid it."

"If that's what you want."

Raymond grabbed her again. "What kind of a monster are you to be able to abandon your children as if they were just so many scales from a fish?"

April stood up to him. "You raped me into having Caroline so she is more yours than mine. As, for Marcus...." She let her eyes slide to Lydia who slowly got up off her knees. "Frankly, I think the children will be better off without me," April said.

Raymond made a guttural sound, like the groan of a caged beast. He ran his hands through his hair. "So help me, April, if it takes the law and the police I will stop you."

"Yes, April," Lydia agreed. "You mustn't leave like this, so brazenly. What you and David plan is very wrong. Wait. Let me talk to David. I'm sure something can be worked out to everyone's satisfaction. I know you are unhappy with Raymond and the way things are."

When Raymond made an angry move to protest she gave him a knowing look and he fell quiet. "Don't run out on your marriage. It would only mean trouble for you."

April said nothing and Lydia saw by the set of her jaw, the steadiness of her eyes, that there was nothing more to be said.

April had shut them out.

CHAPTER TWENTY-TWO

The following evening Raymond and Lydia went together to dinner and then to the exhibit. When they returned to the hotel suite a little before midnight April was gone.

* * * * * *

April had remembered only too clearly Raymond's threats of setting the police after them. She expressed her fears to David when she slipped out the trade entrance of the hotel, where his carriage was waiting.

"They won't find us in time," he said, his eyes puffy from lack of sleep. "All we have to do is have enough luck to get us to the rail station by seven-thirty. I think we'll be far gone before they even start looking for us."

"Rail station?"

"You did bring your travel permits?" he asked ignoring her question. She scrambled around inside her reticule and held them up for him to see

David said, "I doubt if anyone will guess we've gone east. Your mother will surely be expecting us to take the train directly to the coast and sail as we'd planned the last time."

April snuggled against him. "You're so very clever," she said. He put his arm around her and she felt a slight swelling in his chest.

"My sister gave me the idea, actually," he admitted.

"Susan?" April said, looking up at him. "Is she here in Paris?"

"No, but two years ago she, Efrem and Mother were touring Europe and Susan mentioned the Orient Express train which they took only as far as Vienna. We can get on here in Paris if we make it in time." He took out his pocket watch and noted the hour. "It leaves Gare de Strasbourg in twenty minutes."

"Vienna isn't a seaport."

David gave her a tolerate squeeze. "Well go by train all the way to Constantinople. Susan said the train is really comfortable, luxurious in fact. I booked us a compartment."

She hugged him. "Oh, David. Constantinople," she sighed. "How wonderful."

He nodded eagerly. "We'll sail the rest of the way from there."

By the time David paid off the carriage at the depot, they felt sure they had made a clean escape. It was with a tremendous sense of excitement and relief that they hurried down the platform scanning the numbers on the scrubbed rail cars, trying to match them with the ones on their tickets.

They found #17 on a wagon-lit carrying a sign on its side that read: DIRECT-ORIENT and then its itinerary.

The compartment was elegant, paneled in inlaid walnut with framed mirrors between the windows, embroidered chairs, polished brass fittings lavishly used on lamps, toilet fixtures and doors. A deep pile carpet of rich maroon covered the floor.

"Oh, it's fantastic," April breathed. "Like a fairy tale."

"Look," David said enthusiastically. "The backs of these chairs are built in such a way that they can be lowered at night and covered with a mattress and bedding." He gave her a sly smile. "We'll be sharing the same accommodations unfortunately. I hope that doesn't shock you. You are a married woman, after all."

"We will be married once we reach China," April told him softly. "And in my heart, you are already my husband—my only husband."

They had hardly settled themselves in when there was a blast of whistle and a huge cloud of steam puffed up like billowing thunderheads. The train gave a lurch, groaning and wheezing and they started to pull out of the station.

"David," April said happily. "We are finally on our way home." She snuggled closer and put her head against his chest listening to the slow beat of his heart. After a few minutes she heard the beat grow slower and in another moment he was fast asleep.

Home, April said to herself as she watched the houses of Paris gradually dwindle and give way to wide fields where cows grazed and farm folk, busy with their early evening chores, stopped to wave or gawk at the lumbering smoke-breathing monster.

A dull, quiet ache suddenly began deep inside her as she began to realize that each click of the steel wheels was bringing her closer and closer to Kalgan but farther and farther away from her child. She sat up, careful not to disturb David and leaned her forehead against the window pane, seeing none of the swift moving scenery. She hadn't thought she would find it difficult to leave Caroline behind, but now the full impact of what she was doing washed over her like a cold spray. She shivered and lay back against David who stirred but did not open his eyes.

Caroline was better off left behind, April kept telling herself. She had done right, she told her conscience as the noisy, rattling train sped along carrying her deeper and deeper into her dreams. Here beside her was the romance she'd sought and ahead lay all her perfect tomorrows. There was nothing behind her except a little girl whom she'd never wanted and who belonged where she was.

* * * * * * *

It appalled Lydia to think that April was so selfish, so callous that she could pick up and leave without a moment's concern for her infant daughter, to say nothing of the bargain they'd agreed upon concerning Marcus.

What kind of a daughter had she brought into the world, Lydia asked herself as she listened to Raymond giving a description of the young people to the District Prefect of La Sûreté Nationale, the national law enforcement agency. Lydia thought she'd at least instilled a sense of wrong and right into the girl.

As she heard Raymond arguing in the other room, Lydia tucked the light blanket carefully around Marcus and walked out of the nursery.

"Monsieur," the Prefect said. "I know she is your wife, but she is obviously in love."

"Love, bedamned!" Raymond swore. "She belongs to me and I want her found and brought back."

The Prefect rolled his eyes. "We will do what we can, Monsieur Andrieux, but you yourself are a Frenchman; you should understand how clever a woman can be when she wants to avoid a husband to be with her lover."

"Find her!" Raymond shouted.

"Hush, Raymond. You'll wake the children."

The Prefect bowed respectfully, put his notebook back into his pocket and left the room.

Lydia said, "You know it's useless, Raymond. They are well on their way to some harbor where they can find a ship bound for China."

"That's what I told the Sûreté. They'll search the seaports. They'll find them."

"And then what?"

He gave her a blank look. "What do you mean?"

"You are planning on remaining here to run our Paris office. Do you honestly think April will content herself to remain with you? Every day when you are away from her you'll never know for certain if she'll be there waiting for you when you return home. You will never be able to trust her. You'll make her a prisoner and she'll hate you all the more for it."

"Then we'll return to America."

"That won't solve anything. She'll only leave you. She'll divorce you if she can and then go to David MacNair whichever way you turn your life."

His irritation grew. He pounded his fist on the table and

whirled around, running his fingers through his slicked back hair. "And just what in blazes do you suggest?"

"Let her go to China," Lydia said softly, as if resigned. She saw him start to object. "I know, I know. I once thought that it would be the last place where she'd be safe, but I've changed my line of thinking on that score. She's older now, more experienced in so many things. When she first wanted to run off with David she was just a child, doing a childish thing. She is still doing a childish thing but this time, somehow I think she'll be more capable of seeing through the dream to the reality of it all."

"But China? Dear God, Lydia, what are you saying? One reads every day about the unrest there. If those yellow devils aren't trying to kill off all the whites, they're trying to kill off each other."

"You forget, Raymond, that April is the daughter of a very powerful Manchu prince. I believe her father, Ke Loo, will protect her if she goes to him, which I believe she will." She smiled weakly. "The Chinese are a strange people. They put a daughter out to be eaten by the dogs at birth, but when the girl is grown they pride themselves on her beauty...and April is indeed beautiful. The Mandarin prince will take her in, I'm certain of it."

She had turned it over in her mind for hours. In the end she had shrugged off her fears. April would see to her own protection; April thought like the Chinese and would cope very well.

Lydia said to Raymond, "All of her life April has had a dream of the China I carried her away from. I protected her from all its horrors. She never saw the tortures, the death, the terrible subjugation of the people. All she remembers are perfumed gardens, silk robes and ribbons, servants to wait on her, an amah to feed her and clothe her, bathe her, put her to bed. She never knew her father wanted her killed when she was born, or how he tried to poison us both when he took a fancy to another woman. Let her go and find out what China is really like. If I'm right, she'll come home and be happy to get there. If I'm wrong, we've lost nothing because we never had her in the first place...either of us, Raymond."

He thought for a long while. The vision of her stepping from the coach in her yellow silk gown with the strands of pearls in her hair, her eyes painted so seductively, haunted him. Raymond shook his head. "No," he said emphatically. "I want her returned to where she belongs...to her husband and daughter."

"Right now she belongs to China, Raymond."

"I want what is mine," he said half to himself. His mind started to race as a new desire took hold of him.

"However," he said softly, after a moment, "If I cannot have April...."

She saw the telltale glint of lust shining in his eyes. "We made a bargain once," she said. "You got what you asked for."

"But I have not," he said. "I said I wanted April, but I don't have her. In truth, I never have. Now you say that I never will. Very well, then I want another bargain."

She knew full well what he meant—he wanted her. It was blackmail, plain and simple.

"I can't stay in Paris," she said.

"You can stay for a while. We were once very good together, Lydia, can you deny that?"

"No," she said, trying to remember. Was it true? So many men, making demands, forcing her to their will—always, just when it seemed at last she was free. Raymond had almost succeeded in taking Peter's place at one time, hadn't he? Or did she only want to believe that?

Seeing her indecision, Raymond came to her, taking her into his arms. She let him kiss her—the cost of refusing was too great. She had lost her daughter. She had never really had Peter MacNair, except for one brief night, in China. It seemed centuries ago.

Nightsong was all she had—*Nightsong*, and Raymond, for without him, she would not have the other.

CHAPTER TWENTY-THREE

The border guards woke them as the train chugged into the station at Munich.

When they again found themselves alone, they sat huddled in one another's arms, watching the high mountains, the glacial fingers still unthawed by the warmth of spring.

They dozed through much of Austria, but when the train crossed into Yugoslavia, they were satisfied they had made good their break for freedom. They got off at the first station and bought coffee and apples from a pushcart.

The trip from Paris to Constantinople took sixty-six hours. They talked about all those things two young people in love find to speak of; mostly they talked about themselves.

They laughed at their own bravery and marveled at the varied countryside.

"It may be beautiful," David told her, "but I hear that bandits very often derail the train to rob the passengers and ravage the women."

He watched her grow pale and snatched up her hand, sorry to have upset her. "I won't let that happen," he assured her.

Their surroundings changed; almost hourly, it seemed, they were viewing a different culture through the window of the train. As they moved east, it seemed there were more and more people; not only on the train, but the stations and the towns seemed more crowded, though the people seemed simpler in their manners. The gaudy epaulettes and braids of the rail inspectors became loose flowing trousers and jackets; turbans and scarves replaced shiny caps.

"It's hard to believe people could live so differently," David said.

"Wait until you see China," was April's reply.

The remark gave him pause. He had felt uncomfortably foreign just being in Paris, where the lifestyle, the clothes and the food were really much similar to America. The further east they had traveled, the more exotic it had all become; his ears were assaulted by a language whose very sounds and rhythms were different from his own. The smells and colors, even the strains of music, fell harshly on his senses.

And China? How different would China seem?

* * * * * * *

"Well," he said when they finally stepped from the wagon-lit into the station at Constantinople, "We've reached the end of the train line."

Outside they passed a row of hovels. Everything to his untraveled eyes looked old and dilapidated, like the spoils left behind by some uncaring conqueror.

April's heart sank at the squalor, the bedraggled children carrying their heavy bales and crates, the strange flat boats with their high flopping sails. Would such a boat carry them across the Sea of Marmara and down the Aegean to the Mediterranean?

Somehow they made themselves understood, and were able to arrange passage to Alexandria. They would have to change ships once or twice, but it was not, they were assured, a difficult journey.

At last they were handed aboard a large ship packed with boxes, and seemingly overflowing with people and animals. There were goats and chickens, dogs and even a monkey in a cage. A cacophony of sound went up as the ship sailed from the dock.

April stood a long time at the rail looking back—not only at the land, but at the cluttered vista of her life until now.

Would she ever return? Even as the shore faded, a part of her was telling her to go no further.

It's too late to turn back, she told herself.

As if reading her thoughts, David slipped his hand into hers and said, "We will be together forever after, my darling."

But would they? She felt suddenly as if they had been cast adrift on some great uncharted sea. She shuddered involuntarily; then, seeing David's anxious expression as he watched her, she snuggled cozily into the crook of his arm and managed a reassuring smile.

"Forever after," she echoed his promise.

CHAPTER TWENTY-FOUR

Peter MacNair looked out at the impressive New York sky-line and bit down on his lower lip. At first he'd been furious with David for not returning home when expected; now, he was worried. And what would he tell Lorna?

"Damn," he swore as he crumpled David's letter in his hand. After a moment he glanced at the balled up letter and smoothed it out. He read it for the hundredth time, searching for a clue that might have eluded him.

"Dear Dad,

I am taking April home where she belongs, and where she is, that is where I must be. David."

Peter cursed himself for being a fool in taking David with him to Paris. But how could he have known Lydia would be there with her daughter? By "taking April home" Peter assumed David meant to China where they had tried to go once before.

Every time he thought of it he felt sick. China was on the verge of a full-scale blood bath. Didn't David read newspapers or listen to what people were talking about? What in God's name were those two young idiots thinking?

They were in love, he reminded himself. "To hell with love," he told an empty study. When a man was in love, he did every-thing possible to protect his beloved from harm, even if she was not aware that it was for her own good.

He started to think of the time in China so very long ago when he had forced April's mother to accept the protection of that filthy Mandarin, Ke Loo.

Yet, though he had done what he thought safest and best for Lydia, she had never stopped hating him for it. Perhaps after all protection was not what a woman valued the most.

Peter sighed wearily and brought his thoughts back to his son. David had always been selfish and hard to handle. It was his fault as well as Lorna's; he had been firm with the boy, but not with the mother. He had let Lorna spoil their son. Even when David was involved with a pistol dueling incident at school, Lorna had made excuses for him.

Hard as Peter had tried, he had never been successful in getting close to David. The boy was an adventurer, without a grain of sense or ambition; if he had his preference, he would be left alone to do nothing for the rest of his life.

Even keeping tight strings on David's money had not seemed to bother the boy. He spent what he had and borrowed liberally without any qualms. With his charm and magnetic personality it was difficult to deny him.

Peter himself had to admire some of David's polite schemes to get money out of him. Like the time he had cut off David's allowance when at school and David had begun polishing the boots of the faculty members in order to earn money. Lorna had been horrified and humiliated. David's allowance had been renewed...and increased.

Peter re-read the note. Perhaps he and Lydia had been wrong in interfering with the young couple's earlier elopement attempt. Maybe this was the way for David to learn to stand on his own two feet

Lydia, he thought with a sigh as he gazed out the window.

Lorna tapped on the study door and breezed into the room with a stack of books. "I have had the strangest feeling all morning that something is wrong," she said as she started replacing the books on the shelves. "The Hearsts cabled that they planned on arriving in New York on the twentieth, but they said nothing about David. I find that rather odd."

"David isn't with them."

She stopped fussing with the books on the shelf. "What?"

"David's run off."

Lorna looked at him with wide, startled eyes. "What are you trying to say?"

He held out the crumpled note. Lorna snatched it from his hand and hastily read the short message. "I don't understand," she muttered. "Taking April home?"

"April Nightsong. Lydia's daughter."

Lorna clutched the note to her breast. "The Chinese girl? Good Lord!" A second later a new horror occurred to her. "Peter, she's a married woman."

Peter shrugged. "With two children, I understand. That obviously doesn't seem very important to either of them."

"Oh God, the scandal."

"To the devil with the scandal," he fumed.

Lorna turned and stared back at the books on the shelf. Ever since Peter had forced her to move to this infernal city things were constantly going wrong. Little Efrem was suddenly too grown up to be with his mother, and Susan was always out somewhere with boys whose families Lorna didn't know. And now David was lost to her. She hated New York with a passion and longed to go home to San Francisco.

She choked back her tears and said, "You're right, of course, Peter. What does a scandal matter? We know so few of the right people here anyway."

"Don't start, Lorna. We are well known in the right circles. You just don't want to adjust. Well, I'd advise you to, because we are not going back to San Francisco and that's final." He glanced at the telephone and added, "However, I may have to go back and try to find out where David and April have gone."

"To that woman?" Lorna sneered.

"Lydia is the only person I can think of who may know where David and April are headed. I assume April is taking David to her father."

"You're going to China?"

"How else do you suggest I find David and April and bring them home?"

"And April?" she slurred. "What do you care about that little harlot?"

"Because China is no place for either of them. They could easily get themselves...." He cut himself off.

"Killed! You were going to say 'killed'."

Peter couldn't look at her because he knew she would see his own fear. "Let's hope I can talk some sense into their heads when and if I find them," he said lamely.

"Killed!" Lorna sobbed as she broke into tears.

In a rare moment of tenderness, Peter put his hands on her shoulders and pulled her against him. It felt so unnatural holding her; it was something he hadn't done in a long, long time.

"It's going to be all right, Lorna," he told her gently. "April's father is a Mandarin prince, very powerful and highly respected. If there is any place in China where they will be safe it will be with him. That's why I must find out from Lydia where I can locate him. His palace is in the north but I don't know where."

"Can't you telephone the woman?"

"She's still in Paris," he said.

Lorna freed herself from his embrace. "Paris? That woman was in Paris with you?" she demanded, her anger again rising.

"I didn't say she was with me, I merely said she was in Paris. Empress Cosmetics opened their offices there."

"You were with her," Lorna accused.

"I saw her, yes. We were both at a party the Hearsts arranged. They invited her. She's their friend as well, remember."

Lorna's eyes flashed. "You slept with her!" she said.

"Don't be ridiculous."

"You did. I can tell. I know you better than you know yourself."

"Stop it, Lorna."

"I won't have it, Peter. I don't mind so much about those places you visit with your friends but I will not have you seeing that Nightsong woman."

"I said stop it, damn it!"

"So help me, Peter, if I ever have proof of your affair with that woman, I'll...."

"You'll what?" he demanded losing his temper. "Divorce me? Well, why don't you? You should have done it years ago," he snarled as he stormed out of the study.

For a moment her world was gone. Then, as the quiet of the room settled about her a terrible fear gripped her. "Peter," she screamed as she ran after him. "Peter, I love you!"

It was too late, the door had already slammed after him.

CHAPTER TWENTY-FIVE

The first night aboard the paddle steamer as they splashed their way across the Red Sea, April found David leaning dejected on the rail, staring out at the reflection of the moon on the water. She touched his arm. "David, what's wrong?"

He shrugged indifferently and shifted his weight. "Nothing."

"No, something is bothering you. Tell me. Please."

Despite her efforts however, David shrugged off her questions. How could he explain to her the doubts that troubled him at this late stage?

With each eastward leg of their journey, he had come to see more and more the enormity of what they had done, and to question its wisdom.

Yet, when he looked at April, every other consideration faded from his mind. Her beauty intoxicated him. His mind was drunk on the sheen of her hair, the fragrance of her body, the texture of her skin.

On their last night in the South China Sea, David found sleep impossible. As he roamed the deck, he heard one bell sound. Once, he thought he heard voices over the water, and the splash of oars, but he could see nothing in the darkness.

The ship was a single-masted freighter, British owned and headed for Hong Kong after repairs in Singapore. The Captain was only too glad to take David's money to help compensate for the lost time and money. He had been frank, though, in his warnings.

"Hong Kong's hardly a place to be heading these days, especially not for a Chinese girl and a white man traveling together. There's too much trouble being stirred up by these so called Boxers—bandits is what I call them—but they don't take too well to whites and yellows mixing."

David paced until he heard two bells. Then, still feeling uneasy, he started back toward the cabin. He noticed a light coming through the louvers of the cabin door, and opened it quietly.

He found April kneeling beside the bed, her palms flat together as she prayed. She was wearing only her shift, the tips of her breasts tight against the silky material, the curves of hips and buttocks plainly outlined.

He could not take his eyes off her. The weeks together had done nothing to diminish his desire for her.

"David," she said, realizing suddenly that he had come in, and interrupting her prayer to get up. "Is something wrong?"

The question irritated him. He felt guilty because of the doubts and fears he had been entertaining, and even more so because he could not bring himself to talk to her of them.

"Does something have to be wrong," he asked, "for me to look at you?"

"No, of course not," she replied quickly, hurt and puzzled.

He came to her and took her in his arms, beginning to fondle her roughly.

"Wait," she said, pushing a hand away. The cabin was stifling hot and even the perfume she had splashed so extravagantly on the furnishings and the bedcovers had not obliterated the stench of its previous occupants.

"Didn't I wait enough before?" he demanded, stepping back.

His unexpected anger mystified her. She too was tired of waiting, but she did not want their love made sordid. She wanted the white marbled bedroom she remembered from her girlhood, with the cooing doves and the cherry blossoms.

"It's only...," she began, but before she could explain, there was a shout from the deck, a brief scream that ended abruptly. A moment later, footsteps raced past the cabins.

David threw open the cabin door. He had bought a pistol in Alexandria, and had kept it on him, tucked into his belt. He paused now to make sure it was there, and loaded.

A sampan had come alongside them, and grappling hooks had been thrown over the railing. As he watched, two Chinese with red sashes tied about their tunics and wicked looking swords leaped onto the deck of the ship. He saw that there were others dressed the same already aboard, fighting with the English sailors.

"Boxers," he said to April, pushing her back into the cabin, but too late. They had been seen, and one of the invaders charged toward them, swinging his sword over his head.

David barely drew the gun in time. His shot was wild, splintering the attacker's shoulder, and causing the sword to fall to the deck; but the man's charge caught him squarely and sent him crashing back into the cabin, to the floor.

He heard April scream, and sat up to find her in the arms of a Boxer, who was trying to drag her toward the waiting sampan. With a cry of rage, David leaped to his feet, sweeping up the fallen sword, and swung it wildly. The man's head seemed to separate into halves; it was a second or two before David realized that it was the blow with the sword that had made it happen.

April collapsed into his arms. David had retrieved the gun, and he fired twice at their assailants, who were fleeing now into the darkness. A moment more and the attack was over as suddenly as it had begun. Swearing, the British sailors ran along the deck, checking the fallen Boxers, flinging the dead ones into the water, and finishing off those who weren't yet dead.

"It's all right, darling," he told April, holding her tightly against him.

She clung to him with a desperate urgency. "Oh, David, you were so brave," she sobbed. "I thought we would be killed."

It was a strange new sensation for him to have acted as a man, to have protected the woman he loved, and it gave him a surge of power and confidence such as he had never known before.

Yet he could not help thinking that they had not yet reached the shores of China, and already they had been made to feel unwelcome.

PART THREE

CHAPTER TWENTY-SIX

Lydia stepped out of the ferry building, thinking that San Francisco looked to her like an old friend. She was glad to be back. It was wonderful seeing the hills, the red, clanging cable cars, the ships in the harbor. She noticed there were fewer of the sailing ships, and more of the large steamers. Times were changing rapidly.

She felt very chic in her Parisian clothes, and especially with the French nurse she had found to accompany her and the children. Nanette was a lovely little thing, not much more than a girl herself, but extremely capable, and devoted to Caroline and little Marcus.

"Magnifique," Nanette breathed, wide-eyed at the sights of the city as the carriage took them toward Nob Hill. Lydia smiled. Everything the girl saw was magnificent to her.

Evelyn Clary looked up in surprise when Lydia breezed in looking ten years younger and the ultimate in fashion. "We didn't expect you until tomorrow."

"The train was on time for a change." She went on through to her office. Evelyn was right behind her. "How is Li Ahn?" Lydia asked.

"Fine. There were some young Chinese fellows here asking for him. They said they were school chums of his and wanted to get in touch."

Lydia looked fearful. "You didn't tell them where he was, did you?"

"No," Evelyn said. "Of course not. You told me you wanted

him kept under wraps and away from everyone so that's what Morris and I did. He's in love with the private school, mad about his chemistry teacher and is constantly telling Morris about some new idea he has for a cream or a powder. I think you have your successor in that boy."

Lydia smiled with pleasure and began going through the stack of papers on top of her desk.

"Peter MacNair is in town," Evelyn said. When Lydia looked up she added, "He's very anxious to see you. Something about April, he claims. Though it might be that other trouble."

Lydia frowned. "What other trouble?"

"Didn't you read it in the newspapers? He's being sued by some debutante's family. It seems the girl used one of his cosmetics and her skin became infected. Now even the government is threatening to get into the act by starting to oversee the cosmetic industry."

"They wouldn't dare. That's socialism," Lydia said hotly.

Evelyn shrugged. "I agree. Still, if things aren't safe...."

"Then it's up to the manufacturers to make them safe," Lydia said, "without government interference."

* * * * * * *

Peter looked haggard and very tired when he dropped into the big leather chair in front of Lydia's desk. "I haven't been sleeping very well lately," he explained when Lydia expressed her concern about the way he looked. "David running off to China with April is worry enough without this blasted dilettante in New York looking for a free ride."

"Evelyn showed me the article in the paper. Was your product really the cause of the infection?"

"Who knows? Perhaps yes, perhaps no. We are both aware that some people react differently to the same things." He heaved a sigh and sat forward. "But to hell with her. I have lawyers that can fight that battle for me. I must know where to find David. It's insanity to allow them to stay in China with all the terrible reports we've been getting from there. I have a friend at the American embassy in Peking. He says the situation is getting worse every day but everybody in any position to do anything about it is just closing their eyes and pretending nothing is amiss. I have got to go and bring those two idiots home where they'll be safe. I don't care if they marry or not, just so they're out of that blasted country."

Lydia told him about April's disregard for her husband and children. "It may prove difficult convincing her to leave China."

Again Peter shrugged. "If I convince David to leave, April will follow. She loves him."

"She does," Lydia assured him. "But she loves China more."

"It's a love that might cost their lives." He frowned. "Perhaps they're already dead."

"Don't even think that," Lydia gasped.

"Anyway, I've got to try to find them."

"The people at the embassy in Peking will be able to put you on the right road to Kalgan. Start with Peking, Peter. Ke Loo may be in residence in the Forbidden City. He has a palace there within the walls." She straightened. "Perhaps I should come with you."

"Not on your life. They'd chop off your head the minute you set foot on Chinese soil. The Empress is still looking for you, remember, and besides, if we have to make a run for it I don't want to have to worry about you."

She stood when Peter got up to leave. As they walked toward the door Peter reached for her hand. "We always seem to be saying goodbye," he said, smiling sadly.

"Perhaps that is for the best, Peter."

"Perhaps it is."

He started to reach for the door knob.

"Peter," she said in a whisper, almost as if a plea.

He kissed her hard and long. "I love you, Lydia," he said; then he was gone.

She stood for a long time with her back pressed against the closed door listening to the pounding of her heart. The tears rolled slowly from her eyes. For a moment she stood there not knowing which way to go. Then she saw the stack of work on her desk and pushed herself away from the door.

"I have a business dynasty to build," she said. She thought of Li Ahn, of Caroline, of little Marcus. Still, with all her heart she wished it would not have to be shared with Raymond Andrieux. If only Peter....

She gave her head a shake and bent over her work.

CHAPTER TWENTY-SEVEN

The fog was beginning to burn off; the sky was gray and close overhead as April and David stepped from the longboat onto the British crown colony of Hong Kong. She wasn't home yet, April reminded herself as they made their way from the trim harbor; and she wouldn't be until she walked on Chinese soil, which this was not. The English taint was everywhere one looked, even in the slant of the oriental roofs in the labyrinth of shabby Chinese shops and houses. They didn't even speak Mandarin Chinese, April noticed as they passed two shopkeepers arguing in pidgin English over two crates blocking the walkway.

She wanted to be on their way. She hated the sterile, white-shuttered club where David left her while he went to make arrangements for their continuing journey.

"Peking is over one thousand two hundred miles north of here," he told her when he returned looking dejected. "It will take weeks to trek that far and no one will even consider guiding us. It seems the Chinese here in Hong Kong are looked on as traitors by the rest of the Chinese. There have been any number of killings by these Boxers."

"If it takes weeks, then the sooner we start out the better," April said.

"But from what I gather it might be suicide."

"No one would dare raise a hand against Ke Loo's daughter."

David cocked his head. "I have a feeling they don't ask for calling cards before slicing off heads."

April gave him a withering look. "Well, we can't stay here. We must reach the Forbidden City. If Father is not in residence there, then we will travel the rest of the way north to his palace at Kalgan."

* * * * * * *

They had no alternative but to be content with passage on a Chinese tea clipper going to Shanghai. It was a low, flat ship with twin masts and triangular sails fitted fore and aft.

As they pushed away from land, leaving the cluster of islands of Hong Kong behind, David felt a strange foreboding, as if he'd never again see his own kind of civilization. His world had been steadily disappearing over the horizon, leaving an emptiness inside him as cold and as dark as a grave.

"You look strange," April said as she joined him at the rail.

David kept watching the empty horizon. "I feel strange," he admitted. "It seems like we've been traveling forever."

She slipped her arm in his and hugged herself close.

"We will be home soon and then there will never be a need to travel anywhere again."

One of the Chinese crewmen yelled something at them. David saw April blanch.

"What is it? What did he say?"

"Nothing. Come," she urged. "Let's go inside. It is getting cool."

Whatever the crewman said had upset her greatly, David knew, but despite his repeatedly asking she refused to translate.

"It was nothing. Just Chinese obscenities." How could she tell him the obscenities were actual threats against David's life...and her own if she did not leave the American white devil. Boarding the tea clipper had been a mistake. They should have waited for some other means of travel.

The common-room aboard the clipper was a cramped, low-ceilinged rectangle with wooden benches and long, smooth tables of mahogany. Opening off the far end of the room was a cubbyhole with half doors, the top one of which was swung back. A plank was laid across the top of the lower door, converting it into a makeshift bar behind which a Chinese with a long pigtail and pillbox hat was mixing various brews of tea. Wicks burning in bowls of oil gave the room an eerie light and an oppressive smell. At one end of the room a small crowd of Chinese sat crowded together eating rice and drinking tea.

David got two cups of tea from the barman in the cubbyhole and he and April sat at the smallest of the wooden tables against the bulkhead, away from the others.

One moment they were sitting alone with their thoughts and the nearly transparent tea; a moment later, a young Chinese seemed almost to have materialized at David's elbow.

"My humble apologies if I disturb you," the stranger said, surprising David even more by speaking in English. "My name is Wu Lien. Would you permit me to join you?" He saw April's disapproval, and added, "I have something of importance to tell you."

"Sit down," David said.

"He only comes to frighten you," April said.

"It was said in Hong Kong that you killed many of the Boxers," Wu Lien said.

"Not many, only one," David replied.

"There are some even here," Wu Lien said, nodding his head to indicate that he meant the ship they were on, "who approve of the Boxers. There are those aboard who speak against the white man who sullies the Chinese maiden."

David glanced instinctively around, half expecting to see one of the Boxers approaching with long, curved sword. Unconsciously, he put a hand to the gun in his belt.

"What has all this to do with you?" he asked Wu Lien aloud.

"I am of the Manchu line," Wu Lien said. "The Boxers have sworn to overthrow the Manchu dynasty. The Boxers are my enemies. They are your enemies. Is it not wise that we be friends?" He smiled and bowed his head deferentially.

David hesitated; for all he knew, Wu Lien might be a Boxer

himself, and this offer of friendship a trick.

Or am I getting afraid of my own shadow, he asked himself. Somehow he had not imagined, when they had planned to come to China, that he would have to live in fear all the time.

He glanced at April, but her manner toward the stranger had changed. David realized of a sudden that it had been Wu Lien's mention of his Manchu blood. He was royalty, the same as she was, and it showed in her expression, in the friendly but regal smile she gave the newcomer, that she felt she had at last found a kindred spirit.

"We're all in the same boat together," David said aloud, but neither of them seemed to appreciate the American slang.

He felt very left out.

* * * * * * *

As the days passed, David had the feeling that he was seeing everything through a mirror, but from the wrong side. It had been so different in San Francisco when he had put his arm around April's shoulder to protect her from the jeers of passersby. Now he was under her protection, and it had struck him that he would be so for the rest of his life. It seemed to rob him of his manhood.

For days he brooded and April, sensing some of what he was feeling, left him to himself. She could not explain, without making him feel worse, that she was indeed trying to protect him. She had struck up friendships among the other passengers, and she had let it be known, until it was now common knowledge on the ship, that she was a princess, daughter of Ke Loo, heir to the throne. The result was that they were treated more respectfully now, but she did not want to humiliate David by bringing this fact home to him.

Most of all she had made friends with Wu Lien, who had discouraged any attempts by the Chinese on the boat to intimidate the young couple in any way. It was true, too, that it was a pleasure to make friends with someone of her own kind, and it was a joy to be able to speak again in her own tongue, at which she had gotten frankly rusty.

None of this was explained to David, however, and by the time the tea clipper had dropped anchor in Shanghai harbor, David's resentment had turned cantankerous.

"Must you be so free with him?" he demanded when he saw April touch Wu Lien's cheek after saying goodbye.

"You need not be jealous of Wu Lien," she said quietly.

David's temper, barely controlled through the course of the sailing, flared.

"Perhaps I wouldn't be," he snapped, "if I knew what you two were jabbering about all the time."

April stopped and looked up at him, her eyes sad. "Oh, David, I didn't realize. I have been cruel to you. It was just that it has been so long since I'd spoken Mandarin."

David felt himself grow a bit calmer. He kicked at an imaginary pebble. "It's just that you two spent so much time talking with the others and I had no idea what you were talking about."

"But you were always there where I could see you."

"Protect me, you mean."

She touched his arm. "That will all be behind us once we have reached my father and you are made one of his family. Then, your name alone will protect you."

"My name?" He screwed up his face.

"You will take the name my father gives you, of course. A Manchu name, a name honored by all and known to be of my father's house."

He didn't like the idea of changing his name, which was what women did when they married. But if it came down to which he'd rather have as his protection, a woman or a name, he opted for the name and decided to content himself with that.

The trip seemed endless to David and he was beginning to wonder if he and April would ever really he husband and wife, and if he would ever feel at home in this strange country. This was a far cry from San Francisco's Chinatown.

When he learned the overland distance still to travel, his

spirits sank deeper.

"Seven hundred miles?" he said, stunned.

"Maybe more, maybe less," April translated as the agent with whom they were speaking bowed and grinned.

It was Wu Lien who came again to their aid. They ran into him in a tea shop, and despite David's reluctance, April told him of their problem.

"I too go to Peking," Wu Lien said. "But I take a shorter route. I will travel by barge along the Yun-ho. It runs from Ningpo all the way to Peking."

"The Yun-ho?" David asked.

"A transit river," April explained. "A canal, you would call it in America." She seemed already to have forgotten that she had ever lived as an American. He noted that she said "you" and not "we." Even she had begun to look upon him as an outsider.

"It will make our journey easier and faster," Wu Lien said.

"*Our* journey?" David groaned.

If Wu Lien felt his resentment he did not show it.

"Yes. We all travel to Peking. I trust I do not intrude by asking you to join my party. It has only five members, all loyal to the Heavenly Empress—which is more than I can say for some."

April said, "What do you mean, Wu Lien?"

"The winds of change are blowing across China. Though there are many who would like to see all whites driven from the land, there are some who would like to see the Manchus annihilated as well."

"But why?"

"Because the ignorant believe that the Manchus are in league with the west and intend opening China's borders completely, thereby destroying our ancient culture."

David found himself wondering now where all those beautiful, bright-colored dreams had gone, those wonderful pictures of everlasting peace and tranquility he and April had talked endlessly about. He had a sudden desire for the noise of New York, where women laughed as if they enjoyed it and where men stood a head taller than himself and never bowed in public.

Then he glanced at April and was ashamed for having any misgivings about their adventure. Away from her anywhere would be a hell.

"The Boxers one sees and hears so much about are just some rebels who wish to overthrow the Empress and her dynasty," Wu Lien continued. "But the imperial lady has skillfully turned their anger against invading foreigners rather than against herself and her family. When they see the futility of their battle against the west, their anger will cool and all will be at peace again."

As they geared up for the long trek to Peking, David was glad he had brought a goodly supply of bullets for his pistol. When he saw Wu Lien's cohorts, he had a sinking feeling that he was going to need them. Rough unkempt fellows, they looked more like hardened criminals, than sailors. The men spoke little, if at all, and seemed to fulfill Wu Lien's every want or need without the necessity of his uttering a word to them.

It seemed to take an eternity to reach their destination. When not traveling on the long, flat reed barges propelled by coolies with bamboo poles, they were trudging across narrow causeways between interminable rice fields.

From dawn to dark they moved northward at what, to David, was a snail's pace; but Wu Lien was pleased with their progress and more pleased with the fact that no mishaps had befallen them. David thought Wu Lien was being overly cautious, always stopping and scouting about, checking out every village before entering it.

There was something about Wu Lien that didn't ring true, but he was afraid to criticize him to April, lest it appear he was only jealous.

When convenient, the little party took shelter in wayside inns in one of the many remote little towns that dotted the waterway and the roads. After the first day or two the country began looking much the same as the day before and after a while David found himself traveling across the landscape without really seeing any of it.

April decided the time had come for David to begin speaking Mandarin Chinese. At first none of it made any sense at all, but April and Wu Lien were persistent and proved excellent and patient teachers. Soon he began to recognize an occasional word, and then an entire phrase.

The day before they reached Peking Wu Lien lead the party along a causeway that started at the foot of a hill and ran upward, ending in an archway that stood tall and grand at the top of the rise. At first David could not see beyond the arch but as they climbed higher the land began to level. Huddled behind the graceful stone archway was a picturesque little village.

After sending two of the men to scout the village, the bedraggled troupe passed under the arch. Chinks of light shone through the shuttered windows of the houses lining the street. It was late already, and the street was still and empty.

April felt alive. At last she was among her real people, the roots of her heart and soul, the ingredients of her royal blood. She breathed in the dank air and looked up at the sky with its clustered stars. Now, she thought, her life would begin.

Wu Lien arranged that they settle in the largest of the buildings, dispossessing whoever belonged in the place.

"Something weird about him," David complained to April, nodding to where an old Chinese was arguing and gesticulating, then started to bow and cower before Wu Lien as he moved off without another word of complaint. "I'm beginning to think he's a lot more than what he appears. He orders people about like they're the servants and he's the master."

They ate the raw fish and cooked cabbage leaves which David still found unpleasant, and he wondered if these people ever stopped eating rice. He had to admit, though, that every time he felt a tinge of discouragement he had but to look at April. She represented all the reward he ever wanted out of life.

Wu Lien went outside after finishing his meal and when he came back a long while later he said, "It would be advisable if we all slept in this room tonight."

"But why?" April asked.

"The peasants say some Boxers have been giving trouble. We are not far from Peking where they have what you would call their headquarters," he said to David.

An unearthly quiet settled about them as they lay on their straw pallets and waited for sleep. From the ceiling a lone paraffin lamp glowed dully, letting David see April's beauty. She lay, eyes closed, head cradled in the crook of her arm.

David closed his eyes and tried to think about tomorrow. Perhaps he would have his first meeting with April's princely father and his royal family. Perhaps a life of ease and luxury awaited him at the rising of the sun. He sighed peacefully and thought that after tonight there would be nothing to trouble him ever again.

Sometime well past midnight, voices, low and a short distance away, interrupted David's sleep. He glanced over at April who hadn't moved from her earlier position. Wu Lien's pallet was empty. Outside the hut there was a rumbling, like the sound of wheels moving over stones.

David made certain his revolver was tucked securely in his belt then rolled onto his hands and knees and moved toward the doorway.

Outside he saw a band of three men trussed up and standing in a cart which was being pulled along by the men in Wu Lien's party. Wu Lien was at their head directing the operation. David frowned as the motley little procession started to move into a stand of bamboo just on the other side of the open courtyard.

David suppressed the urge to call out to them, sensing in his heart that something was amiss. Who were the men in the cart? Where had they come from? More interestingly, where was Wu Lien taking them with their wrists tied...and for what reason? With all these questions buzzing about in his head, David glanced again at April to make sure she was still safe and asleep, then quietly crept over the sill and went after the slow moving procession.

The moon was a thin crescent, sufficient only for minimal visibility. David silently tailed the parade of men and creaking cart. A white mist hung over the shallow stream that wound its way through the grove. The huddled group stopped at the muddy bank of the stream and the men were ordered out of the cart.

Wu Lien spoke a few mumbled words to the taller of the captives and the man answered with what to David sounded like an insolent, *HIE!*

Shielding himself behind a thicket of low brush, David watched, mesmerized by the sudden ritual being enacted before his eyes. Like members of a dance, the men moved slowly, evenly, soundlessly, as they formed a close line in front of Wu Lien and his men. The three captives stood straight, heads high. They looked up at the dark sky and spoke words of prayer or ritual unintelligible to David.

Then, Wu Lien motioned to his men, who positioned themselves beside the captives. Without a signal, as if by intuition or impulse, the captives knelt in the mud and bowed forward from the waist, touching their foreheads to the ground. They straightened only slightly and kept themselves bowed, their backs level with the ground, their necks stretched forward. Wu Lien and two men drew their swords and in an instant, three heads were severed from their bodies and rolled into the murky shallows of the stream, spewing trails of blood over the surface of the water.

How long he lay in the thicket David didn't know. He remembered retching until he lost consciousness and when he looked toward the stream the water ran clear, the severed heads never existed and the kneeling corpses seemed to have been the figment of some horrible nightmare.

He got up on shaky legs and started to make his way back to the hut, feeling at his belt to make sure his pistol was there. As he left the protection of the bamboo grove he saw Wu Lien leaning on a long staff staring intently into a low fire. David staggered over to him and slumped to the ground, his eyes still seeing the swift descending blades, the heads falling to the ground and rolling into the water.

"You saw?" Wu Lien asked, after David's breathing became

more even.

David nodded.

"My father is not yet avenged," Wu Lien said bitterly. When David said nothing Wu Lien looked at him. "You do not approve of our ways of justice."

David couldn't speak. The horror was still too real.

"Hsueh-Pan," Wu Lien said nodding toward the bamboo grove. "He led a small party of Boxers against the house of my father, Wu Loo Wen. He and his followers killed my parents and my virgin sister. These three participated in those murders. Unfortunately, Hsueh-Pan was not among them tonight." He spat into the fire. "But I will find him. He is not far away."

"But did...." David felt the bile rise up in his throat and pressed his forearm across his lips and stared into the fire until the nausea passed.

"Our form of retribution is more sensible than your way, David. It is quick and comparatively painless," Wu Lien assured him.

"And how would you know that?" David managed.

Wu Lien chuckled. He was in no mood, however, to engage in a discussion of the differences in their social theories or ideologies. He looked down at David. Then he put aside his staff and seated himself next to David on the ground.

"If you are to become the Princess's bridegroom, David," Wu Lien said, "you had best heed my humble advice and accustom yourself to the ways of her people. The Chinese are an uncomplicated lot. Except for some," he said, again glancing toward the bamboo grove and spitting into the fire, "the Chinese society is a unit. It is the unscrupulous men like Hsueh-Pan who use their sacrilegious hands to tear down our Chinese civilization, the oldest civilization in the world. You are a fortunate man to have been chosen by Ke Loo's daughter, but you must throw off all your western ways and ideas and always remember that no one has surpassed the Chinese in arts and letters, our thinkers are more profound than any others, we were cultured and refined when men in the west still slept in caves and wore bear skins.

Judge us not by western ways for they are the irrational ways. China has been here long before your country and will remain here long after."

David looked at him long and hard. "Who are you, Wu Lien?"

"I told you. I am of the house of my father, Wu Loo Wen."

"But you are no servant," David insisted.

A smile brightened the young Chinese's face. He shook his head. "No. I am of royal blood, just as your prospective bride. I am forced to wear this deception because of my mission."

"This Hsueh-Pan fellow?"

Wu Lien nodded. "He led me along many false roads. I should have known that all rats return to the nest eventually." He sighed. "Hsueh-Pan is here. I feel it. I will find him and send him before his ancestors to be dealt with for his crimes against the Manchus."

"He is an enemy of the Manchus?"

"Hsueh-Pan is a traitor who already has made one attempt on the Empress's life. He is a bold man, a man with ice in his veins. But he knows his days are few, and that will make him reckless."

"Well," David said, the recent horror beginning to fade somewhat; here, in this barbaric country, such acts seemed almost natural. "I only hope I do nothing to dishonor you, having seen the punishment."

He laughed, but Wu Lien remained sober. "It is more important," he said, "that you do not dishonor Prince Ke Loo. He awaits you in Peking."

David was startled. "In Peking? But how can you know that?" he asked.

"In China, news travels on the wind." Wu Lien paused, choosing his words carefully. "You must take special care too not to offend the Empress. She does not like westerners. She puts on a tolerant face for the sake of international peace."

"Surely I won't have to meet her."

"If you intend to marry Ke Loo's oldest daughter, it will be required. Do nothing to cross her or it will be your last act on earth."

David lay for a long while unable to sleep. He watched April's lovely face and wondered if he could shed all his western ideas, all he'd been taught. He didn't much care for the violence of this barbaric land or the callous disregard the people seemed to have for one another. They seemed as likely to kill friends as enemies. Killing seemed to be the solution to everything.

A sound made him sit up. Somewhere a twig snapped or a pebble rattled, he couldn't tell which, but the quiet of the night magnified the sound and for some odd reason it made David wary. Quietly he went toward the door and looked out. Wu Lien was still sitting by the fire but his head was slumped forward in sleep.

David felt something begin to crawl over his flesh. He took the revolver out of his belt and started outside. Just as he eased the door open wider he saw a man step from the bamboo grove and steal noiselessly toward the sleeping Wu Lien. David stood in a shadow and watched as the man came closer. By the faint light of the moon, David saw the oriental face, the scarlet band around his waist and head.

Instinct told him to stay quietly in the shadows of the building and wait for the Boxer to get closer. The revolver felt heavier in his hand.

Half-way across the clearing the Boxer reached into his sash and drew out a long dagger. He raised his arm and it took David only a split second to realize that he meant to kill Wu Lien.

David quickly raised the pistol, not wondering about right or wrong, and fired at the man's head.

There was a moment of deadly calm; then pandemonium broke out. Wu Lien and his men rushed toward the slain Boxer, muttering, gesturing, shaking their heads. Peasants from the nearby huts hurried to see what made the loud noise that had roused them from their sleep.

April came out of the house rubbing her eyes. When she saw David standing with the smoking revolver still in his hand she choked back a scream and ran to him. "What happened?" she asked.

"I killed another man," he said simply. He felt sick.

"Dear God!"

"He was going to kill Wu Lien. I think it was Hsueh-Pan or one of his men."

"What are you talking about?" April asked as she saw the blank stare, heard the trancelike voice. "Who is Hsueh-Pan?" When she saw how completely dazed he was she took his arm. "Come inside, David. Come inside," she said, suddenly fighting down a dreadful fear that David might have killed some innocent peasant or worse still, someone in favor at the court. It would mean his beheading. The chilling prospect made her tremble in terror.

Wu Lien came into the room and April searched his face for signs of censure or approval. He smiled and her heart began to pound less rapidly.

Wu Lien put both hands on David's shoulders and looked hard into his face. "I owe you my life, my brother," Wu Lien said. He shook his head as though displeased with a naughty boy. "But you have robbed me of the satisfaction I would have had in avenging my father's house."

"Then it was Hsueh-Pan?" David asked.

"Yes. You have killed the Manchu enemy. The Empress will be pleased when I tell her. I only wish you had given me the honor."

"If I had waited for that, you would not be here with me now speaking of it," David said smiling.

"The debt of one's life is a difficult one to repay. I only hope I can do the same for you one day."

David laughed and said, "And I only hope the opportunity never arises."

The two men laughed as they embraced. "Come," Wu Lien said, glancing toward the door. "It is almost light. It we start out now we will be in the Forbidden City at noon. Come."

CHAPTER TWENTY-EIGHT

David objected vehemently when Wu Lien told them they must enter the Imperial City by separate gates and was surprised when April did not take up his argument.

Wu Lien said, "The great Tien An Men gate is only for persons of royal blood. Foreigners must use the side gates. It is the law, David."

David looked helplessly at April.

"It is only until we are inside the city, David. We must not offend the Empress before we've arrived."

David saw a slight haughtiness in the way she held her head and was no more pacified when Wu Lien arranged for a palace sedan chair in upholstered red satin, carried by two bare chested eunuchs, to carry him from one world into another.

His depression blinded him to the grandeur and glitter of the palace. He sat slumped in his cushions wondering if this initial separation was the beginning of many. Coming to China had not been a good idea after all, he thought.

April was enraptured. As the parade of servants began thumping their drums and blaring on the trumpets, she found herself swept back in time to an earlier day when she had sat with her mother as they followed Prince Ke Loo and his son into this fabulous city. She remembered the excitement she had felt when she saw the city's imperial glory for the first time.

"It's more magnificent than I remember," April said, enthralled with the golden lions, the marble staircases, the exquisite pavilions and gardens.

"I fear David is upset," Wu Lien said.

She made an indifferent gesture. "He understands. After he sees how well he is attended he will love it as much as I."

"I will go to David. You must go first to your father's house."

"My father," April breathed nervously, clasping her hands under her chin. "At last."

The bearers carried her through gates of ivory and gold into a courtyard of impressive beauty. Peacocks strutted and doves cooed from their perches in the branches of the pear trees. The very air was scented with romance and intrigue.

A young girl, no more than ten or eleven, came hurrying down a long flight of marble steps, stopping short as April stepped down from the sedan chair. She was pretty, with wide, curious eyes, and her hair was pulled back, hanging in a long pigtail.

She wore, April noted, a yellow silk jacket and trousers—the color of the Imperial family.

The girl bowed, but hastily, as if impatient to get on to more important things.

"You are the American?" she asked breathlessly.

April bowed in turn. "I am the daughter of Prince Ke Loo," she said.

The girl beamed for a moment, as if she had a great secret to share.

"I too am the daughter of Ke Loo," she said suddenly, giggling. "I am Mei Fei."

"Mei Fei." April took a moment to digest the news. Yes, of course, her father had taken another wife. "Then we're sisters," she said. "I am April."

Mei Fei's amah came scurrying after her charge, scolding her, and trying to take the girl away, but Mei Fei would not go.

"I want to take my sister to her rooms," she insisted, and in the end the amah had to leave her charge in April's hands.

As she followed Mei Fei up the marble steps, April wondered where David had been housed. She had been given rooms in the women's quarters; it was clear that David had not been intended to share them.

At least she had no qualms about his safety or his comfort. Wu Lien had assured her that word of David's bravery had already preceded them and the Empress had ordered that David be brought to her when he was refreshed. She hadn't mentioned any of this to David on Wu Lien's advice.

"He will be nervous enough," Wu Lien had said, "without knowing that immediately upon arriving he is to have an audience with her Imperial Highness."

Mei Fei ushered April into a handsome room with tall latticed windows that looked out over a garden of jasmine and plum blossoms. A beam of golden sunlight drew delicate patterns across the highly polished floor. April had never seen a more breathtaking room.

Mei Fei clapped her hands and a chattering, giggling flutter of servants scurried into the room. "You will bathe and refresh yourself," Mei Fei said. "Our father will return soon."

As the handmaids bathed her, April relaxed into the warm milk that filled the gleaming porcelain tub. Mei Fei chattered endlessly, asking question after question about the world April would just as soon forget.

"I wish you to teach me to speak English," Mei Fei said. "I know our father will not approve, but he approves of nothing," she said petulantly. "Besides, I am to marry soon, and I wish to make my husband proud."

The thought of so young a child marrying bothered April. She recalled her terrible marriage to Raymond and she had married him when she was years older than this child.

"How old are you, Mei Fei?"

The girl shrugged. "I do not know. Is age important in America?"

"Girls do not marry so young there."

"I am thought of as old here. Our father wanted me married last year to Hsueh-Pan, but he dishonored the Empress and was banished. It was then I became betrothed to Wu Lien." She made a face. "But I do not want to marry Wu Lien."

"Why? He is very handsome and seems very kind."

"He will take me to live in Lanchou; it is so far away," Mei Fei said.

"Perhaps he will live with you here in the Imperial City."

"I hate it here," Mei Fei said bitterly, not caring if she were overheard. "I want to go away from China. I am tired of bowing and cowering like a frightened bird in a cage. The old Tigress hates me."

"Oh, surely not," April said, assuming the child was referring to the Dowager Empress. "Our divine Empress loves all her children."

"She kills them. She cuts off their heads. I have seen it. She wants to cut off my head too, our father tells me."

April gave her a patient smile. "You mustn't make up such things, Mei Fei."

"I am not making it up. He told me. He said that I am a naughty girl who is always getting into trouble and always disobedient and if I didn't change my ways he'd have the Empress cut off my head."

April stepped from the bath and let the women crowd around her with their soft, fluffy towels. They led her into an adjoining dressing room where an elaborately embroidered gown was slipped over her head. Her hair was brushed and worked into an intricate design with braids and bangles and long sticks of inlaid ivory. April felt radiant as she looked at herself in the glass.

Mei Fei said, "Our father cut off my mother's head. He made me watch so that I would always remember to be loyal to my husband, which she was not, he said."

April's eyes widened. "Surely you jest?"

Mei Fei shrugged. "Why would I do that?"

"You saw your mother beheaded?"

"Yes!" Ke Loo's loud angry voice boomed from the doorway. "And you will see your sister beheaded if she does not learn the advisability of a quieter tongue."

The servants fell on their faces as Ke Loo walked into the room. He was an imposing figure in his robes of figured silk and gold trim but he was shorter and stouter than April remembered. A silk cap sat atop his bald head and a long moustache trailed from each side of his mouth. For a moment April did not know what was expected of her. She saw Mei Lei bow low and did the same.

"My father," April said reverently.

He stood over her, hands tucked into his massive sleeves, his small black eyes moving slowly over her. "So this is the female the American woman bore me," he said coldly. He walked around her as the servants crawled out of the room.

"I am not displeased," he said after studying her closely. "It would have been a pity to have fed you to the dogs when you were born. Your mother was right to have pleaded for your life. You are a beautiful woman. What is it you are called? April?"

"Yes, my lord father."

He laughed. "A ridiculous name, but I will allow you to keep it until I decide differently." He scowled at Mei Fei. "Get out!" he snapped.

The child cowered away from him as she backed toward the door, then was gone.

"Yes," Ke Loo said, stroking his long, thin moustache. "You are a very beautiful flower. You do my house honor."

April bowed and humbly thanked him. At the same time there was something about the way he was looking at her that made her uncomfortable. He was studying her as a man would study a woman, not a daughter.

"Beautiful," Ke Loo said again. "Your mother was beautiful too, yet you are not like her. She had hair of fire, eyes of jade."

He ran his hands over April's arms and her flesh grew cold. "Skin as smooth as alabaster," he said. There was undisguised lust in his eyes.

"I am most honored that you approve of your oldest daughter," she said bowing away from him.

"Daughter? You are a stranger," he said with a wave of his hand. His lips curled in a smile. "You are welcome, April. You will stay here with me for as long as I wish."

"And my betrothed," April said quickly. Ke Loo had already started to leave. There was a feeling of dread creeping over her.

"Betrothed?" He stopped and turned back. "Oh, yes. The American who murdered Hsueh-Pan. I heard Wu Lien brought him here." He narrowed his eyes. After a moment he said, "I am not certain I wish you to have a husband. I will think on it and will tell you of my decision when I have reached it." He turned abruptly and walked away.

April stood staring at the empty doorway, her mouth agape. She turned when she heard a sound at her back. Mei Fei stepped from behind a screen.

"My father has taken a fancy to you," the girl said knowingly.

"Don't be foolish," April snapped. "He is my father too."

Her sense of impending dread was so great that she felt numb. The man who had just left her was so vastly different from the picture she'd carried in her mind's eye for so long. She remembered a tall, noble prince with wide eyes and a broad forehead, constantly hovering protectively over her mother and herself as they played together under the trees of the garden.

"He will not want you to marry," Mei Fei said. "It was the way he spoke, the way I saw him look at you."

"I will marry David."

"David," Mei Fei echoed, quickly losing interest in her father whom she both feared and hated. "Is he an American?"

"Yes. He is to be my husband."

"An American," Mei Fei sighed, hugging herself and spinning around. "How I would like to marry an American and go with him to America."

"You would not like it there."

"Oh, but I would. I would read books and go to school and dress like the American girls in the legation."

April remembered her time at the American ministry. "Why would you want to be like the Americans? You are a princess. That is far, far better."

"I am a prisoner. I am not allowed to do anything but sit in the garden with my amah and the other women of the palace.

And all they do is chatter and giggle and sew and talk of silly things. I want to sail on ships and eat when I am hungry and sleep when I like and marry if I choose, which I do not wish to do yet."

April remembered her own childish fantasies and her discontent with her lot when she had been a child in Kalgan.

"You will miss your homeland if you leave it, Mei Fei," she said. "I know. I did."

"Why? There is nothing here but the dictates of the Empress. Everyone is afraid of her. We must all do as she says or lose our heads. It is not like that in America, I hear."

"From whom do you hear?" April asked.

Mei Fei grew flustered and April saw the furtive move of her eyes. Then she giggled and put her hand over her mouth. "You must not tell anyone."

April shook her head.

"She is the daughter of Mr. Towne. He is an American lawyer who works in offices in the Chinese City. No one knows that we are friends, Nancy and I. I sneak out over the wall by climbing the apricot tree," she said in a low voice as she motioned toward the garden. "Nancy—that's her name, Nancy Towne—Nancy said when she returns to America with her father she will take me with her. That's why I don't want to marry Wu Lien and move to his palace in Lanchou. I will run away to America with Nancy instead."

"That would be a great mistake, Mei Fei. You don't belong in America. I was taken there many years ago. We are hated and spit at. Take my advice and do not listen to the flattering stories they tell you about America. None of them are true. It is why David and I have come here, where we can marry and be happy."

April suddenly thought of Ke Loo. A cold breeze drifted in through the windows and she shivered, suddenly wanting David here and in her arms so that he could warm her.

CHAPTER TWENTY-NINE

David felt ridiculous in the long robe and flat-soled slippers with the square toes, but he was bathed and refreshed and anxious to be with April.

"Be patient," Wu Lien told him as he watched David pacing back and forth. Wu Lien picked a pear from the gold platter of fruit. "Eat something. Drink something. Content yourself to relax. We are not permitted to leave these apartments until the Empress bids us to."

"When will that be? We've been here for almost the whole of the afternoon," David said. Already the sun was close to the horizon.

"She will summon us when she is ready to see you. The Empress has many matters to deal with in a day."

"But what did she speak of when she summoned you earlier? You're certain she did not speak of April?"

"No," Wu Lien lied. He let his eyes slide away from David. Wu Lien saw no reason to upset the American by telling him the Empress's chief advisors suggested that perhaps the daughter's blood should be shed in place of the thieving mother's. The Dowager had retired to think on the matter.

"Did she speak of Hsueh-Pan?" David asked.

"I told you, my brother," Wu Lien said with a laugh, glad of the change away from April. He liked the young American girl more than he cared to admit and had almost lost favor with the Empress when he argued in April's behalf. "The Empress is beholden to you for avenging the attempt on her life. She will grant you whatever you ask." He thought of April and added, "Within reason, of course."

David still hurt from the ease with which April had abandoned him when they entered the city. There was a nagging fear that he'd lose her to her royal surroundings now that she was back among them. He was no competition for the luxuries her father and family would shower on her.

Then what? Suppose he lost her to her past? His own past was now a closed door to him. "God," he swore. "I could use a drink."

Wu Lien barked a command and a servant filled a cup with rice wine, bringing it to David. He sipped it, lost for a moment in his own gloomy thoughts.

An attendant in a gold-trimmed tunic and a square fur hat bowed from the doorway. "You will follow me," he said solemnly.

David had never seen so many marble pillars and gold lions, scarlet hangings, ivory balustrades. Their guide led them through dozens of rooms, along what seemed like miles of corridors, up a raft of staircases only to descend others.

Finally they stood before two huge bronze and copper doors, elaborately carved in a profusion of shapes and forms. A powerful, broad-shouldered eunuch beat a muted striker against a golden gong and the twin doors swung silently open.

An old and wizened man beckoned them forward, bowing respectfully to Wu Lien as they moved across one of the most fantastic rooms David had ever seen. It was as tall as a cathedral, as wide as a sports field and every inch of it was occupied by some piece of furniture that appeared priceless, or an exquisite work of oriental art. All the riches of China might have been stored here; their awesome size and number boggled his mind.

Another pair of huge doors, these gold and silver with ivory inlays, swung open and they found themselves in a dark, hushed room where nothing could be heard over the incessant ticking of dozens of clocks, of all shapes and sizes, elaborate, spectacularly jeweled, ticking away with maddening monotony.

Wu Lien prostrated himself when they were led to the foot of the massive, ornate bed. At first David did not see the old woman propped up against the mountain of pillows and when he did he bowed low, feeling foolish. He wanted to smile but her expression told him it would not be returned.

"The American," the Empress said in a crackling voice. "You honored my house by your deed."

"Thank you," David managed to say, completely at a loss.

"Wu Lien," the old woman said and the young man got to his feet. "I still have not come to a decision as to whether you should be censured for not having accomplished what you set out to accomplish."

"It was done before the opportunity was afforded me," Wu Lien said.

"An excuse I do not accept at present," the old woman rasped. She motioned toward a shadow, and a tall woman with a wild design of knives fastened in her high, thick hair stepped forward and keeping her eyes averted, spooned something into the Empress's mouth.

They waited while she chewed, then swallowed. The attendant offered another spoonful but was waved back into the shadows.

"What is your name, American?"

David told her but had the feeling she was marking time, perhaps testing his nerves.

"And you came here with the daughter of Ke Loo. The girl called April?"

"Yes."

The Dowager's eyes narrowed angrily. "The girl's mother is a criminal," she said.

David kept telling himself not to let the old buzzard intimidate him. He and April were both Americans. This woman would not dare harm either of them. The American Legation would see to their safety or China would suffer the consequences.

"April is guilty of no crime. We came here in peace with pure hearts," he told her.

"In China the sins of the parents are the sins of the family."

"But Ke Loo is not punished," David said boldly.

There was an audible gasp from Wu Lien, who was warning David with his eyes.

The old woman cackled. "Your tongue is sharp. Be careful it does not slice itself off."

David bowed to her and tried to ignore the knocking of his knees.

The old woman moved her eyes to an attendant in regal robes standing near the tall doors. "I want the girl brought to me here."

She studied David for a long time. The incessant ticking of the clocks seemed to thunder in the waiting silence; yet it was not a loud enough sound to drown out the thumping of his heart.

The Empress said, "I am not ungrateful, David MacNair, not even to foreigners. It is rumored that my government, the *Tsungli Yamen* and I feel a hostility toward your country and the others of the west. This is not true, even though some of us resent your having invited yourselves to take up residency here in my country and carry on business that is not particularly beneficial to me or to my people."

"I am not here for political reasons, nor to seek monetary gain at China's expense."

"Then why have you come?"

"April, Ke Loo's daughter, was unhappy living away from this, her homeland. I brought her here to find the happiness she'd lost when she was taken away against her will."

"And you wish to marry her, I understand."

"With your permission," David said with another bow.

Wu Lien beamed approvingly. The American was learning.

The doors swung open and David turned as April was ushered into the room. She walked tall and unbending toward the huge bed, not seeing anyone, her eyes fixed only on the Dowager Empress. David frowned as April dropped to the floor, prostrating herself before this diabolical old crone. He had an urge to grab April's arm, yank her to her feet and remind her that Americans knelt to no one.

"You may rise," the Empress told her.

When she stood beside him he was disappointed that she didn't reach for his hand.

The Empress said to April, "Your mother has left San Francisco." It was a statement, not a question.

"She has been to Paris, Empress." David noticed that April's voice was shaking and now that he saw her up close she was quite pale, as if she were afraid of this frail old woman.

"And Li Ahn, your brother?"

"Li Ahn?" She stammered and David saw her lips tremble. "He expressed a desire to go to an American school."

"Then he intends to remain in America?"

"That I do not know for certain," she answered, her voice getting shakier. David could not understand why she was so frightened and nervous. This old woman couldn't do them any harm. They weren't Chinese subjects.

"Where is this school Li Ahn is attending?"

April hesitated. "I do not know, Empress. My mother made all of the arrangements and did not tell me."

"Then you will find out and so inform me."

She didn't answer, or couldn't.

There was a long pause after which the dowager said, "I must repay a debt of honor to this young American. I have decided to repay that debt by giving you to him in marriage."

David's heart leapt when he felt April reach for his hand and step closer to him. She chanced a glance at him and smiled.

The old woman said, "However, I am informed that you already have a husband."

"He is a Frenchman, Empress. I was forced into marrying him by my mother."

"The criminal," she said with an impatient yank at her sleeves.

April said nothing.

Again the old woman fell silent. She raised her beady eyes to April. "Very well," she said finally. "A decree will be issued releasing you from all outside encumbrances. Henceforth you are returned to your family, princess, with all its rights and privileges. You will be married as soon as preparations can be made."

CHAPTER THIRTY

Ke Loo was not pleased with the royal decree that the American marry April. Since first seeing her he found himself consumed with a burning need to possess her. But this was not the best of times for him, Ke Loo reminded himself. The Empress was displeased enough by Li Ahn's disappearance. He would not risk her wrath by opposing April's marriage.

Somehow, however, he vowed, he would have this lovely girl who claimed to be his daughter. Who could say she was? Anyway, it was as he had said, she was a stranger. Wu Lien was friendly with the American boy; perhaps he would help, Ke Loo thought.

April sensed her father's incestuous desires every time she found him looking at her. Another fragment of her dream crumbled away each time he touched her, each time his eyes undressed her.

Much as she wanted to speak of her fears to David, she held herself back, ashamed to acknowledge that her royal father was capable of such unnatural desires. To her, it would reflect on her homeland, a homeland that seemed increasingly to displease David.

As for David, he found himself more in Wu Lien's company than in April's.

"Our ancient custom permits that you see her only from a distance, and you may not speak with her until you are married," Wu Lien explained. "It will only be a matter of time now before you are together for always."

"Time," David groaned. "It seems to be the bane of my existence. All I do is wait and wait and get nowhere."

He reached for the bottle of rice wine and found it empty. In frustration he hurled the bottle against the wall, shattering it. What did he care? A man didn't have to do anything in this infernal place. He never had to wash himself or shave or even walk if he didn't feel like it. Servants did everything. They crept along the floors like vermin, cowering and crawling and letting themselves be kicked and stomped and beaten—whatever gave pleasure to their masters.

As one of the house servants brought in a new bottle of rice wine, a second swept up the debris of the broken bottle. David drank another cupful and said, "When April and I have our own place I'm not going to have any servants. None. We'll do our own cooking and cleaning and even wash our own clothes. And I won't tolerate any sedan chairs either. We'll walk everywhere."

Wu Lien laughed. "You will be a prince then, David. It is forbidden for a prince to act like a peasant."

"To hell with being a prince," David said, a little drunk from the wine. "I'm an American citizen. I'll do what I like."

"Our Empress has decreed that you are Chinese now," Wu Lien reminded him.

David drained the cup and stared at curving patterns across its bottom. "Chinese," he muttered, then shattered the cup on the floor and stormed into the sleeping alcove where he threw himself across the wide bed.

The days followed slowly and David's frustrations grew. Just when he was at the brink of storming April's quarters and demanding to see her, word came that the ceremony would take place in two day's time.

The ritual was brief but conducted with elaborate pomp and ceremony. Attendants and soldiers in uniform were lined up like carved statues, forming a wide aisle strewn with flower petals. A step behind them were the eunuchs and lesser figures of the court. A raised dais contained the court dignitaries, with on either side the royal elephants in spectacular trappings of gold and silver. The mandarins were dressed in their high Manchu boots with thick white soles, embroidered silk robes with voluminous sleeves that touched the ground and black hats decorated in ornate gold patterns.

The Empress sat above all the others on her high throne of gold, over her bejeweled head a gold canopy supported by four massive red lacquer pillars with gilded capitals. Servants bore fans, an orchestra of lutes and cymbals and flutes played exotic music which fell hard on David's ears.

Yet when April entered the pavilion attended by Mei Fei and dozens of other royal maidens and ladies, it seemed to him as if every dissonant note of music was transformed into the most melodic sounds he'd ever heard. All his qualms, all his discontent, seemed to vanish in a twinkling of an eye.

He was speechless as she approached him, her eyes lowered demurely, her wedding robes a rhapsody of white enchantment.

April and David, side by side, knelt before the high throne with Mei Lei and Wu Lien at their backs. The Empress nodded her regal head. April put her hand in his and they were husband and wife.

A high gong sounded in the tower of the Temple of Heaven and attendants and royalty alike began chanting. When the chanting stopped the Empress raised both her hands. In one impressive movement, like well drilled soldiers, the entire assembly kowtowed before her. To David's astonishment he too found himself paying obeisance to this small, crag-faced woman with the eyes of a lizard and hands like the talons of eagles.

This the assembly repeated five times, the Empress sitting impassively, making no acknowledgement of their acts of servitude. As David looked up at her she might have been some golden jeweled idol, all metal and stone.

The royal party abandoned the dais; the eunuchs came forward, lifted the four pillars supporting the Empress's throne and carried her off over the heads of the entire party.

David was too anxious to be interested in the lavish party

that had been prepared, but April teased and flirted until he began to turn surly. Wu Lien warned her not to toy with him too long.

"I haven't been able to speak to you for days and days," David complained. "How long are you going to torture me?"

"We will be alone very soon now, my husband," she told him.

The night came early and as April linked her arm in his and walked out into the garden, soft strings played a haunting melody. David felt that at last his dream was fulfilled. He and April were married and now his life could begin.

The moon painted silvery tips on the leaves of the lemon trees and twinkled across the rippling surface of the reflecting pools. They strolled along the raised walkway that wound its way through the lush green lawns. Dotted here and there were evergreens from all the provinces of China and the grounds were paved with lapis lazuli to intensify the deep green of the trees. At the top of a rise sat a handsome miniature palace of green jade with silver eaves and ivory floors.

"Island of Flowered Jade, they call it," April told him as they stood admiring the tiny palace that sat like a pearl on velvet, glowing softly in the moonlight.

David swept her into his arms, his senses reeling from the heady experience of their wedding. He carried her easily into the large, high sleeping room with its domed ceiling of pink and gilt. There were huge arrangements of chrysanthemums in large bronze vases spaced about the room and the breeze through the arched, latticed windows billowed out the gauze curtains, moving the perfumed air gently to and fro.

He laid her gently on the bed, shaped in the form of a great white swan with a graceful neck curved high and a gold sheathed tail that spread out in a cascade of shimmering opals. The soft mattress was covered in the finest satin, the color of cream, and fur rugs stretched across the floor, deadening all sounds.

April opened her eyes and looked up into his handsome face, her eyes smoldering with a desire that transcended everything else. The intensity of her passion startled him yet at the same time evoked a response in him so devastating it made him tremble.

He pulled her into his arms. Her lips parted, perhaps to speak, perhaps to protest, but in the next instant his mouth closed over hers.

She felt him fumbling with her robe and helped him until they were both naked. Flesh pressed against naked flesh. April whimpered with delirious delight as his hands moved over her. She thrilled at the hardness of his body, the youthful strength of his chest, so smooth, so muscular. She languished in the strength and hardness of his arms.

The first burning touch scorched the center of her passions, gently at first, then probing, insistent, coaxing. Her body spasmed involuntarily as she felt him move deeper, deeper. She fit herself perfectly into the rhythm of his motions and then as his urgency increased she matched it with an urgency of her own.

April heard the peacocks and felt the warm night air on her skin as David moved faster, more violently, carrying her up, up into the darkness of the night sky, blotting everything from her sight and sound, their bodies melting into one. She soared higher, higher as she felt something inside her urging her on... building, building, closer...closer....

The sky exploded into a blinding sunburst, stars shooting in every direction as they left the earth far below and surrendered themselves to whatever paradise awaited them on the other side of the golden, China sky.

CHAPTER THIRTY-ONE

Inside the high Tartar wall that separated the Legation district from the Imperial City, Peter MacNair stepped from his hired sedan chair. The same large houses—set apart in individually distinct walled areas—glowered at him as he stood thinking back to the last time he'd seen them. He'd been almost penniless then, ragged and exhausted from his flight from the marauding Chinese and the deadly cholera.

He stopped at the corner of Marco Polo Street and the Street of Legations where the French legation sat and remembered the kindness and help they'd offered him. There had been an unspoken tie between the east and west back then, knotted tightly together by the opium trade. He knew that same hospitality no longer existed.

It didn't please him to be back in this godforsaken place of yellow heathens who'd just as soon slit your throat as look at you. To Peter, all the Orientals hid some ancient evil behind their sallow, skull-like faces. They were much too clever and too much of a contradiction to be trusted. For every lovely cage of doves, for every tinkling wind chime there was a deviltry, an inner evil.

Turning from the gateway he walked toward the center of the compound, heading for the American ministry halfway down the street. In the dark distance he could see the lighted windows of Prince Su's palace with its courtyards ablaze with torches and lamps and lanterns burning in the branches of the trees.

"I'm sorry, Mr. MacNair," the secretary said, "but the

American minister is in the interior on a diplomatic tour with some dignitaries from Washington. He'll be gone for some time, I'm afraid."

"Damn," Peter swore. "I need his influence to get an audience with the dragon."

"The Empress sees very few of us foreigners these days."

"It's very important. It's about my son. I have reason to believe he may be inside those walls," Peter said.

The secretary stroked his small goatee. "We had heard of an American entering the city some while ago, Mr. MacNair. It is said that he is under the protection of a Manchu prince or princess, it wasn't made clear which."

"Princess," Peter clarified. "Prince Ke Loo's daughter."

"Oh, that old devil. There was quite a big *do* a few nights ago. I thought we'd all go stark raving mad with the drums and gongs and trumpets raising our scalps every time some royal Joe was carried in. They were having a real knock-down pow-wow in there." He nodded toward the Imperial City.

"I've got to get inside."

"Not possible! The gates are closed and heavily guarded. The old lady wants privacy for a while obviously. Orders are, no audiences, no interferences from foreigners. She made it emphatically clear."

"Damn," Peter said again. He tried to think what to do next. He certainly hadn't travelled all this distance just to let an old leather-faced crone turn him around and send him home.

As it was, he had sacrificed everything to come here. He hadn't told Lydia the extent of his problems over that lawsuit. Perhaps if he had been able to devote the time to fighting it properly—but this had seemed more important, somehow, and he had all but ignored the legal hassle, until it was too late.

He had lost his suit, and an enormous settlement. With that, and the money he had paid Hanover to settle his claim against Lydia, Peter was broke. By the time he returned, P.M. Cosmetics might be nothing more than a memory.

He sighed and asked, "Can you still put me up here?"

"We have your rooms ready, Mr. MacNair," the secretary said. "Not too many tourists are visiting here these days. The Peking Hotel is hurting, I hear. I'll have one of the boys bring your bag."

"And water for a bath," Peter added.

* * * * * * *

An hour later, feeling refreshed and scrubbed, Peter left the legation and turned toward the Peking Hotel, a short distance away. The air had turned cooler with the approach of night, and he was looking forward to a drink, and one of the beautiful dinners for which the Peking Hotel kitchen was famous.

It was a large white building with a veranda that ran around all sides of it, slender-pillared with neatly curved eaves that turned up as if in a smile of welcome. A young man in a white tunic and trousers tied at the ankles opened the door with a bow.

The secretary had been right, Peter noticed as he looked at the lone bartender and the empty lounge. "Not many customers," he said to the bartender.

The barman passed over the comment and asked Peter what he wanted to drink.

The man's surliness diminished Peter's thirst somewhat. Instead of the several drinks he'd been hankering for, he had one straight scotch and then went into dinner.

The dining room was a little more populated but there was a stiffness about the room. Everyone spoke in whispers and seemed to be looking constantly over their shoulders. Fortunately the food was as good as ever. After he had eaten, he lit a cigar and ordered coffee and a brandy.

He felt physically better. Mentally, he was very disturbed. He had purposely blanked out all the problems, promising himself that he would come up with a positive plan of action once he'd been fed and was relaxed. That time was now, he told himself as he sipped his brandy.

It seemed impossible for him to gain an audience with the

Dowager Empress—and without her permission he could not visit David, or even enter the Forbidden City.

Perhaps David could get out, though. In China, one could obtain almost anything, for the right price. It would take no more than a few discreet inquiries to find someone to take a note to David inside the palace.

The rest depended on his son's reaction.

* * * * * * *

The barman, despite his surly manner, took the cash Peter offered him, and told him to wait. Within the hour, he had asked Peter to step outside onto the verandah. Peter went out cautiously, fully aware that he might be stepping into some sort of trouble—but the verandah was empty.

He had been there only a minute when he heard a sound, and turned quickly, to find himself facing a stout Chinese in an important looking robe of figured silk.

"You're the man I'm waiting to see?" Peter asked, in the Mandarin dialect.

The Chinese gave a forced smile. "I am called Wang Seng. How may I assist you?"

"I need to get a message into the palace of the Empress. How would I go about it?"

"Everything is possible for a price."

"Could you or someone you know arrange such a transaction?" Peter asked, noting by the man's official dress that he was obviously someone of standing and influence.

"Wang Seng can arrange anything," the fat man said with a bow, "if the payment is adequate enough."

Peter took out his billfold and removed the bank notes inside. He began counting through them and watched Wang Seng's eyes widen with greed.

"My son, David MacNair, is somewhere in the Forbidden City," Peter explained. "He is under the protection of Prince Ke Loo's daughter." He looked to see if the Chinese was listening or just bemused by the bank notes.

"The young American bridegroom," Wang Seng said without moving his eyes from the money.

Bridegroom, Peter thought with a pang. So they were married. "Yes," he said.

"Ke Loo plans to leave for Kalgan with the couple. If you want to communicate with the American I would suggest you do not delay too long."

"And you're certain you can get a message to my son?"

"Wang Seng, your humble servant, is the merchant who supplies the royal kitchens and storehouses. I, or one of my representatives, go daily into the Imperial City. Wang Seng is highly trusted."

"How much would I be expected to pay to get a message to David?"

In a quick, easy move, the Chinese snatched all the notes from Peter's hand and tucked them into his sleeve. Peter made a move to object but the Chinese eyes warned him to take care.

"I will send my eldest son to you here tomorrow morning, Mr. MacNair," Wang Seng said. "Have your note written." He bowed and went down the steps to his waiting sedan chair.

Later, as Peter sat at the writing desk in his room, he took a sheet of stationery with the American Eagle emblazoned in the right hand corner and wrote, "At the American Legation here in Peking. In a lot of trouble. Desperately need your help. Dad."

He didn't have to fret long in the morning. As he finished his breakfast a youth, pallid faced but neatly dressed, asked for him by name, took the note, gave Peter an engaging as well as encouraging smile, and was gone.

There was nothing for Peter to do now but wait. As he lay in his room, hands clasped behind his head, he could not help thinking of his financial troubles.

For a time he had been tempted to ask Lydia to buy back his fifty percent claim to *Nightsong.* He was sure she would be glad to, and surely she could afford it.

In his heart, however, he knew he could never ask Lydia for

money, nor even accept it from her if she offered.

He closed his eyes and saw her face smiling at him as she had that night, in the shabby hut with the painting on the wall. He felt the same familiar stirrings inside himself. He ached suddenly to hold her in his arms, to kiss her lovely mouth, and smell the intoxicating aroma of her body, more maddening to him than any perfume could ever be.

He would gladly lose anything for her—and she was the one thing he had never truly possessed.

CHAPTER THIRTY-TWO

Mei Fei flung the hairbrush against the mirror, splintering it into fragments as the hand servants squealed and scurried for cover.

Her amah said, "A temper tantrum will change nothing, little one. The Empress has decided that you will marry. Object all you chose, fire cat, the order stands."

"I will not marry," Mei Fei fumed, her eyes sparking. "I am learning from April to be an American. I will go to America with Nancy Towne and her father and mother."

"You will go with your father, Ke Loo, to Kalgan and prepare yourself to be a proper bride."

"Never!" Mei Fei broke into tears and threw herself into the silk cushions of the window alcove. April came in and went quickly to the crying child.

"Leave her," the amah said. "It is your fault that she is becoming so difficult—all your western teachings. Mark me, Princess, the Empress will cut out your tongue for the evil things you are teaching my charge."

"I am only teaching her to speak English as Wu Lien speaks it."

The old amah shook her head sadly. "The curse will come true if all these western ways go unpunished by her Imperial Highness."

"What curse?" April asked, piquing Mei Fei's interest as well.

"Prince Gintaisi died cursing his enemy, Narhachi, who wanted to combine all Manchu tribes into one invincible dynasty. Narhachi condemned Gintaisi to death and the Prince swore that if he died at Narhachi's hands the Manchu tribes were doomed. He cursed Narhachi and all his followers saying he and his ancestors would see that the Manchu race would one day perish at the hands of a woman of the Yehe clan." He eyes were wide and staring. "Tz'u Hsi, the Dowager Empress, is of the Yehe clan."

"Begone old hag!" Ke Loo ordered, giving the amah a kick as he came into the room. "You will be the first to perish if I hear again of these old witches' tales. Go!" He turned toward the two girls in the alcove. "Mei Fei, leave us."

Mei Fei stood and walked over to him. "I do not wish to marry," she said. "I wish to go to America."

Ke Loo looked down at her, then raised his hand and struck her so hard she fell backward onto the floor. April screamed and started to help Mei Fei.

"Leave her!" Ke Loo shouted and the fury of his voice sent April back into the alcove under the windows. Ke Loo reached down, grabbed Mei Fei's hair and yanked her to her feet. He slapped her again, holding her upright then shoved her toward the door.

"You will obey me or you will have your feet boiled from their ankles."

April cringed deeper into the pillows. From the tone of his voice she knew it was no idle threat that he made. She'd seen too much evidence of late of cruelty and torture here in this fabled palace with its treasure stores and golden rooms. She thought idly of the priceless riches that went unseen by everyone but those of the royal household of which she was now one and she wondered if all the misery of the less fortunate was worth the idle luxury in which they indulged.

Ke Loo looked at her and his expression softened. "You are wrong to teach Mei Fei English," he said easily, but there was a warning in his voice.

"She only wishes to learn, my father. She has an inquiring mind."

"All the more reason to keep her ignorant. She is, after all, a female."

"As is our Empress."

His cold, steely eyes reflected his disapproval. He stood over her in his stiff silk robes with the heavy blood-red sash. On his feet were high wooden Manchu shoes that added almost six inches to his height. Ke Loo stroked his moustache and reached out to touch April's cheek.

"Like a flower," he said. "I am pleased you have returned to me." He reached inside his sleeve and withdrew a small velvet box which he handed to April.

Her face lit up when she saw the large ruby pendant. Ke Loo fastened it about her neck and gently, lovingly caressed her shoulder.

"It would give me great joy to have you accompany me to Kalgan. I leave here soon. The Empress will journey in a month to the Winter Palace."

"My husband and I look forward to coming to Kalgan," April said.

"Your husband will not be welcome," Ke Loo said bluntly.

April stared up at him. "But I must be with my husband."

"I will be husband as well as father to you." Ke Loo's eyes flashed. He did not wait for a reply, but turned and marched out of the room.

April sat trying to quiet the nausea that seized her. Her head began to pound and cold, frigid terror gripped her. With a maddened, blind dash, she fled the room, her heavy pearl-encrusted robe slowing her steps, the blood red ruby pendant burning her breast.

"What am I to do?" she asked Wu Lien when she found him alone in the West Flower Garden.

"Have you spoken to your husband, to David?"

"I can't find him. Besides, he is so depressed all the time. I think he would rather speak to his rice wine cup than to me."

"David is having difficulty in adjusting, April. Give him time. He does not think as we do...perhaps in time...."

"But until then, what am I to do about Ke Loo?" she asked, suddenly realizing that she was thinking of the man now as "Ke Loo" and not as her father.

Wu Lien looked unconcerned. "You belong to his household. A man has the right to do whatever he chooses with whatever belongs to him."

"But I am his *daughter.*"

"You are his property," Wu Lien reminded her. "You came here of your own choosing. You did not protest when the Empress granted your reinstatement as a Manchu princess. It has all been accomplished, April. None of it can be undone."

When he saw her tears he put his hand on her arm. "Ke Loo is not a constant man. His fancies change quickly, like the seasons. His attentions will not last very long."

April began to shiver with disgust. She felt she would welcome the disdain of those who'd despised her back in San Francisco rather than accept the ugly thing which Wu Lien was treating so lightly.

She said, "I could never give myself to him, Wu Lien. I would kill myself first."

He gave her a wry smile. "Ke Loo might demand it," he said without emotion.

All her terrible fears began to surface. She felt as if a trap was beginning to snap shut. "What am I to do?" she cried. The tears came in a rush and in another moment she found herself in Wu Lien's arms.

"Very touching," David said, staggering into the garden at that precise moment. "They say the husband is always the last to know."

"David!" April pushed herself out of Wu Lien's arms.

"Yes, remember me? The bridegroom?" he asked in a bitter voice.

Wu Lien said, "April is very unhappy."

"Ke Loo...," April started to explain, but David cut her off.

"Ah, the royal father," he snapped. "That old bastard tells me you leave for Kalgan, that the chief cow is off to the winter palace and I am to remain behind."

Wu Lien looked quickly around. "Be careful, David, of what you say even when you are drunk."

"Which I intend to be forever. It's the only way to get rid of the boredom and the rest of the filthy stuff that's going on around here."

He looked at Wu Lien and spoke to him as if April weren't there. "I thought my wife might relieve at least some of the boredom, but she's so busy being a royal princess with her royal servants and her royal tea parties with the other royal asses, she doesn't have time for her commoner husband."

"David," April cried. She went to him but he pushed her away.

David looked at Wu Lien and said, "How do I go about getting the hell out of this damned place?"

"David!"

"Oh, it's only to see my father," he reassured her. "I'm not running home to Mama. Father sent me a note."

"Your father? He's in Peking?" April asked.

"Has been for a day or two. Well, at least somebody needs me," he said drunkenly as he started away.

"David," April said laying her hand gently on his arm.

He shrugged her off. "You don't need me, April. You have your family, your friends...." He turned back and sneered at Wu Lien. "I thought I had a friend here once. I see I was very wrong." He turned again and with dragging steps went back the way he'd come.

"David, wait!" Wu Lien called to him.

David waved his hand in disgust. "I don't need your help, friend. I'll find my own way out of this hellish place."

April started after him but Wu Lien caught her hand. "Let him go, April. He is drunk. No amount of sense or reason will filter into his head. Let him sleep. Afterward he will hear you when you tell him how much you love him."

She saw the love for her in Wu Lien's eyes and broke away. "I must see that David sleeps," she said and ran off.

It was a mystery how these men could be so shallow in their affections, April thought as she hurried after David. Wu Lien was as free with his affections as Ke Loo or the rest of the Chinese men. Women to them were mere chattels that they used to feed their vanities and then disposed of at their amusement. David had been right; she had been neglecting him shamefully, but the Empress relied on her for so many things. It was impossible to split her loyalties and satisfy both Empress and husband. Both were so demanding.

She tried to explain all this to David after he'd wakened but he could not see her side of it...or would not.

"You're my wife, April, plain and simple as that," he said.

April realized that he was as selfish and as self-centered as the rest of the men, but then she cried for having spoken to him so unjustly.

David took her in his arms and pulled her into the bed beside him. He undressed her slowly and they made wild, passionate love and all was right between them again.

"What is your father doing here in Peking?" April asked as she lay snuggled contentedly in his arms. "Does he want to take you home?"

David sighed. "Perhaps I should go home, April."

"No, David," she cried with alarm. "I love you. I'd die without you. It's difficult for me too, getting used to these new ways. But we must both be patient, darling."

He tightened his arm around her. "Yes, I suppose so. I do love you, April. I always will." He kissed her, then relaxed back against the pillows. "Father couldn't force us to go home now even if we wanted to. But that isn't my worry just now...it's your father who's trying to break us up."

"My father," April said with a shudder of disgust. She told him haltingly about the advances Ke Loo had made to her.

David snorted. "I thought that old bastard had something filthy like that swimming around in his sewer mind. I see it in the way he looks at you. Everyone sees it."

"I am going to speak to the Empress about him," April said.

"You're going to speak to the Empress? And I suppose she'll make everything just dandy because you want her to? Oh, April, open your eyes. The old woman is just as bad as the rest of them, even worse—cutting off hands and feet and heads whenever it suits her. God, she's nothing but a damned barbarian. They're all barbarians and they're trying to turn us into barbarians just like themselves."

April didn't heed David, however, because the next day she spoke to the Dowager Empress about her predicament.

"Your father is your lord," the old woman told her. "However, if you choose to accompany me to the Winter Palace instead of to Kalgan you are free to do so."

April fell on her face in thankful servitude, but a moment later another trap snapped shut on her.

"Your mother?" the dowager said. "You have contacted her by letter as I asked? You have found where Li Ahn is in hiding?"

April frowned. "I'm sorry. I forgot. I did not write her as yet."

An ugly expression fixed itself on the Empress's face. "What? I ordered you and you disobeyed me? You will write at once. I will oversee your correspondence personally. See to it!"

April went back toward her own royal suite despondently. She could see no answers to her quandaries. She could not go with her father. She could not betray Li Ahn and her mother to certain death and there was no safe place for her to run.

Perhaps David was right, after all. Perhaps they should go home. She thought of the hateful people in America and all she hated there. No, she must stay here. An answer would be found.

CHAPTER THIRTY-THREE

"David!"

It took Peter a moment to recognize his son. He looked older and very foreign in his peasant disguise, with his dirty face hidden beneath a dome-hat of straw.

Peter embraced him stiffly, having trouble remembering the last time he'd ever physically touched the boy. But David wasn't a boy any longer, Peter thought as he took in the cold, tired eyes, the sullen mouth, the determined thrust of the scraggly chin.

"How are you, David?"

"I'm all right." David didn't move from his stand just inside the door of the room. "You said you needed my help."

"Yes," Peter answered uncomfortably. "But that can wait for a minute, can't it? Can't we talk? How's April? Come, sit down."

David didn't move. "You'll be happy to know, Father, that you were right."

"Oh? About what?"

"We don't belong here. At least I don't. It was a mistake to come."

Peter could tell how difficult it was for David to admit his mistake. "We all pull boners, son. Let's just say it didn't pan out the way you expected. No harm done. You and April are married, so some good came out of it."

David gave him a curious look. "You approve of our marrying?"

"I should never have tried to prevent it. If you want to stay married to her, I personally will do everything I can to straighten out the mess April left back home, and see that your marriage is sanctioned by the laws of America."

"You mean that? This isn't some kind of trick?"

Peter showed empty palms. "No trick. I am deeply serious, David."

For the first time David smiled as his eyes got misty. He hesitated for a moment, then went over and embraced his father warmly, letting the tears come.

Peter wasn't sure he was doing the right thing. He'd try to keep up his end of the deal but he didn't know how he was going to break the news to Lorna and Lydia if it came down to that. They'd both be furious with him. Oh well, he thought, the important thing now was to get them home.

"I hate this place," David admitted when he had regained his composure. "April's an entirely different person than she was back home. Here they treat her like a goddess or something."

"And you?"

"They hate me, just like you always said they would. Oh, I get waited on hand and foot, but they always let me know I'm an outsider, and just the husband of a princess."

"Do you want to come home?" Peter asked.

"Yes," David said simply.

"And April?"

"I can't go without her. And even though she's not truly happy either, she won't admit it. She still trusts and admires these people."

"That's a mistake," Peter said. "I've lived here, and I can tell you, you can't trust that infernal Empress. She'll get her way, or kill anyone who prevents it."

David saw the bottle of scotch whiskey on the tray.

"May I?" he asked, helping himself without waiting for an answer. "This sure beats rice wine."

Peter poured himself a drink, and another for his son, and they toasted one another silently before emptying their glasses.

"Here's to getting the devil out of here," Peter toasted, then emptied his glass. He splashed more whiskey into it and offered more to David.

Peter motioned to a chair. David seated himself and Peter took the chair opposite, their knees almost touching. They sat looking at one another as old memories, both good and bad, ran through their heads.

David took a deep swallow of his drink and leaned back, his eyes firmly fixed on his father. He saw the lines of worry and age and wondered which of them he'd caused.

"What about you, Dad," David asked, "And P.M. Cosmetics? I haven't heard anything yet about how you are."

"I'm well enough, or will be, once I get out of this blasted country. As for P.M. Cosmetics—" He hesitated and downed another drink quickly. "I don't think you'll have to worry about taking over the family business, if that makes you feel any better."

David set his glass down heavily, and met his father's eyes. "You'd better tell me about it," he said.

"You've got enough problems of your own," Peter said, though he felt a wave of satisfaction at his son's concern.

"They're our problems," David said emphatically. "You've heard about mine, now it's my turn to hear about yours."

Grateful, Peter told him about the problems that he had recently faced—the payment to Walter Hanover, the lawsuit, which had virtually wiped him out financially. He was careful not to blame his own absence for the loss of the suit, but David seemed to put the pieces together himself.

"And I've made it all worse for you," he said when Peter had finished.

"I expect I made a great deal of it harder for you, too," Peter said. "At any rate, there's nothing we can do about any of it until we get back to the States."

"But there is," David said, brightening.

"I don't think the Empress is likely to loan me the money I need," Peter said drily.

"She might." David laughed and poured another drink.

"Come on, you didn't sound a little while ago like you were

on good enough terms to ask her for help."

"Maybe I won't ask," David said. "And she wouldn't have to loan you money, exactly, if it was something worth money."

"I hope you're not planning on stealing the Imperial jewels," Peter said, mystified.

"Something more valuable than that—something that made April's mother a rich woman—" He paused, waiting as the meaning of his words dawned on his father.

"Perfume," Peter said. "Cosmetics. Of course, by now she has an entirely new scent to replace the one Lydia stole. She would never deign to wear a scent being marketed around the world."

He hesitated, and the smile faded from his face. "But that's too risky. It almost cost Lydia her life, and they're still sending assassins to try to kill her for stealing it."

"She's a woman," David said. "And she didn't have you here in Peking, to help."

"That's very flattering, but...."

"No buts about it, this time you listen to me," David said stubbornly. "I'll figure out how to get some of those things out of the palace, and how to persuade April to come with me. You figure out how we're going to get out of China."

He offered his father his hand. After a pause, Peter shook it warmly.

"It's a deal," he agreed, beaming; but he grew sober again. "On one condition, that you promise to take no chances with getting this stuff. It's not worth risking your life. Together we can find some way to rebuild the family fortune when we get home."

"Agreed," David said. "Just leave this to me."

* * * * * * *

Wang Seng had promised the guards would not notice David stealing back into the Forbidden City.

Still, David found his heart in his throat as he passed through the gate into the South Garden.

He tried the door to the royal storehouse, and found it locked. The lock was a flimsy affair that he could easily have broken, but it would be discovered in the morning, and the Empress alerted.

The door to the Treasury was, of course, locked also, and far more securely; but he doubted the royal perfumes and cosmetics would be kept there. In fact, he had no idea where they might be kept, he realized, returning despondently to his own quarters.

To his surprise, he found April waiting for him there. "Where have you been?" she demanded.

"I went to see my father," he told her. He explained to her about Peter's promise to help arrange a proper marriage between them if they returned to San Francisco. He did not, however, risk telling her the rest of his plan. It was safer for her if she did not know.

"I don't trust him," April said petulantly. "Or my mother."

"She's not in this," David argued.

"She's there, waiting like a spider in a trap for us to return."

He saw that April was still not able to face the mistake they had made, and he was glad now that he hadn't mentioned his plan to steal the Empress's cosmetics. He would find a way to do that on his own, and get them to his father. Then he would find a way to get April outside the palace, even if he had to trick her. Once they had her outside, his father would know what to do.

For the first time in his life, he was grateful for his father's aura of strength and authority.

* * * * * * *

It was when he saw little Mei Fei sitting under a peach tree the following morning, studying her English, that an idea came to him. Mei Fei was friendly with Soon Gh'ing Ling, wardrobe mistress to the Empress; and an inquisitive child like Mei Fei could almost certainly be counted on to know where all the secret hiding places were, even in a palace.

It helped that the child was friendly with April, and had always tried rather shyly to be friendly with him. David sat down with her and began to help her with the lessons, laughing at the difficulty she had with the R's. They worked on them until they were both rolling with laughter on the grass.

When they had calmed down again, David said, "You know, I bet you're the one person in the whole Forbidden City who can help me."

"Help you what?" Mei Fei asked, flattered that someone needed something of her.

"Hide something. I bought the most beautiful pearl for April, and I want to keep it safe until her birthday, but I know she'll find it in my rooms. She's very much like you," he said, tweaking her nose, "very inquisitive."

"I know a place," Mei Fei said brightly. "No one goes there but Soon Ch'ing Ling, and she's always too busy making perfumes and lotions to look for a pearl."

"If I bring the pearl," David asked, "will you show me where I can hide it?"

Mei Fei was only too happy to get involved in an intrigue. "I can show you now."

She led David to the Pleasure Palace and taking his hand took him inside. The rooms were empty except for several women in ceremonial robes praying before a golden lion. Mei Fei brought him to a small side room which was hidden behind a Nine Dragon Screen. She lifted a key from a concealed niche and unlocked a small bronze door that opened into a storage area. The articles on the shelves were few but carefully arranged according to textures, David noticed...creams, powders, lotions, scents. Sitting in a velvet niche on a platter of silver were several small vials of yellow topaz.

"The royal scent," Mei Fei said, boldly taking down one of the vials. She unstopped it and smelled the perfume. She handed it to David to smell. It was enchanting.

That night, rather than return to his father with the news of his find, he decided to return with the evidence of it. When he stepped into the storage room, he decided he'd better insure his success by taking one of each article from the various compartments. He filled the pockets of his disguise and found it necessary to stuff some into his cloth boots and even under his domed hat. He didn't know which items were the most valuable, but if one perfume could make a fortune, several must be better.

The moon was waxing to full when he stepped from the Hall of Pleasure and Longevity and started toward the Well of the Pearl Concubine and on toward the north gate, the Gate of Divine Military Genius.

Everything clunked and banged when he walked. There had to be another way to smuggle them out past the guards, he told himself. He ducked into the shadows of a stand of apricot trees near the wall. He thought he heard footsteps and froze, pressing hard against the bark of the tree.

When the hand fell on his shoulder a gasp escaped his lips and his whole body went stiff with fear.

"What are you doing here?" Wu Lien asked.

David let out his breath and fought to get himself back into control. "Wu Lien," he stammered. "Thank heaven." David moved and two jars clanked together inside his tunic.

"What do you have hidden there," Wu Lien asked as he felt the bulges.

"I'll tell you later. I've got to get through the gates. My father's waiting for me at the American legation."

"You are stealing?" Wu Lien asked in disbelief.

"Only some cosmetics which the Empress uses. Nothing that can't be replaced. They're for my father's company."

The moon slipped behind a cloud, hiding the frown on Wu Lien's face. "Your father?" he repeated.

David looked at Wu Lien with an earnest expression. "You said once that you were in my debt and that if I ever needed a favor you would do anything for me."

"Yes."

"Well, I never thought I'd have to ask for payment, Wu Lien, but I desperately need your help. Father wants to take April and me back home where we belong."

"To America?" Wu Lien felt a sinking feeling in his heart. The American wanted to take April away from him. "Perhaps it is for the best," he said after a moment. "How can I help you?"

"By getting me out of here with these samples." David still could not see Wu Lien's face, but his voice was oddly hoarse.

Wu Lien peeked around the trees, toward the main gate at the north entrance. "You'll never get past the guards clanking like a utensils peddler," he said. "You sound like a rusty bell. Come, I know a way that might not be guarded. Through here." He took David's arm.

As they skirted along the east wall Wu Lien led David past the great theatre, then across the shadowy courtyard fronting the Palace of Young Princes. As they edged their way along the stream they called a river, hugging the wall, Wu Lien cautioned David to hide himself in the hedge while he checked to be sure the guard house at the East Gate was unmanned as it usually was.

"It's never used anymore. A cat once dashed in the Empress's path when she was leaving by this small gate. She had it sealed and ordered it never used except for escape in the case of a siege. There is a small opening which you can slip through. Wait here," Wu Lien urged and then crept away, leaving David to the night.

David waited, his breath short, the vein in his throat pulsing wildly.

After five minutes Wu Lien was back. "There is no one. Come," he urged.

The guard house was dark and deserted looking, the door ajar. As they passed it Wu Lien stepped behind David and with a quick shove pushed him through the doorway, sending him sprawling on the dirt floor of the guard house. Before David could gather his wits a lamp flared up and David found himself staring up into the angry faces of a circle of palace guards.

With a frightened gasp he leapt to his feet and made a dash

back through the door. But the doorway was now blocked. Ke Loo stood with arms folded across his chest, his eyes like daggers.

"Take him," Ke Loo ordered.

David looked at his friend, dumbfounded. Wu Lien smiled.

CHAPTER THIRTY-FOUR

Peter paced and paced. It was almost midnight and David hadn't shown. He was worried but he tried to keep calm, telling himself that nothing was wrong, that David simply could not slip away. Perhaps he'd gotten involved in some court celebration and was unable to break away. Or perhaps he hadn't found the cache of cosmetics and saw no sense of coming to the legation until he had something definite to report.

Peter slept fitfully with a dull ache that told him that something actually was wrong. In the morning he went to find Wang Seng, the fat Chinese who'd been helping them.

Wang Seng was not in his shop. Peter found instead the young son who'd come for the very first message.

"Honorable father has gone to the Imperial City at the command of the Empress. I do not know when he will return. Very important, the guards told him."

Peter's fears began to grow. "I need to send another message," he told the boy.

"I cannot leave the shop and there is no one else who could pass the guards. I will come to you when Father returns," was the best answer Peter could get.

He waited the whole of the day. The French minister sent a note asking him to dinner. Peter felt in no mood, and declined, angry that the note had been from the minister and not a message from David.

At five minutes past seven o'clock there was a tap at his door. Peter opened it to find Wang Seng standing in the hall, looking very official in black robes.

"Your son is detained. He sends you this," Wang Seng said, handing Peter a large bundle wrapped in silk. He bowed respectfully and was gone like a shadow dissolving into the night.

"The cosmetics," Peter thought eagerly. David had been successful, then—but where was he?

Peter brought the bundle to the table and began to unwind the yards of delicate silk.

As he unwrapped the bundle, an eerie feeling came over him...such an oddly shaped package—and damp, his hands were wet....

He turned his hand over and saw that it was not only wet, but red—with blood. A sudden horror swept over him, and with violent gestures he tore the rest of the silk from the bundle.

A strangled scream tore from his throat as David's unseeing eyes, still wide with horror, stared up out of the sockets of the severed head.

* * * * * * *

April wondered if perhaps she had died, or gone mad. The nightmare that had fallen upon her seemed never to end, it went on and on and on, whether her eyes were open or shut. Every day was as black and terrifying as the one before. There was no way of knowing when darkness stopped and light began.

Through the dimness she heard distant sounds, familiar sounds, like the sounds of human voices.

"April?" Wu Lien said softly.

She wanted to answer him but the nightmare swooped down over her again and carried her back into its horrors, setting her down on the same terrace beside the Empress, looking down at the same courtyard, watching David, bleeding and unconscious, being dragged toward the chopping block. She heard herself scream as the ax blade descended and the blackness returned.

It was always the same. A thousand times she watched it re-enacted at the backs of her eyes. A thousand times she screamed and a thousand times she woke only to dream it all again.

Something cold and wet touched her forehead and when she opened her eyes to see what it was, Mei Fei's pretty face smiled at her.

"Wha...."

Mei Fei put her finger gently against April's lips. "The fever is gone," she said. "You will be well soon."

April had no idea what she meant. Suddenly the horrible nightmare started down over her again but this time she kept her eyes wide, fixing them firmly on Mei Fei's face, refusing to let herself be carried off into the terrifying blackness of that hell. She tried to speak but there was no strength left in her.

"Lie still," Mei Fei said. She took the cold towel from April's forehead and replaced it with a hot one. A moment later she touched something to April's lips. "Try to drink some of this," Mei Fei said.

It tasted sweet and hot and delicious and April suddenly felt very hungry but only managed a few spoonfuls. Then she lost what little strength she'd mustered and slipped back into sleep. This time the terrors didn't come as visibly but the finality of death and devastating loneliness were there waiting for her.

The sun was shining through the latticed windows when she opened her eyes again. Mei Fei was still there, looking concerned but smiling.

"Mei Fei," April managed. "David...." The tears suddenly blinded her and she turned her face into the pillow as her body shook with the pain of her loss.

"You must not think of the past, April," Mei Fei said, sounding old and wise. "It cannot be brought back but the good in it can always be cherished."

"David," April sobbed.

"Try to eat. You must get back your strength if you are to travel with us to Kalgan."

"He's dead," April moaned and again she closed her eyes and raced backward in memory to search for him.

It took a long, long time before she came back into the light and when she did she was alone. "Mei Fei," April called in a faint whisper.

"Mei Fei is gone," her old amah said. "They are all gone, child."

The days became longer and her terrible emptiness deepened. After several days of nodding and waking she found herself able to distinguish morning from night, hunger from thirst, real from imagined.

When she moved her eyes about the room the amah anticipated her question and said, "You alone are here in the Imperial City. You are to join your father in Kalgan if...." She let her sentence go unfinished.

April finished it in her mind. "If I live."

"What day is it?" April asked.

The amah shrugged. "What does the day matter? They are all the same."

"How long have I been here in this bed?"

"A month. Perhaps less, perhaps more."

April tried to push herself up but the amah eased her back. "You have stayed in this bed for some weeks and you will remain in it until you are strong. Go back to sleep."

By the end of the week April was able to sit up. By the end of the second week she was walking about the room. The weather was turning cold and she forced her mind to occupy itself with building her strength, restoring her health and not agonizing over her loss. She refused to ask where he'd been buried, or whether he'd been buried at all. David was gone. She'd seen his execution with her own eyes.

"As a lesson to all those who are tempted to betray me," the Empress had told her as David was led to the block.

A dry, grit-filled wind, cold and penetrating, lashed in from the far-off Gobi desert, reminding April that winter was not far away and she had to be off. She didn't want to go to Kalgan to her father and she never wanted to see the Empress's cold emotionless eyes ever again.

The amah finished feeding her then said, "If you are well enough I will pack your trunks and we will go to Kalgan."

"No," April said firmly.

"Where then? To the Winter Palace?"

"No."

"It must be one or the other, little one. We cannot stay here."

"Why not?"

"Because the snows are deep and the storms fierce. We will freeze in this deserted city and we will starve as no supplies are brought in when the Empress is not in residence. That is why everyone leaves when the Empress leaves. As it is we are already dangerously low on provisions. It is imperative that we leave."

April didn't care. She'd rather starve or freeze than go to Ke Loo or to the Empress. Going to the window she leaned her head against the sash and thought of David again. "Was he buried?" she asked the amah.

"Who?"

"My husband."

The amah threw back the coverlet to air and said, "The father took him."

"Father? David's father?"

"Yes. He took him to the cemetery in the American compound."

April pushed herself away from the window. "I will go to his grave," she said. "Bring me a warm cloak and call bearers to take me."

"You cannot go there. The guards are ordered to forbid you to enter foreigner's territory. By going to the American legation you betray the Empress and automatically become party to your husband's crime and, therefore, are subject to the same punishment. You must not go there, child. You must not. You are a royal princess, remember. You have no business with the foreigners."

"I will go to my husband's grave."

"No. It is blasphemy against the Empress and the gods for

you, a Manchu princess, to pay homage to one who, together with his accursed father, defiled your ancestors and the ancestors of all the Manchus."

"Together with his father?" April picked up. "What do you mean? What does David's father have to do with the execution?"

"Wang Seng told the Empress of their plot to steal from her."

"Steal? Steal what? What are you talking about?"

The amah told all she'd heard from gossip, and as told to her directly by Wang Seng, who had once been her lover. It was she who had delivered the note for him, though she did not say this.

"David's father?" April said again when she had heard the story.

The amah nodded gravely. "Your husband himself said that it was for his father that he took from the Empress." The amah shook her head in disgust. "It is said that the young American deceived you from the very beginning, that he only came here to steal."

April knew that to be untrue but all she could repeat was, "David's father!"

The more it seethed inside her head, the more her hatred of Peter MacNair grew. If he hadn't followed them here, David would be alive. Peter had lured David to the legation and somehow persuaded him to steal the Empress's perfume and lotions just as Lydia had done. But unlike her mother, David had been discovered...and beheaded.

"Peter MacNair," she said, clenching her fists. She never knew herself capable of such hatred. She carefully sketched a picture of him into her mind and vowed with all her soul that one day she would have her revenge.

Her mother too was just as much to blame. The initial sin was Lydia's and she would pay for it.

Now April knew where she must go, and it would be far away from China. But guards blocked every door leading from the palace, she found. She had to get to America. She had to cause Peter MacNair and her mother the same pain and misery they'd caused her. There seemed no escape from this palace prison, however, except by sedan chair that would either take her to Kalgan and Ke Loo or south to the Empress.

The following day while walking in the garden she saw Mei Fei's bare apricot tree that leaned over the wall. Hurrying back to her dressing room, April wrapped herself warmly, took Ke Loo's ruby pendant and the rest of her exquisite jewels and tucked them into a carrying case. She left all her lovely clothes, knowing she would never have need of them where she was going. She had money and jewelry enough to buy everything she'd need.

April slipped into the garden and started to climb the tree. She was still very weak but her determination gave her the strength she needed to scale the wall.

She dropped to the other side and sat huddled against the stones, trying to recapture her spent energy. After a few minutes she forced herself to move on toward the Tartar wall and the foreign legations beyond.

The distance wasn't far but it took the better part of an hour before she reached the entrance to the compound. As she stepped into its protection a deafening roar began to build up inside her head and her stomach turned over. She staggered and almost fell. A foreign gentleman saw her and hurried over.

"You're ill, my dear," the man said.

April found it difficult to see or breathe. She put out her hand, groping for support. "Help me," she said in English.

"Of course. Come." As he helped her along, supporting her with his arm about her waist, he looked closer into her face. "You aren't full Chinese," he said.

"American," April managed. Suddenly her stomach lurched and she doubled over. The man called out something in Chinese and a moment later April felt herself being carried in a litter.

When she opened her eyes a man was leaning over her. He said, "Feeling better, young lady?"

April nodded, but she felt very sick. She opened her mouth to speak.

The doctor answered her question before she asked it. "Nothing too serious. You're a little run down, but it's nothing that can't be rectified by a few days of rest in bed. And you needn't worry; there's been no harm done to the baby. I'd say you should deliver in about seven months."

"Baby?" April said widening her eyes.

"Of course. You're about three months along. Didn't you know, my dear?"

"I've got to get home. I must get to San Francisco," April said urgently after several minutes of letting the announcement fill her head.

"Oh, I think that shouldn't be a problem." The doctor chuckled. "I can well understand your anxiety, my dear. I wouldn't want a child of mine born in this heathen land either."

It wasn't China she was running from, April told herself as her need for revenge grew stronger with every passing day.

On the first day she was permitted out of bed, April went to the American cemetery. "I'll make them suffer as we suffered," she said as she stood over David's grave. "You will be avenged, my darling David. I swear you will. And one day I will come back to you." She thought of Mei Fei and of Wu Lien. "I know now where our true friends are, my darling," she said.

She turned, fists clenched, and slowly went down the hill and to the ship that was waiting in Shanghai to take her to her enemies.

ABOUT THE AUTHOR

V. J. BANIS is the critically acclaimed author ("the master's touch in storytelling..."—*Publishers Weekly*) of more than 200 published books and numerous short stories in a career spanning nearly a half century. A native of Ohio and a longtime Californian, he lives and writes now in West Virginia's beautiful Blue Ridge.

You can visit him at http://www.vjbanis.com

www.ingramcontent.com/pod-product-compliance
Lightning Source LLC
Chambersburg PA
CBHW050355260626
47156CB00003B/746